Copyright © 2025 by Melody Tyden

All rights reserved.

The characters and events portrayed in this book are fictitious. Any similarity to real persons, living or dead, is coincidental and not intended by the author.

No part of this book may be reproduced, or stored in a retrieval system, or transmitted in any form or by any means, electronic, mechanical, photocopying, recording, or otherwise, without express written permission of the publisher.

Cover design by: GetCovers

HIDDEN IN PLAIN SIGHT

MELODY TYDEN

Contents

Previously in the Rocky Mountain Wolves...

Supernatural hunter Calista met Alpha Vaughan while investigating his Crimsontooth Pack for a series of murders taking place near their Montana pack territory. He immediately recognized her as his mate but had recently signed a treaty with the Ravenstone Pack in Alberta to take their Alpha's daughter, Amanda, as his mate. Unable to fight the connection between them, Vaughan and Calista accepted their bond and Amanda returned to her own pack, taking Vaughan's sister Savannah and the pack Beta, Felix, with her.

At the Ravenstone Pack, Savannah was introduced to several eligible men, including genetic scientist Kyle, but soon discovered that her fated mate, Jasper, was a former pack member currently living as a rogue and suffering the effects of a failed experiment on him. Savannah almost fell victim to Kyle's experiments before discovering that he was responsible for both Jasper's exile and the Ravenstone Luna's illness. Amanda claimed authority over the pack after her father betrayed the pack's best interests in favour of saving his mate and asked Savannah to be her Beta.

Felix returned home to the Crimsontooth Pack in Montana, where this story begins.

Chapter One

~**Felix**~

After fifteen minutes of waiting for Vaughan to show up for our scheduled meeting, the impatient clicking of my pen had almost started to sound like music. Before I drove myself crazy, I mind-linked him. *Are we still on? There are only so many times I can count the number of trees outside your window.*

After a short pause, his reply echoed in my head. *Shit. I forgot.*

A smirk tugged at my lips. *Let me guess: your Luna is currently underneath you?*

Based on how often the two of them were going at it, calling my statement a 'guess' was generous. I would have put money on it.

On top of me, actually. Sheepish satisfaction filled every word. *I'm sorry, Felix. Can you review what needs to be done with Leo?*

No problem. Have fun, kids.

Closing the link, I sat back with a rueful shake of my head, the leather office chair creaking beneath me. As happy as I was for my best friend and Alpha, I also hoped the all-consuming honeymoon phase between him and his new mate wouldn't last *too* long. At the end of the day, we still had a pack to run.

Heading down the hall, I ducked into the Gamma's office and found Leo there, hard at work. Stacks of neatly ordered files covered his desk, not a single item out of place. At least *he* would never change. "Hey. Vaughan's busy and I know we need to catch up on everything that we missed while we were up at the Ravenstone pack. Can you run through it with me?"

"Of course."

He tidied up his already pristine desk as I took a seat across from him. Although all the rooms in the pack house were cleaned with the same frequency, his office always had a freshly-cleaned scent that mine never kept for more than a couple of hours.

From his desk drawer, Leo pulled out a long, typed, itemized list. "I kept track of the things that would need your attention while the two of you were away. Now that Savannah has defected from the pack, we'll also need to reassign her responsibilities."

"She didn't 'defect'," I pointed out as I took the paper from him, wincing at the sheer volume of items on it. Any hopes I had of getting through this meeting quickly vanished faster than a vampire at sunrise. "She found her mate. There's a difference."

"The end result is the same."

Since I couldn't argue with that, I started working my way down the list instead. Over the next hour, we managed to get most things taken care of other than a couple of items which required Vaughan's personal attention. Thankfully, when I finished with Leo and headed back down the hall, Vaughan sat at his desk with Calista standing next to him.

"Alpha Marcus called while we were away," I announced from the door, nodding to Calista in greeting as they both looked up. "Says it's important. Do you want to return his call?"

"I should," Vaughan agreed, his brows knit slightly as he beckoned me inside. "Come on in. I'll put it on speaker so you two can hear."

I took my usual seat across the desk from Vaughan, whose arm curled around Calista's waist as she perched on the arm of his chair. Her feminine scent had become mixed with his upon their mating, declaring them a couple as effectively as the physical marks on their neck did.

"Who's Alpha Marcus?" she asked while Vaughan pulled up the number on his computer.

"Alpha of the Vermillion pack, fifty miles northwest of here," Vaughan explained, his tone more patient than usual when he spoke to her. "They're a small pack and under our protection."

His last words told me he shared my concern that Marcus' call had something to do with a threat to his pack's security. After the attack on us and the recent events at the Ravenstone pack, it seemed that strange happenings were on the rise and we should all be on our guard.

The gruff older Alpha's voice filled the room as he answered the call. "Hello?"

"Alpha Marcus, it's Alpha Vaughan from the Crimsontooth pack. I understand you've been trying to reach me."

"Thanks for returning my call, Alpha." The relief in his voice bled through the phone clearly enough that we all heard it. "We've got a problem."

"Nobody ever calls just to say hi anymore," I quipped under my breath. Calista smiled while Vaughan shot me a warning look before speaking aloud into the phone.

"What's going on?"

"I'm not quite sure how to describe it," he answered, stammering over the words as if he knew how strange they would sound. "We keep getting alerts of someone crossing into our territory but we can't locate them. There's no scent, no sign of anyone here, but we're receiving the alerts anyway."

The hair on the back of my neck prickled as I leaned forward and caught Calista's eye.

"Ghosts?" I mouthed to her.

She shook her head as she whispered back, "Not physical."

Good point; without a physical form, ghosts shouldn't trigger a pack's territorial defense.

"Trolls?" she suggested instead.

"Too smelly." My nose wrinkled in such disgust that she had to stifle a laugh, amusement dancing in her eyes.

Vaughan did his best to ignore us both as he continued the conversation with the Vermillion Alpha. "Is that all? Just the alerts?"

"No. That would be strange, and an annoyance, but not really a worry. The problem is that after the last couple of times it happened, we found some of our weapons missing."

Now *that* was interesting. Whatever set off the alarms had to be physical enough to move objects but capable of disappearing with them before being discovered. My pulse quickened as the possibilities raced through my mind and I could tell Calista's thoughts were going a mile a minute too. As a former hunter, she knew more about different species of supernatural beings than anyone I'd met before, including me, and I knew a lot more than the average werewolf.

Vaughan easily picked up on my investment in the situation and gave me a nod. "I've just returned from a trip away and need to stay here for a while, but I can send my Beta, Felix, to investigate with you."

I suspected his desire to stay home had a lot more to do with spending more time alone with his new mate than catching up on pack business, but I didn't mind. Not only did it sound interesting, we had a duty to protect the packs who relied on us. What was a Beta for if not to take on the jobs his Alpha couldn't or didn't want to do?

"We'd sure appreciate that," Alpha Marcus said. "We'll have a room ready for him as soon as he can get here."

After making a few final arrangements, Vaughan ended the call and looked between me and Calista. "Do either of you have any idea what might be behind this?"

Calista went first. "Pixies and goblins like to steal things, but I've never heard of them being invisible."

"I wasn't thinking invisibility," I contradicted. "I'm thinking they might have the ability to appear or disappear at will. If the creature's invisible, won't the weapon still be visible? Meaning the pack's guards would see these weapons walking themselves off the territory?"

The visual image made Calista smile. "It depends on the being. Some can confer invisibility to things they touch, but those ones aren't usually known for being thieves. It's an odd combination of characteristics."

We tossed a few more ideas back and forth before Vaughan interjected. "Do you want to know what I think?"

Curiously, we both turned to him. His knowledge of other species wasn't as extensive as mine or Calista's, but maybe he picked up on something we missed.

He leaned back, his fingers drumming rhythmically on the desk and his tone steady and serious. "I think there's nothing supernatural about this at all. I'd bet this is an inside job and someone in the pack is triggering the alarm somehow. That's why they can't find anyone: because the person they're looking for belongs there."

That could be possible, I had to admit. "But why trigger the alarm at all in that case? Why not just steal the weapons?"

"To divert blame. If the weapons went missing without the alarm, they'd know it was an internal problem. This way, they're busy looking for some outside force when the perpetrator's right under their nose. Sorry to disappoint you but I think you're looking at a plain old werewolf thief here."

"Well, that's no fun."

Calista smiled again at my fake pout. She smiled a lot more now than when she first joined us, and Vaughan seemed more relaxed too. They were good for each other.

What new side of me would *my* mate bring out? After watching first Vaughan and then his sister Savannah find their other halves, a faint ache had settled in my chest every time I thought about my future mate, but I doubted I'd find her at the Vermillion pack. Pack business had taken me there a few times before without a hint of her.

And business called me back there now, starting with packing my overnight bag once again and getting back on the road.

Chapter Two

"Watch out, Lina," my best friend, Keerla, whispered, glancing over her shoulder as she bustled into the kitchen, her arms laden with fruit from the forest. In the waning days of autumn, the berries for which our home was named were almost *too* plentiful and their sweet, tart scent filled the air as she walked past, her springy blonde curls bouncing with each step. "Tarron is on his way down here."

Stifling a groan, I looked over the dishes in front of me, all in various states of preparation for that night's meal. Could I hide for a few minutes without ruining anything? Probably not, even though I would have gladly stuffed myself into a cupboard to avoid another encounter with the high prince. Wiping the sweat from my brow as the fire crackled behind me, I resumed my work.

Not a minute later, his tall, slender frame filled the doorway. The kitchen's warmth seemed to chill as his sharp gaze swept the room, and the heels of his shoes tapped softly against the stone floor with each step he took inside. Keerla and I both stopped what we were doing, bowing our heads in respect as women in our position were expected to.

Not that I felt any respect towards the man; in my view, respect should be earned, not given by birthright, and Tarron had done nothing to earn mine.

"Is everything ready for tonight, Evalina?"

"It will be, Your Highness," I replied, bobbing a curtsey and keeping my head down as I resumed my work. Now that he'd addressed me,

I could safely move again. Poor Keerla had to remain still since her presence hadn't been acknowledged yet.

His smooth, imperious tone grated on my nerves more than a dragon's screech. "Do you know who's visiting us tonight?"

Gossip moved fast in Etta, especially when it involved the royal family. I'd heard the rumours. However, I played dumb, my head still down. All I could see of him were his pointed green velvet shoes. "No, Your Highness."

His deep chuckle filled the room, sending an uncomfortable shiver down my spine that I did my best to hide. "I think you do. You're just jealous."

The arrogance of the man knew no bounds. As *if* I would be jealous of the poor woman whose parents were dragging her there to see if she could catch the Etta prince's eye. If she were lucky, he'd have no interest in her and she could return home with no harm done.

I could only dream of such a luxury. My home, and my mother, were in Etta. I had nowhere else to go.

Burying those thoughts, I acknowledged that I did, in fact, know who the guests were that evening. "I hope that you will find your equal and be happy, Your Highness."

The air thickened as he stepped closer, the sharp scent of Etta blossoms native to his bloodline overwhelming everything else. The cooking food, the fruit Keerla had gathered, and even the fire's smoke all receded beneath the floral aroma that clung to him like a second skin.

Some women found it attractive. I'd even heard it called an aphrodisiac, but it only made me feel a little nauseated when I got too close to any of the royal family. I'd learned to hold my breath when they were in the room or breathe through my mouth so it didn't affect me so strongly, but when he got as close to me as he did then, it became harder to hide the way it made my stomach churn.

As usual, Tarron misinterpreted the reason for me turning my head away and he reached over to hook my chin, pulling my face towards him and upward so I had no choice but to look directly at him.

Calling him unattractive would have been a lie. Lavender eyes the colour of Etta blossoms sat nestled beneath his jet-black hair and above his high, sculpted cheekbones. His lips were a deep shade of red and his straight, white teeth gleamed as his lips parted.

Beautiful.

No other word really did him justice, but he wielded his beauty like a blade, sharp and unforgiving. After tormenting me for sport for years, he'd suddenly decided he wanted me, and the charm offensive was a full-on assault. I couldn't imagine the reason for his interest other than me being pretty much the only woman in Etta who didn't fawn over him.

"Jealousy is unnecessary. Be my amorta and you can have everything you want. You can leave all of this behind."

His hand flicked dismissively over the kitchen and food, my day's work, his nose wrinkling in distaste as if he found it all beneath him.

He'd made the offer before and I'd turned him down. Not just once or twice either. It had become almost a daily routine over the past few weeks, as if he thought I might eventually agree as long as he kept asking. It only proved how little he knew me because I wouldn't be any man's second choice, let alone his. Amorta might be the fancy word that we used for it, but an official lover would always be second to a prince's wife, and I would rather work all day in the kitchens than pledge myself to a man who didn't consider me worthy of being his one and only love.

Tarron knew nothing about what I wanted. How could he when he never thought of anything but himself?

I bit the inside of my cheek to keep from saying as much. "You flatter me, Your Highness, but I can't accept."

"Because of your mother," he said, filling in the rest of the sentence that I left unspoken.

I'd given him that excuse before. Because of my mother's ill health, I needed to devote my attention to her, and he deserved a woman who could give herself entirely to him. It skirted the issue that I simply didn't *want* to be his amorta. Confessing that out loud could have resulted in me losing my job entirely, and that would have been disastrous when my meagre income was all that kept me and my mother from complete ruin.

"Yes. I'm glad you understand."

Turning my head out of his grasp, I returned to my work. My fingers moved mechanically as I sliced my knife through the fruit, the blade thudding softly against the cutting board.

Still, he didn't leave. "What if I told you I've discovered the cure for your mother's ailments?"

Beside me, Keerla stifled a gasp, and I couldn't stop my head from flying back up, turning to face the prince with my mouth agape. "You have?"

None of the healers knew what was wrong with her. She'd fallen ill a few months earlier, forcing her to leave her job in the kitchen and take to her bed. Every day, she got weaker. I'd taken over from her so that the position would still be open for her when she recovered, but as time went on, it seemed less and less likely that she would ever be the way she was before.

"Of course I'll share it with you," Tarron said, sounding almost compassionate until his lips twisted into a satisfied smile. "*If* you agree to be my amorta."

"You have a potential bride dining with you tonight," I reminded him, indignation bubbling inside me on behalf of the woman I'd never met as well as for myself. "Shouldn't you be focused on her?"

"It will be easier to tell her before we marry that I already have a lover than to bring one on afterwards," he replied with a shrug. "Less drama that way."

He was unbelievable, but I ignored his callousness to focus on the more immediate issue for me. "How do I know you truly have the cure?"

His pretty face darkened into a scowl, his hand darting out to grip my arm. Bony fingers bit into my skin like iron clamps, sending a sharp pain radiating up to my shoulder. A cold knot formed in my stomach at his show of strength, but I forced my face to remain impassive.

"Are you calling me a liar, Evalina?"

There was the Tarron I remembered from my childhood, the one who would fling insults with abandon but could never take any criticism. The one who had made an enemy of the more powerful fae courts because he considered himself above them all, requiring his father to seek an alliance with a noble bride to smooth over the feathers he'd ruffled.

"No, of course not," I stammered, hating that I had to make a liar of myself to appease him. "I'm just surprised. None of the healers have been able to find one."

"I have sources," he sneered, his fingers still digging firmly into my arm. "I'm a powerful man, and if you were smart, you would take my offer. It would be a shame if your mother died because you couldn't make up your mind."

My blood ran cold as his words sank in. Was that a threat? It certainly sounded like one.

As if he had caught a glimpse of his ugliness in my eyes, his scowl disappeared and his beatific smile returned as he let me go and took a step back. "Consider my offer. It won't last forever, and any other woman in your position would kill for it. Isn't that right, Kerala?"

He got my friend's name wrong as he glanced over at her, but she dipped her head in agreement anyway as she broke her frozen pose, her shoulders as stiff as her tone. "Yes, Your Highness."

With a smirk, he disappeared out the door, and I slammed my palm down onto the countertop in frustration. "If he were any more full of himself, he wouldn't fit through that door anymore."

Keerla rolled her neck to ease the sore muscles. "Do you really think he knows how to cure your mother?"

If Tarron truly had the cure, and I wasn't at all convinced he did, I would find a way to get it *without* selling my soul. "I have an idea how I can find out for sure, but I'll need your help."

Chapter Three

~Felix~

The drive to the Vermillion pack land took a lot less time than the recent trek I made to the Ravenstone pack. A dirt road wound through dense forest, sunlight filtering through the leaves in dappled patches, until the Vermillion pack's boundary came into view.

Unlike our pack, which looked and operated much like a modern human town, the Vermillion wolves stuck to a more simple, traditional way of life. Their remote location had no electricity and only a basic system of running water, fed from rainwater and a nearby lake. The Alpha had a satellite phone, the one we'd spoken to him on earlier, but aside from that, technology was sparse. Generally, they lived the way werewolves had lived more than a century earlier. The wolves I'd spoken to on my previous visits seemed content with their simpler way of life but I couldn't imagine living without a fridge or a hot shower.

To each their own, I supposed.

With no formal border crossing, I simply pulled over after passing the large 'keep out' sign along the dirt road and waited for their border guards to arrive. Leaves rustled in the wind and I turned my face to the open window to drink in the fresh air. It didn't take long for three wolves to appear, shifting into three bulky men as they approached my truck.

"Beta Felix from the Crimsontooth pack," I introduced myself, holding up my hands so they could see I was unarmed. "Your Alpha's expecting me."

After confirming that with their superior, they let me go, though one of them ran after me in his wolf form, following my truck until I reached the small town at the centre of the pack land. They were taking security seriously which, in light of the recent thefts, could only be a good thing.

"Beta Felix." Alpha Marcus came over to greet me as soon as I hopped out of my truck. "Thanks for taking the time to come and help us out."

I shook his outstretched hand, giving him a warm smile. Roughly the same age as my own father, he always reminded me of a gruff uncle, someone not prone to shows of emotion but with a good heart underneath the cold exterior. "We'll see how much help I can be. Let's start off by looking at where your weapons are kept."

He took me to a concrete shed just outside the town, one of the few buildings on their land not made from the wood of the trees that grew all around us. Two men stood outside, keeping watch, and the Alpha drew a set of keys from his pocket to open the heavy door. Inside, steps led down into an underground vault where guns, knives, and crossbows were arranged on neat, ordered shelves. The air grew cooler as we descended, the concrete walls pressing in around us, and our footsteps echoed in the narrow corridor. A faint metallic scent hung in the air.

"We keep a strict inventory," the Alpha told me as I looked around the well-stocked storeroom. "It's checked every week. That's how we noticed things were missing."

"Who has a key besides you?"

"Only my head of security, Graham. He's on patrol right now but he'll meet us at the pack house later."

Slowly, I circled the room, looking for any other means of entry. There were no windows and no cracks or other flaws in the concrete walls. The only door in and out was the one we came in through.

"Were the guards always posted outside?"

"No," he admitted. "We added extra security once we realized the weapons store had been targeted. Up until now, the locks have been enough to keep anyone else out."

The guards would add an additional layer to get through, but getting past guards wasn't impossible. Anywhere else, I would have asked if they had security cameras inside the facility but I couldn't see any and, given the pack's general aversion to technology, it seemed unlikely.

"So, someone could have gotten in and out without being seen if they picked the lock or had a key," I summed up.

"The door was still locked when we discovered the theft," Alpha Marcus said. "If they picked it, they wouldn't have been able to lock it behind themselves."

That suggested access to a key, supporting Vaughan's theory about it being an inside job, but I still hadn't ruled out a more supernatural explanation.

"Alright, so they had a key or they were some kind of creature who's able to move through solid concrete. What exactly did they take?"

"A few knives, some arrows, and some bullets."

Huh. Looking around at the arsenal, that seemed like a waste of all the effort it would have taken to create the diversion and sneak inside. "They didn't touch the guns or the crossbows?"

Alpha Marcus shook his head. "No. Those are all accounted for."

"Why would someone take the bullets and not a gun, or the arrows without a bow?" I wondered out loud.

"They might already have weapons of their own and only need the ammunition," the Alpha suggested.

I mulled that over for a few seconds but it didn't feel right to me. "Even if they do, why not take more while they're here?"

"Easier to conceal the smaller items?"

"Perhaps."

That only made sense if the person figured they would be seen, which pointed more to someone within the pack being the culprit than someone who could teleport or make themselves invisible. Since I didn't want to accuse any of the Vermillion pack members without some actual proof, I kept those thoughts to myself.

Bending down, I took a closer look at the drawers where the bullets were kept, looking for anything out of the ordinary. No dust covered any of the surfaces, suggesting a recent cleaning. "I'm guessing you didn't find any physical evidence left behind?"

"Nothing," he confirmed.

"No fingerprints?"

"We aren't set up to test for things like that."

The lack of technology would certainly make an investigation more of a challenge, but I still had some other ideas. "What about unusual scents? A lingering sourness or sweetness in the air? Different coloured dust?"

Supernatural creatures left behind unique signatures if you knew what to look for. I knew several of them and Calista would probably know even more if I checked with her.

The Alpha shook his head again. "No, but I did notice one thing. A few arrows were taken out of each of these cases." He pointed at two of the containers where the crossbow arrows were stored. "Just two or three from each one, like they thought it wouldn't be noticed, but none were taken out of the third one."

Intrigued, I went over to the container to take a closer look. "What's the difference between them?"

"It'll sound stupid, but we keep a flint arrowhead in that one."

My pulse quickened but I did my best to keep a neutral expression. That didn't sound stupid to me at all if it were for the reason I suspected. "Why do you do that?"

The older man shrugged. "Superstition, I suppose. An old tradition. My grandfather always insisted on keeping one among the arrows, but I don't know why."

Unlike him, I had a pretty good idea why. European folklore suggested that including a flint arrowhead among the others would protect the weapons from interference by elves or fairies. A lot of that folk knowledge had been passed down with the reasons and meaning behind it becoming muddled until people considered it superstition and nothing more. If the flint arrowhead deterred the thief, it narrowed down the list of potential species of interest significantly.

Unfortunately, my knowledge of the fae realm was pretty limited. My mother used to read me stories about the fae when I was a boy and one pretty little red-haired fairy in the illustrations always caught my attention. I looked for her on every page and usually found her hiding in the background. The memory made me smile, but I'd never imagined I would actually encounter an elf or fairy in real life. Their world existed in parallel to ours with its own rules and laws, and crossing between realms was a rarity.

A consultation with Calista would definitely be required, and maybe I should place a call to Savannah's mate, Jasper, as well. As a detective, he might be able to help with the alternative possibility that we were looking for a perpetrator amongst the pack.

As I followed Alpha Marcus to the pack house to get settled in, the number of questions still unanswered left me with the feeling I'd only begun to scratch the surface of this mystery, and a lingering excitement about the possibility of dealing with a species I'd never encountered before, no matter how dangerous they might be.

CHAPTER FOUR

Gasping, I stumbled against the heavy kitchen counter, gripping it tight as if I needed the support. "What's wrong, Lina?" Keerla asked, right on cue.

With the food all prepared, we'd agreed I would feign dizziness as an excuse to leave the kitchen and account for my absence among the other staff.

"I don't know." My hands rubbed at my temples. "I'm sure it's nothing, I just..."

Stumbling again, I nearly hit the floor, but Keerla caught me just in time. "You need to lie down," she instructed firmly. "We can handle the serving without you, can't we?"

She nudged the nearest server, a lanky young man named Pavla who blushed every time she looked his way, and he readily agreed. "Of course, Keerla. We'll manage, won't we?"

The other servers all mumbled their agreement, more focused on getting through the meal without earning any criticism from the royal family than concerned about my well-being. The kitchen's clatter faded as Keerla helped me to the door. Once we were out of sight, I straightened up and she gave me an encouraging pat on the back. "You'll have at least half an hour before they're done eating. Make the most of it."

Whispering my thanks, I darted down the hall and to the narrow servant's stairs that led up to the royal family's bedrooms on the top floor.

As befitting one of the smaller fae kingdoms, Etta's royal residence was modest compared to the grand palaces I'd seen in books, with only two floors and a basement. The kitchen sat in the below-ground level, the dining room on the main floor, and the bedrooms above. The main stairs would be guarded by the security team but the servant's stairs were empty, allowing me to slip into Tarron's room without anyone seeing me.

Being a creature of habit, Tarron had always kept his most valuable possessions in a locked box beneath his bed which I discovered by chance while cleaning his room one day as a girl of eight or nine years. My mother ran the royal kitchen and I acted as her little shadow, pitching in where I could. Normally, my mother tolerated my efforts with good humour, even though they usually hindered her more than helped, but on that day, important guests were expected and she needed to give the meal her full concentration.

Wanting to spare my feelings and still make me feel useful, she suggested I tag along with the servants who cleaned the royal bedrooms instead. Never having been on the top floor of the residence before, I readily agreed.

"Don't touch anything unless we tell you to," the other women warned me, and for a while, I obeyed. I watched in awe as one of them used her magic to eviscerate all the dust in the room. Even I felt cleaner after the wave of her hands.

Not all fairies possessed magic, and not all magic was the same. My mother's gift added a little extra flavour to her food, making everything she made taste better. The kitchen had been a natural fit for her. I didn't share that talent, but I had a little magic of my own, a talent I never told anyone about.

That day, in the royal family's bedrooms, I used it.

Growing bored of the drawn-out process of cleaning the king and queen's rooms, I wandered off on my own, poking in the other doors until I found the high prince's bedroom.

Four years older than me, Tarron never paid me any attention when he passed me in the halls in the servant's areas, and I never spared more than a passing glance for him either. With his pretty clothes, delicate features and lavender eyes, he seemed not quite real to me, an ethereal spirit drifting among the more down-to-earth servants.

If I thought *he* seemed otherworldly, nothing could have prepared me for his bedroom.

My mouth hung open as I stepped into the space. The high ceiling towering above me was the same as in the king and queen's rooms, but descending from it, on pieces of willowy strings, dangled shiny stones glimmering in the sunlight that streamed through the windows. Blues and yellows and reds sparkled, the light dancing around the space until I began to feel I was floating along with them. It felt like being beneath the night sky in the middle of the day, and when my neck got tired of craning up to look, I lay down on the floor to stare up at them without having to strain my head.

I had no idea how long I stayed there, watching the stones twist and twirl above my head, but eventually, I rolled my head to the side and saw the box beneath Tarron's bed. Dark and mysterious-looking, it piqued my curiosity even more than the dancing stones did.

Rolling over, I rested on my stomach on the floor and pulled the box out. The material forming the box was unfamiliar to me, making it look even more important than if it had been made of simple wood. Curiosity overwhelmed me, and I tugged on the lid only to find it locked. That would have stopped most people, but my gift allowed me to go further. Waving my small hand over the lock, it clicked open, and I eagerly pulled the lid up, excited to see what treasures I would find there.

At first glance, I felt only disappointment. The contents seemed to be pieces of paper and a few dried flowers that I didn't recognize. I almost shoved it back under the bed without a closer look until something caught my eye.

A scribbled word, half-covered by another piece of paper, that ended with 'wolf'. Not familiar with the word, I could have ignored it but something urged me on, telling me it could be important. Why I thought that, I had no idea, but I gave in to the feeling, lifting the paper out of the box.

On it, two drawings stood side-by-side, one of a man unlike any I'd seen before. Men in Etta were tall, slender and narrow, like the Etta trees that grew straight to the sky, but this man had broad shoulders, an unusually bulky chest, and bulges in his legs. Next to him was a large animal of some kind, and underneath them both, the cut-off word I had seen earlier: 'werewolf'.

What did it mean? I'd never seen anything like it before, but I stared in fascination, trying to understand it.

"What do you think you're doing?"

Dropping the paper as I jumped in surprise, my head jerked up to find Tarron at the door, his lavender eyes fixed on me in narrowed slits.

"I... um, I... nothing," I stammered, slamming the box shut, waving my hand over the lock to relock it and shoving it back under the bed, as if that would somehow convince him that he hadn't seen what he clearly saw.

Heavy footsteps thundered towards me as he stomped over, pushed me roughly out of the way and pulled the box back out. Tugging on the lid, he found it locked, and he turned to me with anger burning in his eyes and confusion written into the lines of his brow. "How did you open this? Did you take anything?"

"No, I... I didn't open it," I lied weakly. I'd never been a good liar, and under pressure, I choked.

"You little thief," he sneered down at me. "Give it to me. Whatever you took, give it back."

"I didn't take anything!"

In a panic, I tried to race from the room, but with his longer legs, Tarron caught me easily. Hooking my ankle with his foot, he pulled me down and I hit the ground hard, all the breath in my body forced out in one large whoosh. His angry hands patted me down, looking in every crevice of my dress for anything I might have concealed while I tried to curl into a ball to protect myself.

Finally satisfied that I hadn't taken anything, he stepped back, his eyes still dangerously narrow. "Stay out of things that don't concern you," he said, spitting on me once for good measure.

My cheeks burned in humiliation as I ran back down the stairs and out of the residence, through the woods to the small cottage where I lived with my parents. My mother found me there hours later, still hiding beneath my own bed, terrified that I would be punished for my snooping or, worse, that *she* would be.

Tarron never told anyone about that day, as far as I knew, but for years after that, he went out of his way to make my life difficult. When I served him, he always found fault with it. When he broke something around the house, I got blamed.

The years of torment only ended when I came of age and his interest in me shifted. Now, he made my life difficult in different ways with his demands for my devotion to him. Those demands were what drove me back to his room and back to the box beneath his bed. If I could find out what he knew about my mother's condition without giving in to him, I had to take the chance.

I'd seen the box there several times since that first day, whenever I helped to clean his room. The servants never cleaned it, and I certainly never touched it again, but it often moved, suggesting that Tarron himself must still be using it.

That night, I planned to open it again.

The hanging stones from the ceiling disappeared years ago, as Tarron grew older, but his fascination with different materials never diminished. More recently, he kept them in display cabinets around the room, labelled and categorized.

Those didn't interest me, though; the box was my goal.

Pulling it out from beneath the bed as I sat on the floor, I waved my hand over the lock, feeling the familiar tingle through my fingers as my magic worked like a skeleton key to open the mechanism keeping the box sealed. When it clicked, I lifted the lid, holding my breath and praying that I was right. If I were Tarron and had a secret, I would have put it in there. Hopefully, I understood him as well as I thought I did.

Papers still filled the box, but they had been organized into neat files while smaller containers lined the bottom of the box. Flipping through the files, I looked for any mention of illness, medicine or cures. Towards the end of the stack, a singular word caught my eye.

Antidote.

My heart began to pound as I scanned the paper. Most of it was indecipherable ramblings about the effects of terrestrial elements on fae, but one condition sounded eerily like my mother's illness. In the margin of that section, scrawled in uneven handwriting, it read: 'Antidote: silver.'

What the hell was silver?

Setting that page aside, I flipped through the rest of the notes but nothing else seemed to relate to my current predicament. Frowning, I put the papers to one side and began to look through the small containers at the bottom of the box instead. Each one had a small piece of some unfamiliar material in it, with a label describing it. *Mint. Rose. Saffron.* The words meant as little to me as the material itself.

However, when I opened the second-to-last container, my breath hitched. *Silver*, the label said, nestled beneath a small piece of metal, almost cylindrical in shape, rounded at one end.

It might not be what I needed, but I had no better ideas at that moment, so I grabbed the container and the piece of paper, returning everything else to the box and relocking it before shoving it back beneath the bed.

No sooner had I scrambled to my feet than I heard voices outside the door and I froze, terror sending ice through my veins. If someone found me there, I would be in more trouble than I could imagine. In desperation, I searched the room for a hiding place, and when the door to Tarron's room began to open, I dashed for the only spot I could think of: under the bed, right next to the box.

A woman's giggle filled the air as the door closed. "You don't waste any time, Your Highness."

"Why should I?" Tarron's arrogant drawl responded. "If you're to be my wife, we need to make sure we're compatible."

The bed creaked and I covered my mouth with my hand, trying to stop any stray noise from escaping as I realized what they were about to do. Though I'd never had sex myself, my mother made sure I understood the basics of it, and my suspicions were soon confirmed as pieces of clothing began to fall on the floor on either side of the bed. My heart thundered in my chest as I pressed myself into the shadows beneath the bed, every creak of the bed frame above me sending a jolt of fear through my body.

"Oh," the woman breathed, right on top of me. "You're so hard."

"I have been for hours," Tarron muttered before I heard her gasp and him groan.

The bed above me began to bounce in a steady rhythm as I tried not to listen, or even breathe. The noises emanating from above me sounded unnatural and unpleasant, grunts and the sound of flesh hitting flesh. Closing my eyes, I tried to pretend I was anywhere else, internally reciting the ingredients to some of my mother's favourite recipes to keep my mind occupied.

After a couple of minutes of exertion, the movement above me stilled. Tarron groaned again, loudly, and called out a name.

"Evalina."

My entire body stiffened. Horror roared in my ears, drowning out everything else. Any second, I expected a firm hand to seize me and pull me from my hiding place.

No one touched me, though, and above me, the woman stuttered out a confused, choked whimper. "Th-that's n-not my name, Your Highness."

"What?" he demanded, his feet appearing on the floor next to me as he bent down to pick up his discarded clothes. One stray glance would have given me away, but luck was on my side. He seemed to be in a hurry.

"You... you called me Evalina," she said, her slender feet also appearing from the bed above. "That's not my name. And I don't think we're finished yet. I didn't come."

"Oh." He sounded genuinely surprised for a second before letting out a soft huff. "I guess we're *not* compatible then."

His feet disappeared, heading back towards the door, while the woman's hands appeared in my line of vision, snatching her dress from the floor. "Selfish Etta bastard," she muttered as she slipped her shoes back on and followed him out the door.

I lay there another couple of minutes, making sure they had truly gone and wouldn't be back for something they forgot before sliding out from under the bed with my hard-won prizes. I couldn't be sure if they would save my mother, but one thing had become even clearer than before: indebting myself to Tarron was a risk I couldn't afford to take.

Chapter Five

~Felix~

The Vermillion wolves gave me curious looks as I wandered through their town, waving my cell phone in the air like an idiot to try to get a signal. No such luck, unfortunately. The pack's remote location deep in the forested Rocky Mountain foothills would make gathering the information I needed a bit more of a challenge, but I never let a setback hold me down for long. Rather than wasting time on frustration, I headed back to the pack house and asked to borrow Alpha Marcus' satellite phone.

The Alpha handed me not only the phone but his office as well, a wood-paneled relic of the 1970s that reeked of incense. Who knew anyone still used so much patchouli?

Turning in my chair to face the window and the darkening world outside, I called Jasper up in the Ravenstone pack first.

"Hello?" he answered cautiously, obviously not recognizing the number.

"Jasper, it's Felix. How are you? How's Sav?"

He immediately relaxed at the sound of my voice. "Oh, hey. We're fine. She's off taking the pack by storm at the moment."

We both chuckled, knowing his words probably weren't much of an exaggeration.

"Where are you calling from?" he asked.

I quickly filled him in on my current location and the reason for my visit. "I'm a Beta, not a detective, but I'd still like to help," I finished with a laugh. "What would you do in my shoes?"

"How deep do you want to go?" he replied good-naturedly. "I have years of study and experience I can share."

As fascinating as that sounded, I wanted to make some progress before the trail got too cold. "Let's stick to the shallow end for now. Don't want to drown right out of the gate."

"In that case, remember the ABCs: assume nothing, believe nothing, check everything. For instance, the Alpha told you there are only two copies of that key, right? But could someone have duplicated it somehow? Or taken it from wherever the Alpha keeps it and returned it without his knowledge? Identify all the possible scenarios, not just the obvious ones. At the same time, focus on building your suspect list. Not just who has something to gain from stealing the items but who might benefit from the Alpha being distracted by this investigation. The theft might not be the end game, especially if they're not stealing anything high-value. If Vaughan's right and it's an inside job, how did the alert get triggered? A pack member can't trigger it, so they would have had to recruit someone external to help or tampered with the system somehow. Make sure all the pieces fit before you jump to any conclusions."

Damn. I hadn't even thought of half those questions. It felt like trying to untangle a web without knowing where it started or what kind of spider spun it."You want to take a road trip and come help me with this?" I asked him, only half-joking.

He laughed again. "We're a little busy up here right now with our new Alpha and Beta getting settled, but call me anytime you get stuck and want to talk things through with someone."

Calling him 'anytime' would be a lot easier if my phone worked, but I'd figure it out somehow. "Thanks, Jasper. Give Sav my best."

"Will do. Good luck."

After scribbling down a few notes to make sure I didn't forget everything he just told me, I called home.

"Did you miss me already?" Vaughan asked after I got put through to him.

"Who is this guy making jokes and what did you do with my grumpy best friend?" I teased him. "If I knew you just needed to get laid, I'd have gone in search of your mate years ago."

"You're just jealous."

He wasn't entirely wrong but that had nothing to do with why I called. "Speaking of your mate, you think I can borrow her brain for a few minutes? Unless her mouth is currently occupied?"

Vaughan chuckled. Actually *chuckled.* "She's free at the moment, but don't go giving me ideas for later."

"Like you need any encouragement from me."

He gave a grunt of agreement before giving the phone to Calista, who must have been right beside him.

"Felix."

Her mildly disapproving tone made it pretty clear she'd heard every word of that exchange and I rubbed at the back of my neck sheepishly. "Hey, Calista. Would you believe I was temporarily possessed for the last minute or so?"

"By the spirit of an adolescent boy?"

Busted. Vaughan's laugh in the background made it impossible for me to keep a straight face, but I tried to sound sincere as I offered a simple apology. "Sorry."

She exhaled a small laugh too, confirming she hadn't taken any real offense. "Don't worry about it. What do you need?"

Getting down to business, I told her about my visit to the weapons store and about the flint arrowhead in the container that remained untouched. Her sharp inhale confirmed that she thought it could be just as significant as I did. "I'm thinking elves or fairies, but I'm sure you know a lot more about it."

"I've dealt with fae a couple of times," she confirmed. "They're slippery to track down. I agree that the flint points in that direction, and so does the invisibility. To most people, fairies are invisible."

"Most people?" I repeated curiously. "Not all?"

"No. If someone from our world travels to the fae realm, they're able to see all fae creatures when they return. *If* they return. Many don't ever come back."

"So, I could literally be looking for an invisible thief," I surmised. "That could make this tricky. How do I get myself to the fae realm to get this super-special fae vision?"

She laughed at my tongue-in-cheek question that, just like with Jasper, hadn't entirely been a joke. "Generally, you can only get there in the company of a fairy or elf."

"Which... I can't see."

"Right."

I blew out a long breath. "Sounds perfectly straightforward."

"Actually, it's not as impossible as it may seem. If you think your thief will come back, you can set a trap for them. From there, you can put a tracker on them and follow them."

My eyebrows raised in curiosity, the movement reflected in the glass of the window in front of me. Calista had lost me so I tried to take things one step at a time, questioning everything like Jasper suggested.

"What do you mean 'if' they come back?"

"Well, it depends what they wanted the weapons for," she elaborated. "Maybe they already got what they needed and won't return again. Honestly, I'm a little puzzled about what you said they took. Fae don't usually use guns, so why would they want bullets?"

That seemed odd to me too. "Maybe it's not the bullets they wanted? Maybe there's something that..."

I trailed off as a new thought came into my head. *Assume nothing*, Jasper said, but we'd all been assuming the thief took the ammunition and weapons to use *as* weapons. Maybe that wasn't right. Maybe they wanted them for another reason entirely.

"Would fae have any use for silver?" I asked.

"Silver?" Calista repeated thoughtfully. "I'm not sure, but generally, elements are different between the two worlds. They probably don't have it in their realm, so if they needed it for some reason, they'd probably have to come here and take it. Were all the things that were taken made of silver?"

"I think so."

I'd have to ask Alpha Marcus to confirm, but generally, werewolf weapons would contain at least a small amount of silver since it would do the most harm if another pack attacked. Silver could be far more deadly to werewolves than just about any other type of weapon. Bullets, arrows and knives, all the things that were taken from the weapons store, more than likely contained silver.

That felt like my most solid lead so far, so I moved on to the next part of what she said. "How do I set a trap?"

"It's a common item used against a lot of supernatural species," Calista told me. "Want to guess?"

"A pop quiz, huh?" I was always up for a challenge. "Does it have to do with the flint?"

"No. They avoid flint, as you already know, but it won't trap them."

"Not silver, I'm guessing, since they're stealing it," I mused. "Holy water? Garlic?"

"No, but you're getting closer with food."

"Salt?" I guessed, thinking back to the countless hours I'd spent lurking on supernatural forums over the years. Salt worked on demons, ghosts, and hellhounds, so why not fairies?

"Bingo." Calista's approval pleased me as much as a child getting praised by a parent. "Sugar also works. If salt or sugar is spilled in front of a fairy, they have to count every grain of it. It's a compulsion. While they're counting, you can place a tracker on them and follow them back to their fairy ring or whatever space they're using as a portal between realms. Just make sure that when you're in their realm, you don't eat or drink anything or you'll end up stuck there forever."

"Do you really believe all of this?" Vaughan asked in the background. "It sounds made up."

"You can literally change into a wolf," she answered him, completely deadpan. "I don't think you can talk."

I didn't have any doubt about the accuracy of her information, but I did still have another question. "What do I use as a tracker?"

"There are several options, but I've used paint. Glow-in-the-dark paint, specifically."

I didn't expect that answer. "Come again?"

Patiently, Calista explained it to me. "Even though you can't see them, the elf or fairy will have a physical form. If you run into them, you'll feel them. Splatter some paint in the direction of the salt when they start counting the grains, and that paint will stick to them and stay visible to you. Glow-in-the-dark paint works better in case it's nighttime when they move again. Remember how you said the weapons would seem to be walking by themselves if someone invisible picked them up? You weren't wrong. It will literally look like that, like specks of paint moving on their own in the air."

Well, now I really hoped that would happen because I would love to see it. "Have you been to the fae realm?"

"No." Her voice went quieter as she answered. "My father said it would be too dangerous for me, but he went. I saw him disappear into the fairy ring and come back again. That's how I know this will work."

A second later, Vaughan came back on the line. "Listen, Felix, if this is really what's happening, I don't want you going anywhere on your own. Find out if that's what you're dealing with, and if it is one of these fae, Calista and I will come for backup."

The genuine concern in his voice, even if he didn't fully buy into the fae theory, warmed my heart. We might give each other a hard time, but when push came to shove, we were still friends above all. "I understand. Let me do some more investigation and I'll get back to you."

We hung up and I went to join the Vermillion pack leadership for dinner, my head swimming with all the new information I'd learned and the enticing possibility of visiting a whole new world. The thrill of discovery overruled any potential danger, and I'd be very disappointed if there turned out to be a non-supernatural explanation for all of this.

Chapter Six

~Evalina~

The items I took from Tarron's box seemed to burn a hole through my dress, their weight pressing against my skin as if they carried the prince's wrath with them. I did my best to ignore it as I returned to the kitchen to clean up following the evening's meal. Tarron and his 'guest' must have slipped away during dinner because the servers were just taking dessert up when I returned.

"Did you get anything?" Keerla whispered, keeping her voice low enough that it couldn't be heard by anyone else over the hum of activity in the room.

"Maybe," I whispered back, subconsciously clutching at my dress where the hidden items lay. They might be nothing or they might be exactly what I needed. "I'll check my father's library when I get home to find out for sure."

It took another hour to finish my work for the evening, every second dragging with the heavy weight of the stolen items brushing against my skin. Every unexpected noise sent a jolt through my chest, my heart pounding so hard I feared it might give me away. What if Tarron discovered something missing? If I were found to have stolen from the high prince, justice would be swift and brutal.

It always was in Etta.

At last, the kitchen was tidy with everything ready to start on the next day's breakfast first thing in the morning. Pavla lingered outside the kitchen like a shadow, straightening to attention when we appeared.

"May I escort you ladies home tonight?"

"Do you think we'll get lost?" Keerla demanded, and a deep red stain crept up the young man's cheeks.

I hid my smile, understanding the situation clearly even if Keerla didn't yet see it. He hadn't been waiting there for *my* benefit. "That would be nice, Pavla. Thank you."

Outside the servant's entrance, blue stars dotted the inky sky above us. Mindful of nighttime dangers, we walked briskly down the well-trodden path through the trees that led to the servant's quarters. A semi-circle of small huts with grass roofs appeared before us, the first of which belonged to me. I waved Pavla and Keerla goodbye before opening the door of the small house I shared with my mother.

"Mama? I'm home," I called out softly as I entered, not knowing whether or not she'd be awake. Lately, she slept more and more.

"Lina?" A quiet croak of my name answered me. "Help." The one word sent a chill down my spine, and I bolted into her room, my heart pounding as I found her crumpled at the foot of her bed. A pale light from the window cast shadows over her frail form, making her look even smaller than usual.

"What happened?" I gasped as I bent down to help her up.

"I tried to... go... fell."

Even speaking sounded too difficult for her, and I checked her body for injuries after lying her back in the soft bed, thankfully coming up blank. "You know you shouldn't get up on your own. How long were you down there?"

She shrugged, which I knew meant it had been longer than she wanted to admit. While I'd been lying beneath Tarron's bed, my mother had probably also been on the floor in an unintentional parallel.

"I'm going to make you a drink and some food. Stay here."

"No. You work... all day. Rest."

"*You* need to rest," I argued, resisting the tears that threatened to overtake me every time I took in the sight of my strong, capable mother reduced to this helpless shell of a woman. My chest tightened with helpless frustration but my voice remained steady. "I'll be right back."

In the kitchen, I prepared a broth and put it over the fire to warm up before slipping into the small nook that contained my father's books. A teacher with a fascination for other realms and creatures, he had the biggest collection of books I'd ever seen outside of the library at the royal residence. When he died, my mother left them in place. The nook still smelled faintly of aged parchment and ink, as if he'd only stepped away a moment ago.

Luckily, I knew exactly which one to look for: *A guide to terrestrial materials.* One of my father's favourites. With the thick volume in hand, I flipped through the pages of elements, listed in alphabetical order, until I came to the page titled *Silver.* The word leapt out at me like a beacon, and I skimmed the rest of the text eagerly, my index finger underlining the words as I went so I didn't miss anything.

Silver is a light-grey element found in the terrestrial realm's crust. Often impure, it can be refined by a simple dismelding process. Humans use it for currency and decoration. It is harmful to several other species, including genies, gorgons and various shifters, including werewolves.

Old memories stirred at the sight of the word 'werewolves'. Though years had passed, I could still vividly remember the drawing I found in Tarron's box as a child and the strange fascination I felt towards it.

At the moment, though, my focus needed to be on my mother, so I pulled out the small container and page I'd spirited out of Tarron's box that evening. With more time to peruse it, I read through the information about the condition that bore significant similarities to my mother's illness, and how silver might reverse it.

Boil twenty plins of pure silver and add to a standard healing potion. Upon drinking it, the patient will make a full recovery.

My heart leapt at the possibility. With trembling hands, I opened the container holding the small, grey cylinder. If it were pure, it should give me about twenty plins when melted, plins being a standard unit of measurement that I used in my cooking, but I remembered that my father's book said the material was more than often not pure.

It also said I could refine it by dismelding, which could easily be done over the fire. Returning to the kitchen, I added a second pot next to the broth that had almost begun to bubble and set the pot's control to 'dismeld'. While that began to work, I filled a bowl of broth for my mother, along with a glass of fresh Etta berry juice. By the time I returned from taking them to her, the dismelding had finished.

In dismay, I looked down into the pot at the results. The cylinder had melted and separated into small puddles of liquid, but the light-grey one, which I assumed to be the silver, was only a tiny fragment of it, perhaps two plin's worth at best.

I would need a lot more silver.

Pouring the precious material into a vial, I went back to my father's book. Perhaps it had some further information on where to find it that didn't involve breaking into Tarron's room again. Eagerly, I flipped the page, but the next page went on to a new material. In frustration, I turned another page, and another, hoping that somehow, more would appear, but that one page seemed to be all there was.

With a sigh, I closed the book, but as I did, a folded page sticking out of the front of the book caught my eye. The heavy creases suggested it had been folded and unfolded many times before. When I unfolded it, a small, hand-drawn map appeared with notes in my father's handwriting. My heart panged at the familiar sight and the weight of his loss bore down on me again, heavy and solid compared to the fragility of the worn paper in my hands.

Pushing that pain down, I focused on the map. The royal residence, clearly recognizable, sat near the middle and our own house had also been drawn onto it. Down a path, away from the residence, my father had marked a small circle.

Terrestrial portal, it said. *Danger: werewolves.*

My pulse quickened once again. Did the map really show a portal to the terrestrial realm? What danger did the werewolves pose? Would there be silver there too?

It might be a long shot, but at that point, my options appeared to be dwindling. Tarron might have more silver but I couldn't ask him for help, not if I wanted to keep the small amount of freedom that I had.

If I wanted to cure my mother on my own, I would have to take another risk. That night, once my mother had gone to sleep, I would see what lay on the other side of that portal, no matter the danger.

Chapter Seven

~Felix~

Several hours later, with theories and questions simmering in the back of my mind, I sank into the guest bed in the Vermillion pack house. My body begged for rest even if my brain wouldn't stop spinning. At least the mattress wasn't straw; it seemed the Alpha did allow for *some* modern luxuries.

The quiet didn't last long, however. Before I could even start to drift off, a sharp knock sounded at my door.

"Beta Felix?" came a muffled voice from the other side. "The border alert has been triggered again."

Excitement and frustration spurred me back out of bed and I threw a t-shirt on to go with the flannel pants I wore to bed. After shoving my feet into some sneakers, I followed the pack member downstairs. "I'm heading to the weapons store. Bring me some salt."

"Salt?" the man repeated, as if he couldn't be sure he heard me correctly.

"Or sugar," I added. "Either will do."

I dashed out the door before he could ask any further questions.

The Alpha had beaten me to the weapons store, his silhouette stiff under the pale moonlight. The earthy scent of fallen leaves hung in the air, and though his grim expression shifted as I approached, the tension in his shoulders and the clench of his jaw betrayed his frustration.

"My men have been here the whole time," he told me as I came to a stop in front of him. "No one has been in or out, they swear to it."

"Have you been inside to check if anything else has been taken?"

"Not yet. I came over as soon as I got the alert, and it would take even the fastest creatures longer than that to get from the border to the weapons store. If they're coming back here, they haven't arrived yet."

Unless one of the pack members was behind it and they'd been there all along, I added in my head. Although, if that were the case, he or she would be aware of the extra security the Alpha had ordered around the building. How did they plan to get past it?

Too many things still didn't make sense.

The man from earlier came running up behind me, holding out a small bag. "Here's the salt you asked for, Beta."

I turned to thank him, the words on the tip of my tongue, when my nose twitched and every other thought fled my mind.

Crisp apple with a hint of caramel drifted over to me from somewhere out of sight, rich and tantalizing. My mouth watered, and I had to swallow down the extra saliva as I inhaled more deeply.

What the hell is that? I asked my wolf, knowing his sense of smell was even more refined than mine. Kai and I were opposites in many ways, him being introverted and stoic, speaking only when necessary, whereas people often said they couldn't get me to shut up.

Kai growled low in my head before saying the last word I expected him to say: *Mate.*

The word rang in my head, disbelief warring with a burst of excitement. *What?*

I spun around, searching the shadows for any sign of her. Moonlight filtered through the trees, blending with the cold beams of the guards' flashlights. My wolf-enhanced eyes scanned every flicker of movement, every rustle in the dark. If there were anyone lurking in the shadows, I should have been able to see them.

I didn't see anything.

"Beta?" the man who brought me the salt asked in confusion, still holding onto the bag that I hadn't taken from him.

"Do you see something?" the Alpha asked, also scanning our surroundings.

"No, but I... I smelled something," I forced out. "Do you smell it?"

Noses all around me wrinkled, each of the men inhaling deeply.

"I don't smell anything out of the ordinary," the Alpha replied, and all the others murmured in agreement.

*They don't smell her because she's not **their** mate,* Kai pointed out.

You're sure about this? I pressed him. *Where is she?*

I don't know where she is, but I'm sure. Go find her.

The need to do so nearly overwhelmed me. I'd heard about the strength of the mate bond, watched Vaughan and Savannah both struggle against it, and even so, I never imagined it would consume me the way it did. I could barely think straight.

"I'm going to check the area," I offered to the Vermillion pack members. "Keep watching the door."

"The salt?" the man asked from behind me again, but I ignored him. At that moment, finding my mate trumped all my other concerns.

Why is she hiding? I asked Kai as we headed into the trees, sniffing the air to try to follow the scent. It seemed fainter that way, so I turned around and headed in the other direction instead.

Maybe she's shy? She doesn't know us. She might even be afraid.

The idea of my mate being afraid to meet me brought out a protective instinct I'd never experienced with such intensity before. *She never needs to be afraid of me.*

I know that but she might not, he answered wryly.

The scent grew stronger as I headed deeper into the trees, wrapping around me like an invisible tether. Each breath filled my lungs with its richness. It seemed to come from everywhere and nowhere at once, until it felt as though she were standing right on top of me

"Hello?" I called out into the night, hoping to draw her out since I couldn't seem to find her.

No answer came. Tiny animals scurried along the forest floor, the wind rustled through the trees, and in the distance, a coyote howled. But from my mate, from the woman who must have been close enough to hear me if not see me? Not a single sound.

I tried again, doing my best to cajole her even though I still didn't know where to look.

"My name is Felix. I'm a visitor to this pack. What's your name?"

Again, I heard nothing, but the fine hair on the back of my neck seemed to tingle, as though someone stood right behind me. *Watching* me. I spun around, hoping to spot her at last, but I only found empty air. Why wouldn't she answer?

"Don't be afraid. I only want to talk to you."

That might have been a white lie, but I would settle for talking, at least to start. Her silence unnerved me like nothing else ever had. Bushes rustled to my left, and my head snapped toward the sound. Branches rippled like a wave, and my heart leapt. Someone had been there. Sprinting after the movement, I pushed through the undergrowth, hope and desperation pounding in my chest.

"Stop. Wait. Please."

I called out the words in short bursts, desperation starting to claw at me as I emerged on the other side of the tangle of bushes and found my-self in an empty clearing. The scent began to fade. Rather than heading in another direction that I could follow, it dissipated completely.

"No. No!"

The word tore from my throat as I spun in frantic circles, sniffing in vain for a trace of her scent.

Where did she go? I asked Kai even though I didn't really expect an answer.

I don't know. His helpless reply made me feel even worse. *There must be a tunnel or something here.*

A tunnel in the middle of the forest? Unlikely, but I didn't have any other ideas. Had it all been some kind of trick to distract me? Were there supernatural creatures that could mimic the mate bond?

I'll come back and investigate in the daylight, I offered to appease my wolf. *You want to mark the spot so we can find it again?*

After stripping off my clothes, I shifted into my wolf form and let Kai mark the bushes, the scent making it distinct enough that we could locate it in the morning. When I had dressed again, I took one last look around the empty space. There was no one there, and an ache settled deep in my chest. Had she ever really been there at all?

Chapter Eight

~Evalina~

My breath came in short spurts as I inhaled the familiar scent of the Etta trees, safely back in my own realm. The night sky still glimmered with blue stars, but although they remained unchanged, the world around me felt subtly, irrevocably altered.

Or perhaps something inside *me* had changed.

Common lore suggested that none of the terrestrial beings should have been able to see me. Only those who had been to the fae realm could see its inhabitants, and yet, the towering, light-haired man seemed to notice me anyway. It defied everything I'd been told, everything I thought I knew, but the way his piercing blue eyes sought me through the darkness left no doubt that I hadn't gone unnoticed.

I barely had a chance to register the tingling sensation that raced through my body when I saw him, barely had a chance to take in the broad, muscular bulk of him and the way his tight shirt seemed to cling to him as if it had been painted on, before he began to head in my direction. In a panic, I ran, and he ran after me. His voice, when he spoke, was somehow both gruff and kind, vibrating deep within me as he told me his name.

Felix.

A name I'd never heard before, it sounded exotic, dangerous, and somehow inviting.

Nothing about him was like any man I'd ever seen before, and yet, everything about him felt familiar. When he said I didn't need to fear him, something deep within my soul believed it. Despite being a total stranger, something urged me to trust him. The sound of his voice lingered in the air like an unfinished melody, resonating in a part of me I hadn't realized was empty.

I had no words to fully explain it and nothing I could compare it to.

"Evalina."

The soft voice in the darkness nearly made me jump out of my skin. Heart pounding, I turned to find Tarron's lavender eyes fixed on me.

"What are you doing here?"

His gaze flicked between me and the portal entrance, making it clear he already had it figured out. He must know about the portal and he must have guessed where I'd been.

"Your Highness." I fought to keep my panic hidden beneath the practiced bow, knowing how much Tarron would relish my fear if he sensed it. "I'm gathering some heffa seeds for my mother. They help her sleep."

The lie that sprang to mind slipped off my tongue easily enough, but Tarron didn't buy it for a second. His voice turned sharp, his lips curling into a faint sneer. "In the dark? Even the most skilled forager wouldn't see the pods in this darkness."

"My work keeps me in the royal residence all day," I said, and those words carried the ring of truth. "This is the only time I have."

"Hmmm." His noncommittal hum suggested he still didn't believe me and his gaze sharpened as he took a step closer. The scent of Etta blossoms intensified as his shadow swallowed the space between us. "Have you found any seeds?"

He gestured down to the pouch at my side, the one I took with me to keep any silver I discovered in the terrestrial realm. Since I didn't have a chance to find any with Felix chasing me, the pouch remained empty, so at least Tarron wouldn't find anything there to incriminate me further.

Visiting the terrestrial realm without the royal family's permission went against our laws and, depending on the circumstances, could be met with the harshest of punishments. I only had to look at my father to know that was true. Most people didn't have any desire to leave our beautiful home for the dirty, messy alternative reality that lay on the other side of the portals anyway, so it didn't usually pose a problem. However, if Tarron found any proof that I'd been there beyond the suspicions he already had, it would give him one more thing to hold over me.

I couldn't let that happen.

"Not yet, unfortunately." My fingers trembled as I turned the pouch inside out, silently willing him to believe me. "I better get back to my search if I want to get any sleep tonight. Good night, Your Highness."

I bowed to him again before turning to go, but at the last second, something else crossed my mind and I found myself turning back again, even as my self-preservation screamed at me to get as far away from him as possible.

"What are *you* doing here?"

In the dim light, I almost missed the way his eyes widened in surprise and, unless I was much mistaken, a touch of guilt. "I... uh..."

He struggled for an answer, obviously not as accustomed to thinking on his feet as I was. He rarely had any reason to lie. When his word was law, he could say whatever he wanted, so why not speak the truth?

But at that moment, whatever he had come out to the forest for, he didn't want me to know about it.

"I need some quiet to clear my head," he finally settled on for an answer. "The woman I met tonight proved... disappointing. She can't give me what I need."

Memories of the grunting and panting as the bed creaked above me flooded my mind. Apparently, she'd been good enough to give him *that*. Tarron used her, just as he wanted to use me.

I pushed away the thoughts of him saying my name while inside the other woman, still not sure what it meant and not sure I wanted to know. Besides, I felt pretty certain he hadn't come out for a walk to 'clear his head'. He had a different motive, and though I knew I should let it go, I wanted to find out what it was.

"I'm sorry to hear that," I told him, infusing my voice with as much sympathy as I could muster. "I'll leave you alone, then."

With a nod of acknowledgement, he dismissed me, and I turned once again to go. That time, I did walk away, but I didn't go far. Thick bushes concealed me as I circled back around to watch him from another angle.

As I suspected, Tarron stayed where he was, waiting until he thought he was completely alone. Glancing over his shoulders to make sure no one else lurked in the night forest, he stepped forward. A faint hum echoed as the portal shimmered to life, the air around it rippling like water disturbed by an unseen stone, and Tarron vanished.

A chill shivered down my spine, though I didn't know exactly why. Given the items in the box under his bed, perhaps it shouldn't have surprised me that our high prince was making clandestine trips to the terrestrial realm, but the way he lied to me and the fact that he waited until he could proceed under the cover of darkness suggested that he didn't want anyone to know about it.

What exactly was he up to?

Part of me itched to go after him and see but I knew that would be unwise. With Tarron on the other side and the possibility of running into the unusual man who'd followed me, returning that night presented too many risks. Bravery was one thing and recklessness another. My questions would have to wait for later, and so would my attempts to find the silver I needed, but when the new day dawned, it would find me ready. My mother's life, and perhaps my own, depended on it.

Chapter Nine

~Felix~

When I returned to the weapons store, the guards and Alpha Marcus were still there, their faces tight with frustration that mirrored my own though for very different reasons

"The alert stopped," the Alpha told me. "Whoever set it off has left our land, and as far as we know, they didn't get anything this time."

Compared to potentially meeting my mate, the situation with their weapons barely registered as a concern anymore, but I forced myself to feign interest. "Looks like the extra security is paying off. Can I use your phone, Alpha? I'd like to get some backup."

His confusion showed in his face, no doubt wondering why I needed backup when nothing further had been taken, but thankfully, he didn't argue. Together, we returned to the pack house, and I called home to the Crimsontooth pack, waking a grumpy Darius.

"This better be good," our pack's head of security grumbled.

I'd woken up my fair share of people in my time, but Darius sounded particularly unimpressed. It would have made me feel bad if I weren't so focused on my own problems. As Beta, I outranked the Delta, and I pulled that rank now. "I need you at the Vermillion pack. Get here as soon as you can."

His bed creaked in the background as he sat up. "Vaughan cleared this?"

"No," I admitted. "He told me if I needed help, he and Calista would come. They're needed there, though, and to be honest, I'd rather have you."

Calista would be best placed to help with supernatural beings, but we still didn't know for sure what we were dealing with, and when it came to my mate, I needed Darius' tracking abilities more. No one got away from him when he set out to find them. If I wanted to find her, Darius would be my best bet.

"Alright, I'll head out now." He yawned loudly in my ear before signing off. "See you soon."

I returned the phone to Alpha Marcus, letting him know to expect Darius, and was just about to head back to bed when the Alpha's eyes glazed over.

"Another alert," he informed me grimly.

Looked like I wouldn't be getting much sleep that night. "Let's head back out, then. But first, do you have a small tube of paint or something?"

His furrowed brow suggested he thought I'd lost my mind, but he had a staff member bring us one anyway and I shoved it into my pocket before we headed back out again.

For the next hour and a half, we searched the pack's land, looking for any sign of an intruder. Not only did I not see or smell anyone, I didn't see or smell my mate again either. One of the Alpha's men reported that a wolf had marked some bushes, but knowing that was actually *my* scent, I kept my mouth shut.

"Has the intruder left the land yet?" I asked the Alpha when we all reconvened again in front of the weapons store. The guards reported there still hadn't been any activity.

He shook his head. "No. It seems they're still here but we've searched everywhere. I'm starting to think they must be invisible."

The words were a joke to him, but I knew it might be possible. Alternately, it might be someone from his own pack. I still didn't know what to believe.

"We do have another visitor, though," the Alpha added.

He gestured with his head to the space behind me, and I turned to find Darius walking over to us.

"Alpha Marcus." He lowered his head to our host politely before turning to me. "Hey, Felix. Didn't think you'd still be up. What's going on?"

Not wanting to tell him about my mate in public, I stuck to the facts about the intruder and the weapons store.

"Have you been inside to check if anything's missing?" he asked.

"Not yet. That was going to be the next move. And just in case..."

I grabbed the bag of salt from where it had been left earlier, leaning against the wall of the small building.

Darius cocked a curious eyebrow. "What's that for?"

"You wouldn't believe me if I told you."

Along with Alpha Marcus and his Beta, we went inside and waited while they inspected their supplies. The cool, damp air of the under-ground room seemed heavier than before, almost oppressive.

You really brought me all the way over here for this? Darius asked through our mind-link, his voice echoing inside my head so the other men couldn't hear.

No. I need your help to track someone else in the morning. I was following a scent but it disappeared.

The thief's scent? he clarified, and a moment of realization hit me. In my excitement and confusion over possibly finding my mate, I hadn't actually made the connection that my mate and the thief might be one in the same. I thought the thief might be fooling me with the mate scent, but somehow, it hadn't occurred to me that it might not be a trick.

Maybe my mate *was* the thief.

What would that mean? Would I be forced to punish someone I was meant to protect? Would I have to choose between the woman intended for me and my duty as Beta?

Before I could answer, a movement over his shoulder caught my eye. A long strap dangling from one of the bags of arrows on the wall suddenly swayed as if something had bumped into it, despite there being no one around and no wind in the underground room.

Calista's words came back to me about how someone from the fae realm might be invisible but would occupy space. Was there someone invisible standing there right now? Was it the thief? It couldn't be my mate because I didn't smell anything.

What the fuck was going on?

"Everything seems to be in order," the Beta announced, and Alpha Marcus nodded.

"I think we all need to get some sleep. We can reconvene in the morning."

They both turned back to the stairs, and I made a split-second decision. If all the information Calista gave me was true and there really *was* an invisible fae being in the room with us, I had all the tools needed to track him or her. If it didn't work, I'd look like a lunatic. But if it did...

I had to know.

Reaching into the bag of salt, I grabbed a large pinch and let it fall to the ground in the middle of the room as I walked out.

Go up the stairs with the others and stall, I instructed Darius through our link. *I'll explain everything soon, I promise.*

You never do anything the easy way, he grumbled but he also followed my instructions, herding the Vermillion Alpha and Beta up the stairs while I turned back and pulled the tube of paint out of my pocket. Squirting it in the direction of the salt, I watched as strings of paint spurted out, hitting the floor.

Most of them hit the floor, at least. For a second, I thought I must be imagining it, but when I blinked, there they were: a few splatters hanging in the air, sticking to something I couldn't see, and my chest swelled in triumphant pride.

It worked. It actually fucking worked, which meant there *was* an invisible being right there from a species I'd never encountered before. All the hypotheticals Calista and I discussed earlier were now a reality.

Gotcha, Kai crowed in my head, as pleased as I was with this revelation.

Now, we just had to wait for the creature to leave so we could follow it. After losing track of my mate earlier, I wasn't going to let anyone else slip through my fingers.

Chapter Ten

~Felix~

As soon as we were back outside, I pulled up short. "Alpha, I'm going to catch Darius up on everything we know so far. Go ahead and get some rest and we'll hit the ground running tomorrow."

The older man gave me a grateful nod. "You can see now why we're so frustrated. We appreciate you being here, and hopefully, we can figure this out together. See you in the morning."

He and the other members of his team walked away, all except the guards who remained in place outside the door, and I pulled Darius a safe distance away where we could speak without being overheard.

"There's some kind of invisible creature inside that building right now. We're going to follow it back to its realm."

He blinked at me so slowly, I wondered if I actually short-circuited something in his brain. "Come again?"

Like most werewolves, Darius never cared much about other supernatural species. Unless it attacked us, it didn't concern him. I was going to need to go back to basics.

"You ever heard of elves? Fairies? Lord of the Rings doesn't count."

He scowled at my teasing. "What about them?"

"They live in a parallel dimension to us and there are portals through which they can access our world and vice versa. When they visit us, they're invisible to everyone who's never visited the fae realm."

I made it sound as though this should all be common knowledge, even though I hadn't put all the pieces together myself until speaking with Calista the day before.

"The thief seems to be one of these beings, and he or she is inside the building right now, counting the grains of salt I dropped on the floor."

Another long blink followed before he squinted over at me. "Is this supposed to make sense?"

"It doesn't need to. All you need to know is that when I ask the guards to open that door in a little while, our invisible friend will probably sneak past us to return to the other realm. We're going to follow and go through the portal with him."

"We're going to follow an invisible man?"

His look shifted from confusion to concern, as if he feared that staying up all night had messed with my head.

"Yes, but right now, he's only *mostly* invisible because I squirted some paint on him."

Darius' eyebrows raised so high, I thought his forehead might snap. His mouth opened and closed a few times, as if he couldn't figure out what question to ask first.

I put him out of his misery. "Never mind. Just do what I say when the time comes, alright?"

He shrugged, too tired to ask any further questions.

Well, *almost* too tired. He did ask one more: "This sounds more like Calista's kind of thing. Why did you want me here?"

Fuck. With my excitement over potentially catching the thief, I'd almost forgotten about my mate.

"There's someone else I need to find, someone other than the thief. I think... well, I think I might have found my mate."

His eyebrows shot up again, but this time in appreciation. "That's awesome, Felix." A second later, his brows dropped and scrunched together instead. "Wait, what do you mean you *think* you found her?"

"I smelled her, and my wolf recognized the scent. He told me it was her but I didn't actually see her. I tried to follow the smell, but I couldn't find her. You're here to help me figure out where she went, but it'll have to wait until after we catch the thief."

His expression didn't clear. If anything, his face wrinkled even further as his lips pursed.

"Let me get this straight. We're going to track an invisible being who's stealing from this pack."

"Right." At least I'd managed to get that much across successfully.

"And you smelled your mate, but didn't see her?"

"Yes."

He stared at me meaningfully and I returned his gaze, uncertain what point he was trying to make.

When I didn't say anything further, Darius sighed. "Really? You don't see any connection between this elf or fairy being invisible and you not seeing your mate?"

"What are you..."

I paused, something clicking into place in my head.

"That's.... that can't be..."

I couldn't even force a complete sentence out of my mouth as my brain finally connected the dots that I'd been too close to the subject to see. What Darius suggested actually made an awful lot of sense.

What if I didn't see my mate because she *couldn't* be seen?

What if my mate wasn't a werewolf at all?

"I thought it might be some kind of trick," I admitted when I regained the power of speech. "I didn't consider she might be another species."

Darius shrugged. "I don't know for sure, obviously, but that's what I hear you saying. Wolves *do* get mates from other species. Not often, but it happens."

I knew that. Humans were the most common ones. Occasionally, I heard about the odd witch or vampire, but someone from the fae realm? I'd never come across that before. How would that even work? We lived in completely different worlds, quite literally.

"Well, whoever's inside that building right there is *not* my mate," I stated with confidence, about the only confidence I felt at that moment. "I don't smell anything from this one. Let's deal with them first and worry about the rest later."

We waited another twenty minutes or so, until I felt pretty certain that the creature would have had time to count all the salt and be free of the trap I set, before I approached the guards.

"I need you to open the door in a minute," I told them. "Don't go in, don't do anything other than open it."

They exchanged baffled glances, but their Alpha had told them to do as I said, so they didn't argue. Darius and I went into the surrounding trees and shifted to our wolves, ready to follow the intruder when he or she fled. Dawn had just begun to break, the light barely streaking across the sky overhead, but in the darkness that still lingered, our wolf vision would be better for tracking.

Per my instructions, the guards unlocked and opened the door, standing out of the way, and we almost missed the small splatters of paint that seemed to float through the air. In the rush to get something to use, I hadn't been able to follow Calista's suggestion for glow-in-the-dark paint.

Luckily, I made the right call in asking Darius for help and he picked up on the movement just in time. Darius' gaze flicked between the floating paint splatters and me, eyes wide with surprise. Even he couldn't deny that something beyond our understanding was happening. *Follow me*, he instructed in my head.

Together, we moved quietly through the trees, stalking our invisible prey without giving ourselves away. Branches swayed as invisible limbs brushed against them and dewy footprints formed in the dirt in front of us, making it clear we were on the right track. It took several minutes before we reached a familiar spot, familiar only because of the scent I'd left there earlier.

The thief was heading straight for the spot where my mate vanished. That couldn't be a coincidence. She'd disappeared, which meant our thief was likely about to do the same. Following them might lead us straight into a trap; what if we weren't able to return?

There were risks, without question, but the alternative was losing our chance to get any answers about both the thief and my mate, and I couldn't accept that. Remembering that Calista said we needed to go through the portal accompanied by the fae being, I gave Darius the order. *Now. Catch him.*

We both sprinted forward, abandoning our stealthiness, barrelling straight towards the specks of paint that picked up their pace at our approach. The cold air bit at my lungs as I propelled myself forward with every ounce of energy I possessed.

My fur brushed up against something solid in the empty air and I heard Darius' low growl beside me as the world around us rippled. Colours blended and blurred together like oil on water, and in the blink of an eye, the forest disappeared.

Chapter Eleven

~Felix~

The ground changed beneath my feet from one second to the next. Leaping from the dirt of the forest floor, I landed on something as soft as velvet, cool and almost spongy beneath my wolf's paws. The pink streaking the pale blue morning sky reversed, leaving blue streaks across a sky of pastel pink. The scent of pine disappeared, transforming into something I'd never smelled before, something bitter that stung my nose and left my mouth feeling dry.

Where the hell are we? Darius asked in my head almost before I could form the question myself.

At a glance, I took in our unfamiliar surroundings until my eyes landed on the man who had tumbled onto the ground next to us. The very *visible* man, staring up at the two wolves above him in disbelief.

The fae realm, I imagine, I answered Darius before shifting into my human form and hauling the man in front of me back to his feet. One hand bunching the fabric at the neck of his velvety clothes kept him in place. Lean and slight, he only came to my shoulder standing up.

"I think you've 'accidentally' taken something that belongs to my friends. Care to explain why?" I kept my tone light but my hands firm as I held him with my left hand and used my right hand to search for items stolen from the weapons store.

It didn't take me long to locate a small black pouch tied around his waist on a green-coloured string. The string snapped easily when I tugged it, and I tossed it over to Darius who had shifted behind me, my eyes never leaving the man in front of me.

"A few bullets and a couple of arrowheads," Darius confirmed, itemizing the pouch's contents. "Looks like we found our thief."

The man in my grasp bristled at the word but he didn't deny it. How could he when we caught him red-handed?

I lowered my face to his, noticing the unusual purple colour of his eyes. Pointed tips of his ears poked out through the strands of his long, black hair. I couldn't tell whether he was an elf or a fairy, but he clearly wasn't human or werewolf. "Why did you take them?"

"I don't answer to you." His voice had a slight lilt to it, not quite an accent, but nearly. It made his speech sound more melodic. Under the right circumstances, it might even be called pretty.

These weren't the right circumstances.

My fist tightened in his shirt. "Right now, you do. What do you want with our weapons?"

"Weapons?" His frown suggested a genuine uncertainty. "I didn't realize they were weapons."

It seemed my theory about the thief being more interested in the silver than the items itself might have been dead on. "So what *did* you want them for?"

"Felix, let's go."

Darius' voice over my shoulder barely registered until he placed a hand on my shoulder, pulling me back from the fae man.

"We retrieved the stolen items, let him know that we're onto him, and we'll see him if he comes back. We don't know anything about this place. We should go home."

Our pack's head of security couldn't help looking at things through a security lens, and I had to admit he had a point. We didn't appreciate people turning up on *our* land uninvited and we had no idea how the people in charge of this realm felt about it.

Reluctantly, I dropped the man's shirt, or whatever the hell he wore. It might have all been one piece of clothing, I couldn't really tell. "Stay out of our realm," I warned him, jabbing a finger into his chest to emphasize my point.

We turned back towards the portal, ready to step through it again, when the scent hit my nose. Much fainter than before, but undeniably familiar, I recognized the scent of my mate immediately.

My feet stopped, my body unwilling to move forward, and I looked back over my shoulder at the man glaring a hole in my back. "Was there someone else with you? A woman?"

His unusual purple eyes narrowed. "I still don't answer to you."

"Felix." Darius tugged at my arm as a wind rippled through the unusual trees around us, but I shook him off to try again.

"Did someone else go through this portal last night?"

"I can't tell you that, but I will tell you one thing."

My heart leapt at the possibility that my mate might actually be nearby, that I could really find her. That it hadn't been a trick after all. "What's that?"

One corner of his mouth lifted into a smirk. "You should have left while you had the chance."

From the trees, men emerged in similar garments to the man we followed, their weapons strange and angular, glinting faintly in the pastel light. Apparently, that hadn't been wind moving the trees after all; with every scent and sight new, we hadn't known exactly what to watch for.

The air vibrated with an eerie hum as they aimed their bowed weapons directly at us. The strings glimmered as though they were made of pure energy.

Darius' voice rumbled in my head through our mind-link. *We need to run for it. We have no idea what those weapons will do to us. The portal's only a few feet away. Shift and run.*

I ran the calculations in my head. Only a few feet separated *him* from the portal. I had a few feet more. He had a much better chance of making it through unharmed than I did. More than that, my mate was here, she had to be, and the thought of leaving without meeting her felt like tearing off a piece of myself.

Staying meant immediate danger but leaving would slowly tear me apart. Every instinct screamed at me to stay, to fight, to find her, no matter the cost.

You go. I'll distract them.

Felix...

I didn't give him a chance to voice whatever protest he had. *Let Vaughan and Calista know what happened. You know where the portal is, and since you've been here, I think you can come back. Maybe you can bring them with you. If I don't come back on my own, you can come and get me.*

I'm not leaving without you, he growled.

And I'm not giving you a choice.

With no further warning, I shifted and sprang not towards the portal but away from it, further into the fae realm. Every pair of eyes followed me, every weapon aimed in my direction, and though I heard a grumbled *shit* in my head from Darius, I knew without looking back that he took advantage of the situation to make his escape.

"Stop him," the man I'd been speaking to ordered, his posture shifting with the ease of someone who knew he had the upper hand.

"Yes, Your Highness," they replied almost in unison.

Your Highness? Darius had it right: *Shit.*

I only made it a few more steps before a sharp, searing pain exploded in my side, and I stumbled, my breath hitching as warmth trickled through my fur. My legs faltered, the ground tilted beneath me, and before I even had time to regret my decision, my vision blurred and the world around me went black.

CHAPTER TWELVE

~Evalina~

First thing in the morning, I returned to the kitchen of the royal residence, ready to start another long day. Before long, the aroma of baking bread filled the small space as I moved from one task to the next in an orderly, methodical rhythm. On the surface, it seemed like any other day, but though I might have appeared calm on the outside, my mind whirred with everything I'd learned and the potential opportunities and pitfalls ahead of me.

So far, Tarron didn't seem to realize the items I stole were missing from his locked box. Since I couldn't count on that being the case forever, I had to make my next move quickly.

What that move should be, I still hadn't completely decided.

The way I saw it, there were two potential avenues to locating the silver I needed. First, Tarron must have more of it somewhere. He told me he knew how to cure my mother, and assuming he read the same directions I did, he would know how much the treatment required. There were other places besides the locked box beneath his bed where he could hide it, and I'd never met a lock that could keep me out. All I needed was the time and opportunity to explore his room more thoroughly.

The other option would be to return to the terrestrial realm and look for it there myself. That seemed less risky on the surface, but it still posed some danger. I could be caught using the portal or I could run into Felix, the man on the other side who seemed to sense my presence even though he shouldn't have been able to.

Both options would have to wait until the royal family had their breakfast, and no sooner had I sent up the dishes than Keerla came rushing into the kitchen.

"New orders from Tarron," she said in a hushed whisper. "There's a prisoner in the pens. He wants food taken to him."

The mere mention of the prison sent a shiver down my spine, knowing how easily I could end up there myself if I chose the wrong path. "A prisoner? Who is it?"

"No idea. He only said to be sure that the prisoner ate something. He said to make it irresistible."

Why would Tarron care whether a prisoner ate or not? It wasn't like him to show concern for anyone, least of all someone locked in the pens. Prisoners usually ate scraps if they ate at all.

"Fine," I agreed reluctantly. "If you can help me with lunch, I'll put something together."

Working together, we managed to prepare the royal family's lunch and make one of my best dishes for the prisoner at the same time. *My* mouth watered at the smell of it, so I didn't imagine someone locked up would be able to resist, though I still had no idea why getting this person to eat something mattered so much.

When the last dish had been taken upstairs for lunch and Keerla had begun to clean up, I took off my apron. "I'll take this over to the pens before I head home to see my mother on my break."

Keerla's expression softened in sympathy. "How is she?"

"No change, or at least not a good one. I have a lead now, though. I just need to figure out how to make use of it."

"Just stay out of Tarron's way today," she advised. "Pavla told me the prince is even grumpier than usual."

"Are you and Pavla a team now?" I half-teased. "Did something happen after I left you last night?"

Keerla rolled her eyes. "He wishes."

Despite her answer, I thought I detected a hint of a blush in her cheeks before I slipped out through the servant's entrance with the plate of food for the prisoner balanced in one hand, covered by a thin layer of gauze to keep it fresh. The warm orange sun shone down on the velvety forest floor, my slippers sinking into the ground with each step. The pens, as everyone called the royal prison, sat a short distance into the forest in the opposite direction from the staff quarters. A round, domed, circular structure with doors only on the outside, it required no guards since the holding cells were magically sealed. Food and drink were sent through a long, narrow passage in the wall, much too small for a person to get through. I'd been asked to feed prisoners before but never to ensure that they ate. Curiosity quickened my steps as I drew nearer.

A small flag post outside each cell announced its occupancy status, and at the moment, only one showed a green flag. That must be the hungry prisoner, so I headed to the small opening I would need to use to send the food through, rapping sharply before raising the barrier. My chin barely reached the bottom of the window.

"Hello? I brought you some lunch."

A deep growling sound came from inside, making me take several steps back, the plate teetering dangerously in my hand as my heart thumped heavily in surprise. What in the world made a sound like that? It didn't sound like any fairy I'd ever heard. A dragon, maybe? Or one of the strange creatures that lived in the elven lands?

A moment later, the growling stopped and a male voice spoke instead. "Come closer."

The voice sounded vaguely familiar, and I stepped forward in spite of my concerns to repeat my earlier greeting. "Hello?"

When I peered into the darkness, I could just make out a face at the end of the passage, shrouded in shadow. No distinct features were visible other than two wide eyes which stared at me as if I were not quite real. Honestly, I kind of felt the same. What kind of man could make a noise like the one I just heard? What *was* he?

"What's your name?" His voice came out softer than before, almost reverent, and a blush started to heat my cheeks, completely against my will. Why was he staring at me like that and speaking to me that way?

I could only think of one reason, so I tried to let him down gently. "If you think I can get you out of here, I'm sorry, but I can't. I just came to bring you some lunch."

I placed the plate into the small passage and removed the gauze covering it. Immediately, the rich scent filled the small space and I heard another growl from inside, but this one, I recognized. It came from the stomach of a very hungry man.

I used the small stick left near the opening to push the plate towards him, close enough that he could reach out and take it. "Please, eat. I made it for you."

"*You* made it?" His voice still held that same reverent tone, and despite the gurgling of his stomach, he never once looked at the plate. His eyes remained locked on me. "Please tell me your name."

"What's *your* name?" I shot back, trying to get the focus off me while I waited for him to eat. Tarron would want to know if he had.

"It's Felix. I told you that last night."

Cold shock slid through my veins as I realized exactly why his voice sounded familiar. *Felix.* The man who chased after me in the terrestrial realm, the one who knew I was there even though he shouldn't have.

How did he end up in Etta? Did he follow me? Did Tarron capture him? How? Why?

A dozen questions sprang up, leaping over each other to get to the tip of my tongue to be asked first, but Felix spoke again before I could ask any of them.

"Now, it's your turn. What's your name?"

"I think you have bigger things to worry about than me," I pointed out gently. "You're imprisoned and you're starving. Please eat."

Finally, his eyes dropped to the food, and he let out a regretful groan. "It smells fantastic, and knowing that you made it only makes me want it more, but I can't eat anything here." He hesitated a moment, his voice softening as he added, "If I do, I won't be able to go back."

"Back?" For some reason, the thought of him leaving pulled at something inside me, something that didn't make any sense when I didn't even know this man.

"To my world. My home. I'll tell you all about it, if you like, but first, will you please tell me your name?"

My mind raced again, just like it had that morning, but suddenly, the possibilities seemed new. This man came from the other realm. He might know where I could get silver, and maybe if I helped him to escape, he would help me in return.

How I would manage to free him, or how I could avoid Tarron finding out about it, I didn't know yet, but it seemed worthwhile to at least tell him my name and try to find out a little more. For reasons I couldn't fully understand, I *wanted* to trust him.

After glancing over my shoulder to ensure we were still alone, I leaned forward with my hands on the ledge in front of me, my chin resting on top of my fingers, and offered him a smile down the passage between us. "I'm Evalina."

Chapter Thirteen

~Felix~

Perfect.

That one word kept going around my head as I stared down the bright passage towards my mate on the other end.

She was perfect.

Tiny, but perfect.

All I could see was her head, while on my end, I had to bend down to look through the opening. She must have been a foot shorter than me, at least. If the prince who captured me was anything to go by, people in this realm seemed to be shorter in general, so it didn't really surprise me that Evalina would be on the short side too.

Evalina. Even her name sounded perfect.

I couldn't even see her all that clearly. The sun behind her created a backlit effect, blocking out the details of her delicate features, but my chest still constricted with near-boundless joy at every little glimpse I did get. Those small pieces were enough to confirm how lucky I was.

Perfectly lucky.

Unfortunately, she also seemed to have no idea we were mates. I knew that could happen with other species, so I tried not to take it personally. Hell, even Calista didn't recognize Vaughan as her mate until her wolf broke through. Fae didn't have wolves, so Evalina might never feel the mate bond in the same way I did, but she felt *something*, I'd have put money on it.

And *damn*, could she cook. My stomach growled unhappily as I pushed the food away from me, trying to get rid of the temptation.

Calista's words rang in my ears, reminding me that eating food in the fae realm would bind me there forever, and even though my mate lived there, I had no intention of remaining permanently. Wherever we made our home once I convinced her to accept me, I'd still like to be able to visit the other realm.

Was I getting ahead of myself? Maybe a little.

I would have to tell her about our connection eventually, but during my incarceration didn't seem like the best time to break that news. I could think of a hundred better places to do it.

She stared at me while my mind wandered, a shy smile sprouting on the corners of her lips. "Well?"

"Well what?" I'd completely forgotten what we'd been talking about.

"You said you'll tell me all about where you come from."

Right. I did say that, but first, I had another question for her. "It was you I spoke to last night, wasn't it? You came to my world through the portal."

Her head swivelled left and right, checking to see if anyone else might be listening. Seemingly satisfied, she turned back to me and lowered her voice to a whisper. "Yes, but I'm not supposed to. Please don't tell anyone you saw me there."

"I would never do anything that would put you in danger," I assured her fiercely. "And besides, I *didn't* see you."

Her head tilted to the side curiously, giving me just a glint of her pretty eyes. I couldn't even tell for sure what colour they were, but damn, they were pretty. "Then how did you know I was there?"

"I have a very good sense of smell and you smell... so good." The last words came out a little strangled, probably making me sound like some kind of pervert. Clearing my throat, I hurriedly moved on. "What were you doing there?"

She looked to the side again and I could see her chewing on her bottom lip, debating whether or not to answer me. I waited as patiently as possible and eventually, she nodded to herself and turned back. "Have you ever heard of something called silver?"

It took a great deal of effort not to laugh but I forced my lips to stay straight, not wanting her to think I was laughing *at* her. "Yes. It's relatively common where I'm from. What does it do in this realm? Your prince was after it too."

Even with the light from the sun obscuring her face, I could see her eyes widen. "Tarron got more silver?"

"Is that his name? All I know is that he stole from some friends of mine and locked me up in here. I'm not his biggest fan."

I could have sworn she smiled, but it vanished so quickly, I couldn't be certain. "He's dangerous. You should try not to upset him."

"I think it's a little late for that." I tried to keep my tone light, but the way she described him as dangerous concerned me. The walls around me seemed to hum with a faint magical energy, a constant reminder that I was out of my element. My wolf stirred uneasily. "What has he done to you?"

She glanced away again, double-checking no one lurked nearby. "Nothing too bad yet, but I'm afraid of what he *might* do. I need silver and he's the only one I know who has any, but what he wants in exchange, I'm not willing to give."

What the fuck does that mean? Kai growled in my head. *What does that skinny little twerp want from her?*

Taking a deep breath, I tried to stay calm despite the leaden feeling in my stomach. If I let out another growl like before, I might scare her off right when she was opening up to me.

"I can get you any silver you need," I offered, the words tumbling out even though she still hadn't told me what she needed it for. I just knew I couldn't let her rely on someone who made her feel afraid. "You don't need him."

Evalina stiffened at the other end of the passage. "And what do you want in return?"

It broke my heart that she assumed my intentions were anything less than pure, but I had to remind myself that I was still a stranger to her and she didn't feel the connection between us the same way I did. She didn't know yet that I would never ask anything of her that would make her uncomfortable.

Saying I didn't want anything might make her suspicious, though. Why would a complete stranger offer to help her? I would have to think of something to ask for, and it didn't take me long to land on something I actually needed quite desperately.

"Can you get me out of here? Stuck in this cell, I can't do anything, but if you can break me out, I'll be free to help you."

Again, that bottom lip disappeared beneath her teeth. "There's magical protection over the prison and I don't have the power to break it."

Damn it. I might have to wait for Vaughan and Calista to show up, but I had no idea how long it would take or what Tarron might have in store for me in the meantime. If nothing else, I needed to eat eventually.

Evalina hadn't finished yet, though. "I have an idea, if you're sure you don't want to eat that food."

"I'm sure," I said, reluctantly pushing the plate further towards her. Fuck, it smelled good.

She had to jump up to reach far enough into the passage to grab it, rather adorably. How could someone so small already hold so much power over my heart?

When she had the plate in hand, her eyes flicked to my shoulders briefly, almost as if measuring me in return. "I'll be back as soon as I can. Wait here."

"I'm not going anywhere."

A flash of white teeth answered me, and she disappeared from my view, her scent fading with her as she went. Kai sighed in my head, both of us just as smitten as each other with our mate that we'd still only barely seen. How could we not be?

She was absolutely perfect.

CHAPTER FOURTEEN

~**Evalina**~

It would be a risk. I couldn't pretend otherwise. If Tarron found out that I helped Felix escape, I would pay for it one way or another. He could lock me up, or force me to accept the position as his amorta that until now had only been an offer, or worst of all, he could take his vengeance on my mother, knowing that would wound me the most. A hundred different, awful scenarios ran through my mind, pressing down like a stone on my heart as I hurried down the path back towards the royal family's home.

And what guarantee did I have that Felix would even help me like he said he would? Once he got free, he might disappear back through the portal and I'd never see him again.

For some reason, though, I didn't think he would lie to me. He seemed sincere. Even through the distance between us at the pens, something connected us, something I couldn't put into words. It made no sense but if I couldn't trust my gut, what hope did I have?

Given the choice between asking him for help and relying on Tarron, the decision practically made itself.

Rather than going back to the kitchen when I reached the royal residence, I went straight to the guards' room instead. Jermyn, the head of the guards, always had an after-lunch nap there, and sure enough, I found him passed out in one of the chairs, his head leaning against the soft wall as if it were a pillow.

"Jermyn, wake up." I nudged his shoulder hard, knowing I had no time to lose. The older man snuffled and snorted as he jolted awake, his brow furrowed in annoyance at being disturbed until his eyes fell on me.

"Evalina? What are you doing here?"

Pulling himself up, he swayed unsteadily on his feet for a moment before he drew himself up to his full height, a head taller than me and nearly twice as wide. His bushy hair stuck up on the side where it had rested against the wall, and he ran a hand roughly through it to try to tame it.

The way to Jermyn's heart had always been through his stomach and he often visited me in the kitchen to steal any leftovers I might have. As a result, I'd earned a bit of a soft spot in his otherwise gruff demeanour, one that I would have to exploit for my plan to work.

"Tarron asked me to take this food to the prisoner in the pens." I held up the plate and Jermyn licked his lips as the smell hit his nostrils. "The problem is: he refuses to eat it."

The whiskers surrounding his lips pulled down into a frown. "Tarron insisted that he eat."

It seemed we'd both been given the same instruction, which would make things easier. "He said it didn't smell good. I think it might have something to do with the magic protecting the cells."

Keeping my expression neutral, I held my breath as Jermyn thought that over, hoping he would believe the lie. His particular magic controlled the pens, which explained how he became head of the guard.

"Maybe it's because he comes from the other side," he eventually mused. "The magic might affect him differently. That's all I can think of because that smells as good as anything you've ever made."

He cast another longing look at the plate in my hand while I pressed my advantage. "Do you think you could remove the magic, just long enough for him to eat?"

Instinctively, he shook his head. "I can't do that. Too dangerous."

"But the door will still be locked," I reminded him. "No matter how strong he is, he can't break through a lock like that."

His frown deepened, his fingers tapping against his arm as he weighed my suggestion. 'I don't know, Evalina. Tarron would have my head if something went wrong."

"I'll take full responsibility," I promised. "It will only be for a minute and there are no other prisoners to worry about."

For a long moment, he considered my proposal, his tongue darting out subconsciously every time his gaze fell on the plate in my hands. I forced myself to remain silent so I didn't betray just how personal the request was to me.

"Alright," he finally agreed, and my heart leapt in delight. "But I'll stay with you the whole time to make sure there's no trouble."

Sugarlumps. That hadn't been part of my plan, but I couldn't think of any reason to disagree as Jermyn called down the hall to his colleague to tell him he would be back in a few minutes. When he turned back, his gaze fell to the food in my hand again, and an idea sparked in my mind.

"I'll be right back."

Racing to the kitchen, I grabbed an extra plate, slid it under the one I already had, and returned to the door where Jermyn waited. Together, we walked the short distance back to the pens and once there, he lowered the magical protection over the facility, as I requested.

"You know, this is quite a lot of food for one person," I said, holding up the plate in my hand. "Tarron only said he had to eat *something*, right?"

Jermyn nodded, his eyes tracking the plate's movements with longing.

"Why don't you take half of it, and I'll give the prisoner the other half? I brought two plates to make sure I didn't drop it."

That didn't make a lot of sense, but since it meant he got some of the food for himself, Jermyn didn't seem to notice. His eager eyes watched as I divided the food between the two plates and handed one to him. "It would be a shame for it to go to waste," he justified, and I nodded in encouragement.

"Exactly. I'll take the food to the prisoner and be right back. You can stay here. I'll be in sight the whole time."

He might not have even heard me as he placed the first bite in his mouth and groaned in delight.

My feet skipped across the short distance back to the passage into Felix's cell. He already stood at the other end, waiting for me.

"The barrier around the cells has been dropped, and I can open the door for you. Unfortunately, I had to bring the guard along. Can you take care of him without hurting him? He's not a bad person."

Felix's smile seemed understanding. "Of course. Stay right where you are, I don't want you to get caught up in the fight."

Nodding, I placed the plate of food in my hands down onto the passage ledge and closed my eyes to focus my magic. When I couldn't see the lock in front of me, it took a little longer, but eventually, I could hear the mechanism in the door grind open.

"What's that behind you?" I called to Jermyn, hoping to distract him, and it worked as his head spun around to check over his shoulder.

Moving faster and quieter than any man I'd ever seen, Felix burst through the door and reached Jermyn in seconds. He rammed straight into him, the two of them tumbling to the ground and sending the plate and its few remaining bits of food splattering onto the soft velvet forest floor. The downed guard never even saw the punch coming before he went completely still.

With my heart in my throat, I raced over to the two men. "Is he okay?"

"He'll be fine," Felix assured me as he got back to his feet. Higher and higher he rose until he reached his full height, his body completely obliterating my view of the sun.

He was *huge*. I'd never seen anyone so big before.

And he was wearing...

Against my will, a giggle erupted from my lips as my gaze travelled down his body and I saw his broad, strong frame squeezed into clothes meant for a man almost half his size. The sleeves of the tunic's arms only reached his elbows, the leggings barely touched his knees, and most of his midsection remained completely uncovered.

His firm, sculpted stomach didn't look like anything I'd ever seen before. Nothing at all like Tarron's slim, lean lines.

My laughter died as I took in more of him, the sheer bulk of him that went against every definition of masculine fae beauty but somehow, on him, looked more attractive than anything I'd ever seen before. That didn't even account for his face: kind blue eyes beneath sandy blond hair, a firm, stubbled jaw line, and a beaming smile that made me smile back out of sheer instinct.

If Tarron was beautiful, I had no words to describe Felix. He defied any category of man I'd ever seen before, and he was looking at me like he felt just the same.

"It's okay," he said, his deep, warm voice pulling me out of my head. "You can laugh. I look ridiculous."

He gestured down to the clothes he wore with a self-deprecating grimace.

"I don't think they make werewolf sizes here."

"You're a werewolf?" Something tugged inside me at the word while images of the pictures I saw in Tarron's box on that long-ago day flashed through my mind. The way I felt when I saw them wasn't so far off the way Felix made me feel. That didn't seem like a coincidence.

"You know about werewolves?"

We did that, I'd noticed already in the short conversations we'd had. Both so eager to know more about the other, we answered questions with more questions. I made sure to answer him this time before repeating mine. "I don't know much other than that they exist. Is that what you are?"

"Yes." He said it softly, like a confession. A hopeful one. "I hope it doesn't scare you. I won't hurt you, Evalina."

My name sounded heavenly on his lips. "I'm not afraid of you," I assured him, even though I couldn't say why not. Perhaps I should have been, but despite his size, he put me at ease. "But you should go before they find out you escaped. You'll still help me get some silver, won't you?"

"Of course. I promised I would." He stretched out his hand towards me, palm up, and offered me another blindingly beautiful smile. "Come with me and I'll make sure you have everything you need."

Chapter Fifteen

~Felix~

Once I got out of the cell and got my first real look at my mate, I couldn't stop staring. The strange daylight of this world bathed her in a soft glow, and for a moment, I forgot how to breathe. The things I'd guessed about her from my glimpses through the tunnel - her petite stature and the beautiful gleam of her eyes - turned out to be true, but those things barely scraped the surface.

Auburn hair, streaked with all the shades of reds and browns, curled delicately over her shoulders. Eyes of icy blue, the blue of mountain streams or the sky in winter, gazed up at me from beneath long lashes, and pink lips formed a perfect bow beneath her slender nose. I'd never seen a bone structure so delicate or ears quite so pointed at the tips. The tops of her ears poked up adorably through the cascades of her hair. She wore a dress that would have been suitable for a ball, much more formal than anything I normally wore, and soft slippers covered her little feet. At least, they looked like slippers in the small glimpses that I got of them when her skirt swished from one side to the other.

The only thing I didn't love about her on sight was the frown that pulled her lips down when I offered her my hand and asked her to go through the portal with me.

"I can't leave," she said, taking a step back as if to stop herself from taking my hand. "It's not that I don't want to go, but Tarron would be suspicious, and I have to work. I have to look after my mother."

Since she had multiple reasons for turning me down, I tried to go through them one by one. "Tarron is your prince?"

Her head bobbed up and down in a quick nod. "He is, and he ordered me to bring you food. If I go with you, he'll figure out that I helped you escape."

"Not necessarily," I countered. "He might think I kidnapped you."

I offered her a smile to let her know I wasn't being completely serious, but Evalina's frown remained. "That would make matters worse. He might follow us and try to get me back. It could put you in danger."

"Are you that important to him?" Jealousy undercut my words despite my best efforts to hold it back. The idea of her being important to another man, especially one like Tarron, flooded my chest with an uncomfortable heat. I remembered what she said before, that he wanted something from her she didn't want to give, and my imagination threatened to conjure all kinds of dark and disturbing scenarios.

"Our interaction is... complicated," she said, which didn't explain much at all. "He's looking for something he can hold over me. I don't want to give it to him."

I didn't want that either, though I still didn't understand exactly what she meant. Reluctantly, I turned to the second part of her refusal. "Where do you work?"

Her honest, open expression held nothing back. "In the royal family's residence. I cook for them. That's why Tarron ordered me to cook for you."

That explained why her food smelled so delicious, and it raised a host of other questions in my mind. How did she learn to cook? Did she like it? What were her favourite foods? Had she ever tried a cheeseburger?

There were so many things I wanted to know and no time to ask any of it, so I stuck to the matter at hand instead. "So, you'd be missed if you didn't turn up to make dinner?"

"Exactly."

With a firm grasp on that objection, I moved on to the third thing she mentioned. "Is your mother alright?"

Worry flashed across her face, pinching the corners of her mouth tight. "She's sick and I need the silver to make her better. There's no one else to look after her so I can't leave her alone."

Putting those three things together, I could see why she refused to go with me at that time, and though I didn't like it, I wouldn't force her into a potentially dangerous situation for herself or her mother. "How should I get the silver back to you, then?"

The worry in her expression cleared, replaced by hope, and I had never seen anything so beautiful. "I can sneak through the portal at night, like I did last night. Can you meet me on the other side?"

"You're sure that won't get you in trouble?" She mentioned earlier that she wasn't supposed to go through it.

"I'll be careful, and it's probably safer than you coming back here. Tarron won't be happy when he realizes you escaped."

Her concern for my safety sent a flush of pleasure through me. *She has a good heart,* Kai said in my head, and I readily agreed. The way she cared for her mother, the way she trusted me despite not knowing about the bond between us, and the way she asked me to make sure I didn't hurt the man she tricked into freeing me all pointed to an empathetic and compassionate soul, someone I could admire as well as adore.

First, I would get her the silver she needed to help her mother. Afterwards, we could figure out the rest.

"Do you need help to find the portal again?" she asked, and although I would have loved her company, I put practical considerations first.

"Point me in the general direction and I'll find it. It has a distinct smell, similar to my home world, so once I get close, I'll be able to sniff it out."

Her head tilted to the side, curiosity filling those gorgeous blue eyes. "You can *smell* it?"

She said it as though navigating by scent had never occurred to her. It probably hadn't. "I can. My nose will lead the way and I'll attract less attention if I travel in my wolf form."

"Your... what?"

Her gaze travelled down my body, searching for clues, and I smiled as a pink blush spread across her cheeks when her eyes rested on my exposed stomach and hips.

"My wolf form. As a werewolf, I can shift into a wolf."

That didn't seem to make things any clearer for her, and her eyebrows drew together in an adorable furrow as she looked back up at my face. "What's a wolf?"

Goddess, we had so much to teach each other, so much to explore together. Some werewolves might have been upset to get a mate outside their own species, but other supernatural beings had always fascinated me. Finding a mate was supposed to feel like coming home. With Evalina, it felt like an adventure: unfamiliar, but exhilarating.

"I'll show you in a moment if you like. First, let's finish making plans. You should stay here and pretend to be unconscious so it looks like I knocked both of you out. That'll deflect suspicion off you for my escape. Tonight, when you can, come through the portal and I'll be waiting for you with the silver. How much do you need?"

"Twenty plins."

She stated her answer quickly and confidently but she might as well have been speaking gibberish for all the sense it made to me. "I have no idea what a plin is, but I'll bring you as much as I can. If you don't come tonight, I'll return and find you."

"But Tarron…"

I didn't let her finish. "It's more important to me that you and the people you love are safe. If I don't see you tonight, I'll find a way to get back to you. Don't worry, Evalina. You're not alone."

She blinked up at me rapidly, my words obviously meaning something special to her. *Good.* She already meant everything to me, so I had my work cut out for me to make her feel the same.

"The portal is that way. Be careful." She pointed to our right, and I held out my hand again. Tentatively, she took it and the warm, electric tingles of our bond spread through my body for the first time as our skin connected, her small hand disappearing inside the grip of my larger one.

Fuck, that feels good.

Evalina's eyes widened as she stared down at our joined hands, but she didn't pull away. When I bent down to lay a kiss on the back of her hand, her cheeks flushed even pinker than before, but still, she didn't resist. If anything, I could have sworn her fingers tightened around mine, just for a second.

"I'll see you soon. Please, take care of yourself."

With those parting words I released her hand and took a couple of steps back before shifting to my wolf. A ripple of energy coursed through my body as my muscles stretched and shifted, fur erupting across my skin in a rush of heat and shredding the ridiculously undersized fae clothes in the process.

Evalina's lips parted, her eyes shining with wonder as she took in my animal form, and Kai gave her a wink before we bounded off in search of the portal and the way home.

Chapter Sixteen

~Evalina~

Of all the strange things I'd seen in my life, nothing came close to this.

Not just seeing Felix turn into an animal, although that had certainly registered high on the crazy scale, but the whole encounter with him. The way he made me feel safe and comfortable despite his size and unfamiliarity. The way I blurted out things to him, like my mother's illness, that I hardly told anyone else. The way my body lit up when his hand touched mine and the tingles that zipped straight to my core when his lips pressed against my skin. He seemed to see right through every wall I'd ever built, straight to my heart.

It felt like something out of a dream.

Did all werewolves cause that kind of a reaction, or was it unique to him? Since I'd never met another one, I couldn't be certain, but more than ever before, I wanted to know about his species. I wanted to know about his world, and his life, and every single thing about *him*.

Unfortunately, all of that would have to wait. Pushing away those thoughts as the furry, four-legged version of him disappeared into the forest, I found a spot on the ground not far from Jermyn's prone body and lay down, doing my best to mimic his unconscious state. I had no idea how long it would take until he woke up or we were discovered, but it ended up not being very long at all. No more than five minutes passed before the ground bounced beneath me from the pounding of approaching footsteps.

"Over there," a man yelled. "Check the pens!"

Voices drew nearer as another man shouted back. "Empty! He's gone!"

"Jermyn? Wake up, sir," another voice said from nearer to me, and a few seconds later, someone poked at my shoulder.

"Miss? Are you alright?"

Squeezing my eyes tight, I raised my hand to my head and did my best to look disoriented as I slowly blinked. "What... what happened?"

"You were assaulted," the young man at my side said grimly. "Are you hurt?"

Every ounce of me wanted to say that Felix hadn't assaulted me, would *never* assault me, but that wouldn't accomplish anything. Instead, I forced myself not to argue and focused on the soldier's question instead. "I'm okay. Where's Jermyn?"

He glanced over his shoulder to where the older man had started to get to his feet too. "He's alright. We'll take you both back to the prince."

My hand went to my chest, not part of the act that time. Tarron was the last person I wanted to see. "Actually, I'm a little dizzy. Maybe I should go home."

"After you speak to the prince."

His tone, though kind, left no room for argument, and reluctantly, I allowed them to lead me back to the residence.

Tarron sat in his formal reception room, on his large armchair that resembled a throne as much as it could without actually being one. Suspicion clouded his eyes when he saw me come in, but he focused his attention on Jermyn first.

"What. Happened."

He bit the words out, each a complete sentence and barely even a question. He must have already known that Felix escaped, he just wanted to know how.

Jermyn's face had bruised where Felix punched him, and he hung his head in shame. "We were trying to get the prisoner to eat, as you ordered, Your Highness. He said Evalina's food didn't smell good, which couldn't be right, so we thought the magical shield might be affecting the smell. I lowered it to see if that made a difference but I don't know how he got out. The door should have still been locked."

Tarron's lavender eyes slid over to me and I held my breath while doing my best to give nothing away. Would he connect the dots between his locked box that I'd opened all those years ago and the locked door?

When he spoke, his words were measured. "It seems that every time I turn around lately, I see you, Evalina."

It felt that way to me too, and I didn't consider it a good thing. Holding his gaze, I answered as politely as possible. "You ordered food to be taken to the prisoner, Your Highness. I followed your orders."

I should have left it there, but I couldn't stop myself from asking a follow-up question.

"Did the prisoner get away?"

Since neither Jermyn nor I had alerted him to what happened at the pens, something else must have tipped him off about Felix's escape. I hope that didn't mean he'd been spotted or recaptured.

Tarron didn't answer me. He turned back to Jermyn with a sneer. "Five days in the pens for your stupidity, with only Etta juice for sustenance."

Jermyn's jaw fell slack as he blinked at his prince, and guilt stabbed at my chest. He'd only been trying to help me, and now he had to suffer for five days without food. Etta juice would keep him alive, but wouldn't help with the hunger pangs. The pens were a cold, damp circle of misery, not to mention the shame incarceration would bring.

What would my fate be if Tarron suspected I'd purposefully let Felix go?

Apparently, he didn't want to announce it in front of the others. "You can all go," he dismissed everyone else before crooking an elegant finger at me and beckoning me towards him. "Evalina, you stay."

With no other choice, I remained still while the room emptied until only Tarron and I were left. The click of the door closing behind us sent a chill down my spine.

For a long minute, he simply looked at me, his eyes roaming over me before resting on my face, and repeating the action when I didn't speak. He seemed to think that I would eventually find the silence unbearable and start talking, but he didn't understand that I would happily stand there for hours in the quiet rather than say a word to him that I didn't have to.

He didn't understand me at all.

Finally, he spoke, the words sounding louder than they should after the forced silence. "Strange how the prisoner escaped through a locked door."

My heart thudding was the only reaction I allowed myself to have. Externally, I betrayed nothing. "Very strange, Your Highness."

"Did you speak with him?"

My fingers tried to curl into fists at my side but I resisted it, not wanting to make any move that would suggest anything other than open honesty. "As Jermyn explained, I offered him the food and he said it didn't smell good. I went to Jermyn for help since I was told the prisoner needed to eat."

"That's all you spoke about?"

I stuck to my lie, hoping it would convince him. "Yes, Your Highness."

"Hmmm."

Did that mean he believed me or not? Since I couldn't tell, I fell silent again, waiting for him to say something else.

That time, I didn't have to wait long. Tarron suddenly changed the subject to something I wanted to discuss even less than I wanted to talk about Felix.

"Have you considered my offer to cure your mother?"

"I have considered it," I answered carefully. "But I have another treatment option I would like to try first."

"Why would you waste time on that when I told you I have the cure?"

"I would prefer not to bother you with my personal problems. You're a busy man."

Tarron's expression darkened to a scowl. The air in the room thickened and my palms grew damp against my skirt. Outside, a bird called out, sharp and sudden, sounding a warning.

"Don't toy with me, Evalina. It's a simple proposition: agree to be my amorta and your mother's life is saved. It will be hard for you to cure her yourself from prison."

A gasp flew out of me before I could stop it. "Prison?"

"Jermyn just got five days," he reminded me, gesturing towards the door the others had gone through. "Do you think you're immune from punishment?"

"No, but..."

"But nothing," he cut me off. "Make up your mind. The pens are waiting, or you can accept my offer and be the envy of every woman in Etta. Honestly, I'm beginning to think there's something wrong with you if you consider this a difficult choice."

In his words, I caught a hint of the old condescension he used to show me, and I couldn't help wondering: if that distaste for me still lingered, why did he care so much about having me at his side? The contradiction gnawed at me.

Even if I knew the reason, meeting Felix had made the prospect of binding myself to Tarron even less appealing than before, and I wouldn't have thought that possible. I couldn't agree, but how could I leave my mother alone either?

Wavering between both sides of an impossible choice, I took too long and Tarron's scowl turned stony. "One night in the pens should make things a lot clearer for you."

"No, please, Your Highness..."

If I had to spend the night in prison, not only would my mother be on her own but I wouldn't be able to meet Felix as I promised and get the silver I needed. That assumed he had even made it safely back to his world at all.

Tarron sprang to his feet, coming to stand right in front of me, his eyes intense as they stared down into mine. Behind the lavender, something darker flickered, a hunger that went beyond any interest he'd ever shown me. "Say the word and I'll have you and your mother moved into the residence tonight. She'll start her treatment and you'll never have to work again. We'll both have what we want."

He made it sound so simple, but it wasn't simple at all. My stomach twisted at his words and I clenched my fists at my sides, forcing myself to meet his gaze. He wanted me to feel powerless, to break under his scrutiny, but I refused to give him that satisfaction even if I had no other power in this situation.

"I..."

I tried to think of something to say, anything that would change his mind and give me more time, but when no further words came, Tarron turned away and stormed out of the room, calling over his shoulder.

"Think hard about your answer before tomorrow, Evalina. I won't wait forever."

Outside, I heard him order one of the guards to take me to the pens to join Jermyn, and my shoulders slumped in defeat. I had absolutely no idea what to do next. Tarron expected my answer in the morning and I could only hope that hours alone in the pens would provide some inspiration.

Chapter Seventeen

~Felix~

It didn't take me long to find the portal thanks to both Evalina's directions and the fact that several fae warriors stood guarding it, their scent strong and unmissable now that I'd become more accustomed to the scents of this world. Maybe they wanted to be sure no one else would be coming through it after Darius and I showed up unannounced, or maybe they wanted to stop people from leaving.

Either way, I had no intention of letting their presence impede me, so I employed a little old-fashioned distraction.

From my spot to the left of the portal, I let out a loud howl that had them immediately scrambling in my direction while I made a wide circle, ducking through the trees until I had a clear shot at the barrier between this world and my own. Readying myself like a runner at the start line, I broke into an all-out sprint.

The fae warriors' footsteps thudded against the velvet forest floor as they spun back around, their shouts cutting through the air. I pushed my body harder, weaving between trees and keeping low, my heart pounding as the portal shimmered in the distance like a lifeline.

Thankfully, no arrows hit me that time as I dove through the portal and emerged back on the Vermillion pack land. It didn't take long for their wolves to find me, and I shifted and identified myself before they let me head back to the pack house.

I arrived just as Vaughan's truck pulled up, Calista in the front seat next to him. While I pulled on some spare clothes, they both got out and came over to me, relief written clearly across their faces.

"I'm glad you're okay," Vaughan said before giving me a rough shove to the chest. "What the fuck were you thinking? Calista said not to go through that portal without her."

I rubbed at the spot where he'd pushed me. "Nice to see you too, Alpha."

He shot me a warning glare I'd seen used on many pack members over the years, a look I knew was rooted in genuine worry. As Alpha, his concern extended to everyone in his care, even if he sometimes had a funny way of showing it.

Calista stepped between us to defuse the tension. "Let's go inside and talk. I want to hear what happened."

We found Darius waiting inside, pacing the kitchen, and his shoulders relaxed when he caught sight of me. "Thank the goddess. I honestly thought we were going to have to go back for you."

"It's not over yet. I'll tell you everything, but I really need something to eat first."

Just the thought of Evalina's food had my stomach growling again. The others waited patiently while I grabbed a bottle of water and some food, scarfing it down as we made our way to a small, unoccupied meeting room. Other pack business had called the Vermillion Alpha away, giving me a chance to bring my own Alpha up to speed first.

"It looks like you didn't eat anything in the fae realm," Calista remarked, trying not to smile as I shoved another bun in my mouth.

With a hard swallow, I cleared my throat as much as possible to answer her. "I didn't, but the temptation was there. More importantly, my mate was there."

The room went deathly quiet as all three of them stared at me.

"Say that again with your mouth empty," Vaughan ordered. "It sounded like you said you found your mate in the fae realm."

"That's what I said." I took a long drink from the water bottle to make sure they didn't misunderstand anything else. "She's a fairy, I think. Elves are taller, right?"

My eyes went to Calista with that question and she nodded. "Elves would be the same height as you or taller. Fairies are shorter. So I've been told, anyway; I've never seen either."

"Because you haven't been to the fae realm."

"Right."

"Are we seriously just going to skip over the fact that your mate is from another world?" Vaughan interjected, looking between me and his mate incredulously. "How did you find her?"

"I actually smelled her first. I know it sounds crazy, but trust me, her scent hit me like a lightning bolt. There was no mistaking it even though I couldn't see anything. I tried to follow her, but I lost her when she went through the portal. I didn't realize what happened at first; I thought she just disappeared."

"Why did she come here?" Calista asked.

"She's looking for silver."

"So, she's the thief?" Vaughan guessed.

"No. The thief is her prince, the guy Darius and I followed through the portal."

Our Delta nodded his agreement. "We caught him red-handed. Like I told you on the phone, he called for back-up and Felix drew their attention so I could escape."

"Then what happened?" Vaughan and Calista asked the question nearly in perfect unison.

I summed up the day's events as succinctly as I could. "They shot me with something and put me in a prison cell. They sent food from the kitchen and my mate was the one who brought it to me. That's when she told me she came here looking for silver but didn't get any. She helped me escape and she's going to come and meet me here tonight so I can give her the silver she needs."

Although I covered all the important points, Vaughan still looked confused. "What does she need silver for?"

"To heal her sick mother, apparently." It didn't make much sense to me, but there were probably a bunch of things about my world that wouldn't make sense to her either.

"So, you get her the silver, and then what happens?" he pressed. "Is she going to come and live here with you? How would that even work if nobody can see her?"

He made a good point, but I couldn't help grinning at the image my mind conjured. "An invisible mate would be pretty cool, don't you think?"

Calista tried not to smile while Vaughan raised his eyes to the ceiling in exasperation, "Seriously, Felix. What's your plan?"

"I don't have one," I admitted. "Every instinct I have says we belong together, but first, she needs this silver and I promised to get it for her."

"I can call some of my hunting contacts," Calista offered. "Someone somewhere might have heard of werewolves and fae mating before."

There was one small problem with that idea. "There's no cell service here. Aside from the Alpha's satellite phone, we're on our own."

"What about the prince?" Darius chimed in. "Is he going to be angry that you escaped? Will he try to come back and find you?"

"I think he knows he doesn't have any authority outside of his own territory and that's why he wanted to keep me there. He was really eager for me to eat something so he must know that would have bound me to their realm. But no, I don't think they'll come for me here. Honestly, I'm more worried about what he might do to Evalina."

Glancing around the room at my three friends who had dropped everything at a moment's notice to come to my aid, my heart swelled with the recognition of how lucky I was to be part of such a close-knit pack. Did Evalina have others who would help her if she ran into trouble before our arranged meeting time? Every moment that passed was another where Tarron might discover her role in my escape, or where her mother's condition might worsen, and my need to help her gnawed at me as fiercely as the hunger I'd ignored in the fae realm.

A soft smile spread across Calista's face. "Is that her name? Evalina? It's pretty."

"It really is." Pride accompanied my words, even though I had no idea if she'd accept being my mate, or how we would make it work if she did. So much was still up in the air, but I knew one thing for certain: I would see her again that night no matter what I had to do to make it happen.

Chapter Eighteen

~**Felix**~

When Alpha Marcus returned, I filled him in on what I'd managed to figure out so far: namely, that their thief was an invisible fae prince.

He stared at me for a long moment before his eyes moved to Vaughan, who sat on my left with his arm resting on the back of Calista's chair. "Is this some kind of joke?"

"Do you have another explanation?" The calm authority in Vaughan's voice gave no indication that he'd doubted the fae realm's existence less than twenty-four hours ago. "Your men confirmed nothing had been taken from your weapons store, no one else was seen going in despite the guards posted at the door, and now, additional items are missing. What else could it be?"

Since the Alpha had no answer for that, he bent his head in concession. "How do we stop him from coming back, then?"

Calista fielded that one. "We can disable the portal between the two realms."

Panic spiked in my chest and I leaned forward, my mouth already open, but she held up her hand to stop me.

"*After* we take care of some other business. There are plenty of passages between the two realms; this is only one of them, but if we disable it, at least they won't have direct access onto your land."

"What business?" Alpha Marcus pressed.

Calista's eyes flicked to me. "Felix followed the prince to the fae realm last night and they temporarily held him there. We need to find out what impact his presence might have had."

She didn't say anything about Evalina, and I kept my mouth shut too, understanding that she must have her reasons for skirting the truth. However, I did have another request. "I also need some silver, as much as you can spare. We'll replace it."

The Alpha's brow furrowed but when he looked at Vaughan, my Alpha nodded his consent, and Alpha Marcus relented. "I have a few bars in storage that we haven't used yet."

"Perfect, thank you."

When the meeting ended, Vaughan ordered me to get some sleep. "We'll rest too since we got up early to get here and we'll want to be alert tonight, just in case."

"You're coming with me?"

His elbow nudged against my side, playfully jabbing me. "I need to meet your mate, don't I?"

He might be my Alpha, but he was also my best friend, and I appreciated his support more than I could say. "Thanks, Vaughan. I can't promise you'll be able to see her, but thanks."

With a roll of his eyes, he pushed me towards my temporary room and I gratefully fell into bed.

Eight hours later, as the sun started to go down, the four of us walked through the forest back to the location of the portal. The trip would have been faster in our wolf forms, but I didn't want to be naked when Evalina arrived and scare her off. Along the way, Vaughan asked Calista for more information about the connection points between our two worlds.

"How many of these portals are there? How do we know if there's one on our territory?"

"You wouldn't know, and it might not ever be a problem if there is one. Since you have to travel through it with someone from the other realm, nobody's likely to accidentally go through, and for the number of fae there are, they don't often come over here either. Usually, it's only the ones who want something that make the trek, like this prince. Do you have any idea why he wanted the silver, Felix?"

Everyone turned to me but I could only shrug. "Not a clue. I feel like if he wanted it for the same reason Evalina does, for healing, he would have sent someone else to get it rather than putting himself in danger. My gut says he didn't want other people to know about it."

After what Evalina said, I had no intention of giving Tarron the benefit of the doubt, and the way he captured and imprisoned me didn't exactly scream innocence either. He was up to something, and the idea of Evalina being in his orbit created an itch of discomfort in my chest, like ticks burrowing their way into my skin. Hopefully, when she showed up that night, I could find out more about the whole situation.

We found the spot easily enough, following my scent in the bushes. Calista's nose crinkled at the smell while Vaughan rubbed a hand across his face. "Seriously?"

"It worked, didn't it?"

Calista and Darius tried not to smile while Vaughan glared at me, but it didn't last. All three of us broke into wide grins, and eventually, Vaughan cracked too.

Even if we hadn't been able to follow the scent, I would have found it eventually, because as soon as we stepped into the glade, the shimmering outline of the portal hung in the air, fractals of light glinting in the forest's darkness.

"Do you see it too?" I asked Darius.

"Yeah." His wide eyes and hushed tone told me he found it just as impressive as I did. "It didn't look like that yesterday."

"What do you see?" Vaughan asked, his eyes scanning the area and brushing right over the spot that had our attention.

"They can see the portal because they've been through it," Calista ventured. "And they can go back through it now too, on their own. Once you've seen the other side, it all becomes visible."

That made it easy to know where to look as we waited for Evalina to appear, but an hour went by, and another one, without any sign of her.

"Something's not right," I muttered, my arms crossed tight over my chest. "She really wanted that silver. She should be here."

A dozen worst-case scenarios popped into my head that might explain her absence, everything from her mother dying to Tarron discovering the part she played in freeing me to her being in a relationship I knew nothing about. I hadn't even asked if she was single, and it would have been a very weird question to ask her anyway. Did fairies wear wedding rings?

"I'm going in to find her."

I didn't plan for the words to come out of my mouth. They were an instinctive reaction I couldn't control but I meant them completely.

Thankfully, nobody tried to argue with me. "What are the risks?" Vaughan asked Calista instead.

"We don't know anything about their weapons, what they wanted the silver for or what they wanted Felix for. If he's recaptured and they force-feed him, he'd be stuck there forever."

"So, it's not a holiday," I acknowledged with a shrug. "I'll stay out of sight. Evalina thought it was strange I could smell the portal and I managed to travel through their forest without attracting attention, so I'm pretty sure their sense of smell isn't as developed as ours. I'll be careful."

"Do you even know where to start looking for her?" Darius asked.

"Not exactly," I admitted. "But I've always had a good sense of direction. I'm pretty sure I could get back to the prison and go from there."

My friends all exchanged looks, and their concern for me genuinely touched me. It wouldn't stop me from going, though.

"Alright," Vaughan finally agreed. "We stick together as much as possible. If we need to separate for safety, I'll give the orders through our mind-link. If I say to abort, we all come back without question or argument. Understood?"

It took me a second to catch up. "You're coming too? All of you?"

Three solemn heads nodded in confirmation before Vaughan added gruffly, "We're family, if not by blood then through the pack. And family doesn't let one of their own walk into danger alone."

To punctuate his point, Calista lifted the leg of her jeans to reveal a small pistol strapped to her calf. "Just in case. And what the hell, I've always been curious about the fae realm too."

I grinned back at her. Having seen her aim first-hand, having Calista for backup gave me a lot more confidence. "You can take the girl away from the hunters, but you can't take the hunter out of the girl."

"I'd prefer to know more about them before we charge in again," Darius admitted, always looking at things from a security angle. "But I understand why you need to. I'm with you."

"Don't get all sappy now, you'll make me cry."

My teasing managed to draw a smile from all of them and I faced the portal with renewed confidence. Although I didn't want to put any of my friends in danger, four of us would be more effective than one, especially if Evalina really had run into trouble.

Whatever kept her from coming to meet me, I wasn't going to let her go that easily.

"Alright, then, let's see what we can find. Follow me."

Chapter Nineteen

~Evalina~

In the quiet, dark cell where the damp air clung to my skin, I whispered a silent thanks to the heavens for Keerla. When she found out I'd been locked up, she stopped by to see me, bribing the guards that Tarron posted with a sweet treat from the kitchen.

"I'm alright," I told her through the same type of passage Felix and I communicated through earlier that day. "But can you please go check on my mother? She needs to eat."

She promised she would before disappearing into the darkening night, and I stepped back, breathing deeply to try to calm the swirling storm of disappointment and anxiety inside of me.

Stuck in the pens, I couldn't meet with Felix, which meant I had no easy way of finding the silver I needed. I could try to find some on my own by going through the portal another time, but based on what I saw during my abbreviated visit the night before, they seemed to be prepared for any kind of intruder. And even if I somehow managed to find enough of the material and bring it back with me, I would still have to evade notice when going through the portal.

It seemed impossible.

Too many odds were stacking up against me, leaving Tarron himself as the only viable option to get the silver I needed. He made it that way by design, I knew that, but it didn't make it any less true. Stuck in the prison with time running out, I would have to give him an answer sooner rather than later.

My stomach twisted uncomfortably at the idea of being tied to that boorish, selfish man for the rest of my life and I sank down onto the floor of the cell, pulling my knees tight to my chest to try to keep the nausea at bay. Maybe it wouldn't be *so* bad? My mother would be healed, and I could stay close to her and Keerla. I wouldn't have to work anymore, though what I would do with my time instead, I couldn't be sure. The king had an amorta but she was rarely seen in public. Her whole life seemed to be confined to the residence, and my chest tightened at the prospect of being so restricted.

The world had much more to offer than that, I knew it did. Felix's kind blue eyes flashed through my memory, asking me to go with him, and even though I knew it would have brought its own challenges, I wished I'd agreed.

The noise outside didn't immediately make me get up. Voices drifted down the passage, sounding like the guards talking to someone, but I didn't pay any attention. It might be time for a shift change or there might be new orders from Tarron. If it had anything to do with me, they would let me know, I had no doubt.

Nothing pierced through my internal debate until I heard my name, not shouted in anger but whispered urgently down the passage.

"Evalina?"

My head snapped up at the sound of the deep, warm voice I'd just been listening to inside my head. "Felix?"

It couldn't be. My mind must have been playing tricks on me, but when I scrambled to my feet and pressed my chin against the bottom of the passage, there he stood, bending down to see me, just as kind and handsome as he'd been in my memory even though the moonlit shadows obscured most of his face.

"What are you doing here?"

I still couldn't believe my eyes. Maybe I'd started hallucinating? It made more sense than that the werewolf would have returned to our world after escaping earlier that day.

"You didn't come to see me," he said simply. "I had to make sure you were okay, and obviously, you're not."

The words, so simple and direct, warmed something deep inside me. His eyes scanned the wall, looking for a way in, but with the magical field in place, there wasn't one. Unlocking the door wouldn't do me any good.

"There are guards out there," I warned him. "Be careful."

A warm smile spread across his face. "My friends have taken care of them, don't worry."

Friends? More of his kind? How did they 'take care' of the guards?

Who *was* this man?

"I brought the silver you wanted," he continued, and my heart swelled with all the hope that had abandoned me earlier, rushing back in. "Now, we just need to get you out."

"Don't worry about me. Please get that silver to my mother's house. Tarron will let me out eventually and I'll figure out a way to put him off a little bit longer. The most important thing is that my mother gets better."

Deep furrows creased his brow as he processed what I said. "Put him off? From what?"

That would take too long to explain so I stuck to my instructions instead. "Go down the path to the left, past the residence, and you'll find a small settlement. The houses form a semicircle and ours is the first one on the left. My friend Keerla might be there, but don't worry about her, just tell her I sent you. In the kitchen, there's a small pantry, you can hide the silver in there and I'll find it when I get home. Once it's there, please go back to your own world before you're captured again. It means so much to me that you kept your word, but I don't want you to get in any trouble."

It meant more to me than I could possibly express in the limited time we had, so hopefully, he could hear the sincerity in my words.

"I'll send my friends there now," he promised. "But I'm not leaving you here. You got me out, so we can get you out too."

He stepped away from the opening and I could hear more murmured voices, others that were deep and masculine, like his, and one that sounded like a woman. The words weren't audible but I could hear firm tones, not arguing but debating, until Felix returned into my line of sight.

"Alright, I passed on your directions. They've gone to your house and will wait for us there. Now, tell me what I need to do to get you out."

He made it sound so simple. "I told you earlier: there's a magical force field surrounding the building. I can open the lock if the magic is removed, but with it up, there's nothing I can do."

"What about the man who lowered it before?" Felix pressed. "Where can I find him?"

"He's being punished as well. He's..."

I trailed off, wanting to smack myself in the head for not thinking of it earlier.

"He's in another one of the cells. I'm not sure if he can work his magic from inside the field, but..."

"... it's worth a try," Felix finished for me. "I'll be right back."

He disappeared again and I could hear him calling out "hello" down some of the other passages. Jermyn might be in any of the cells. From the inside, I couldn't tell, even if he occupied the one right next to me.

The seconds ticked by as my mind raced. Would Jermyn be able to help? Would he be *willing* to, knowing it might bring an even greater punishment down on him? Would he recognize Felix as the one who knocked him out earlier that day and refuse to help him for that reason? What if the guards had somehow managed to get a message to Tarron about Felix's arrival? If Tarron found out, he wouldn't just lock me up again. My punishment would be severe and I didn't want to think about what might happen to Felix. The more I thought about it, the less possible it seemed that we'd be able to succeed, but when Felix returned a few minutes later, a grin lit up his face. "He says it's done. Can you try the door?"

Closing my eyes, I focused my magic, and sure enough, the lock clicked, the mechanism springing out, and the outline of the door appeared in the wall. I ran for it, pushing the handle outwards and stepping out into the freedom of the Etta night. Fresh air hit my face, a welcome relief from the cell's cold, damp staleness, but that comfort paled next to the warmth of Felix's smile.

"What did you say to him?" I asked Felix, staring up at the big, brawny man in awe.

"I kind of promised you'd cook for him," he said, shrugging his broad shoulders in a sheepishly adorable way. "He seemed to really like your food earlier."

"That's perfect." Obviously, he paid attention to details to remember that from our earlier interaction. I was impressed.

Together, we circled the pens and I repeated the process to release Jermyn from his cell. As we walked over to where the unconscious guards had been deposited, one of the men lifted his head, letting out a soft groan.

"Felix!" I hissed in warning but he'd already seen it.

"Sorry about this," he apologized to the man before knocking him out cold with another well-placed blow.

Felix and Jermyn dragged the guards into the cell Jermyn had just vacated, and I relocked the door before Jermyn raised the magical field again. Hopefully, they wouldn't be discovered until someone came to relieve them, so it would buy us a bit of time.

Not intending to waste a minute of it, I instructed Felix and Jermyn to follow me as quietly as possible down the path to my house before Tarron realized we were gone.

Chapter Twenty

~Felix~

Vaughan's voice sounded in my head as soon as we left the prison behind, slipping through the nighttime shadows on the way to Evalina's house.

Ten more minutes and we need to go, Felix. I'm serious.

Understood, I responded since I couldn't say anything else. We'd already left a trail behind us. Guards had been waiting as soon as we entered the portal, but between the four of us, we managed to get them subdued. From the small bag she carried, Calista produced rope and duct tape.

"A hunter is always prepared," she explained with a shrug when Darius and I exchanged impressed looks.

With that group of men tied up and their mouths taped over, we proceeded towards the prison since I remembered the way from my earlier escape. From there, I planned to find the prince's residence, remembering that Evalina worked in the kitchen, but it turned out we didn't need to go any further than the prison. As soon as the circular structure came into view, I could smell her.

She's in one of the cells, I mind-linked the others, and we quickly incapacitated those guards too.

No one had been seriously injured but we were definitely not flying under the radar and Vaughan didn't want to stick around to find out what kind of trouble it might cause for us. Neither did I, so I had to make the next ten minutes count.

"Why were you being held?" I asked Evalina, keeping my voice down so as not to attract any unwanted attention in the dark forest. Every creak of the trees whispered of potential danger.

"Tarron guessed that I helped you escape," she explained, her eyes staying forward as she darted gracefully down the narrow path, her steps light and sure on her tiny feet. "He doesn't know how I did it, but he doesn't need proof. It's one more thing he can hold over me."

That wasn't the first time she made a comment about Tarron trying to manipulate her, and each time, I liked it less. "What does he want from you?"

Evalina didn't answer, but to my surprise, the other man with us did. "He wants what any man wants from a beautiful woman. It's obvious."

"Don't go saying things like that, Jermyn," Evalina hushed him. "You're in enough trouble already and you don't know anything about it."

"Is he wrong?" I asked, guessing from her reaction that Jermyn had hit the nail right on the head. When she didn't deny it, that certainty grew and so did the possessive, protective urges inside me that were part and parcel of the mate bond.

The fae prince wanted *my* mate? Not happening. Not in this world or any other.

"You're not married, then?" I followed up, trying not to sound too eager. Was that even the right word? I didn't know how her species marked their commitment. "Or in a relationship?"

She glanced over at me but the nighttime light wasn't strong enough for me to make out the expression on her face. "No," she answered simply before pointing ahead of us. "We're almost there."

I let a smile break across my face as she hurried the last few steps towards the small settlement she'd described earlier and the house where her mother and my friends were waiting. She wasn't in a relationship. That eliminated one potential obstacle to us being together. Next, I just had to figure out how to get around the whole living-in-two-different-worlds thing.

How hard could it be?

Evalina dashed through the door of the house, as gracefully as she did everything, while I had to turn sideways and duck to get through the door, smiling as I imagined Vaughan and Darius doing the same thing. Inside, my friends had gathered in the small living room that sat to the right of the kitchen we walked into, only a half wall separating the two rooms. The men sat on the floor since they were too large for any of the chairs and would have had to bend over to stay standing, thanks to the low ceiling. Only Calista had found a spot to sit without breaking any of the furniture.

"You put the silver in the pantry?" Evalina asked the others, not stopping for an answer as she ducked into a small room to the side of the kitchen, barely bigger than a cabinet.

"It's on the top shelf in a red box," Vaughan answered, his deep voice almost making the walls of the house vibrate. On the spongy ground, even the foundations of the buildings seemed flexible.

I took a step closer, ducking even further to avoid a light fixture at eye level, and found Evalina on her toes, trying to reach the red box on the top shelf. I reached over and grabbed it, and her grateful smile when I handed it to her filled me with warmth from head to toe.

"Thank you." She glanced down, hiding a blush as she took it from me and squeezed past me, back into the main part of the kitchen. "You should go. If Tarron realizes I'm not in the prison, he'll come looking for me here and I don't want him to find you."

"What happens if he finds *you*? We're not leaving you to face him alone."

If he imprisoned her for helping me to escape earlier, I didn't want to think about the punishment that might await her for breaking out.

Picking up some kind of pan from a pile by the fire, Evalina opened the red box, her eyes widening as she saw the bars of silver inside. Since I had no idea how much she needed, I'd brought as much as I could.

"Felix is right," Calista said, getting up from her seat and stepping into the kitchen to join us. "If you're going to be in danger here, you should consider coming with us."

Evalina's hands stilled for the first time since we walked into the house, her pretty blue eyes glancing between me and Calista warily. "I can't leave. My mother's here."

Her hand waved towards a closed door that must lead to a bedroom, but that didn't seem like much of an objection to me. "We'll take her too, then."

"She can't walk," Evalina protested. "She's barely conscious most of the time."

"Then we'll carry her."

She sized up me, Vaughan and Darius, calculating that I meant it literally. If her mother was the same size as Evalina, none of us would break a sweat carrying her.

"Can I come too?" Jermyn asked, the first words he'd spoken since we arrived at the house. He'd been hovering by the door, trying not to draw any attention, but when he spoke, every head in the room turned to him.

"You don't even know where they come from!" Evalina pointed out.

"It's got to be better than the pens," Jermyn retorted with a shrug before turning to me. "Is there food there?"

"Plenty of it," I assured him.

"Count me in."

Evalina let out an exasperated sigh at the man's easy abandonment of his entire life. "We can't just..."

"We don't have time for this," Vaughan interrupted, curtly but not unkindly. "Here are the facts: we're leaving. If you stay, you may be in trouble. If you come with us, we'll protect you as well as we can."

"Why?" Evalina asked, her eyes searching his face for answers before turning to me. "Why are you helping me?"

Because you're ours, Kai answered in my head. *Because there's nothing we wouldn't do for you.*

True as they were, those words would only confuse her, so for the time being, I stuck to a simpler explanation. "Because you need help and we can give it. After everything you went through to get this silver and help your mother, do you want to risk being separated from her if you're put back in prison?"

Or worse, I added in my head, but since I still didn't know exactly what Tarron wanted from her, I left it at that.

Evalina chewed her bottom lip, the silver and the pan still in front of her, while everyone in the house leaned forward to wait for her reply.

"Will I ever be able to come back?" she finally asked, her voice barely louder than a whisper.

I turned to Calista for help with that question since she intended to disable the portal, and she quickly stepped in. "If you really want to, we'll find a way for you to return. But for now, I think it's safer to come with us."

My lungs forgot their job as I waited for her to speak, but finally, Evalina gave a tiny nod. "Okay. We can go."

Instantly, everyone sprang into action.

"Darius, check for activity outside," Vaughan ordered. "Calista, help Evalina pack anything she needs. Felix, you and I will figure out the best way to transport her mother."

I nodded, moving with him towards the closed door as I whispered my appreciation. "Thank you."

He clapped me on the back, his expression still serious but with understanding in his eyes. "She's your mate. I get it."

If anyone would understand, he would.

Just before going in, I glanced over my shoulder at the woman whose life we were about to completely upend, and found those beautiful blue eyes of hers fixed on me. I gave her what I hoped was an encouraging smile and nod, and when she nodded again in reply, everything felt right with the world.

No matter what, I'd make sure she never regretted deciding to trust me.

Chapter Twenty-One

~Evalina~

Upon receiving their orders, the werewolves moved with a quiet, calculated efficiency that felt alien to me, almost unnatural. Had I completely lost my mind? Nothing else explained my agreement to travel to the terrestrial world with people I'd only just met. Felix was one thing; for reasons I couldn't fully explain, I felt safe around him, and when he said he wanted to help me simply because he could, I believed him. The others, I knew nothing about other than that Felix trusted them.

Most people would agree that throwing my lot in with these strangers qualified as insane.

On the other hand, what choice did I have? Tarron's patience had been wearing thinner, and the memory of lying under his bed while he bedded another woman, saying my name, had been haunting me no matter how much I tried to forget it.

Would escaping from the prison be the final straw? If he found me, would he force me to accept the position as his amorta?

Would he force more than that?

I didn't want to find out and so I agreed to go, ignoring the pang of regret I felt about leaving Keerla. She would be worried when she found me gone, and I hated disappearing without a word, but the werewolves were right: going with them had to be safer than staying in Etta, at least for now. Of the two uncertain paths stretching in front of me, the one Felix would be on seemed by far the more appealing one.

"What do you need to bring with you?" the pretty blonde woman asked as she joined me in the kitchen. The largest man had called her

Calista, a name I'd never heard before. It seemed to suit her since I'd never seen a woman like her, not one so tall, or one wearing pants like a man. All of their clothes were very unusual, including Felix's, though I rather liked the way the garments looked on him. They certainly fit him better than what he'd been wearing in the prison earlier. "Do you have some bags we can pack things in?"

"There are satchels here." Returning to the pantry, I pulled out the silken bags my mother had made for us to carry food that we gathered. "My room is this way."

The narrow space next to my mother's room didn't hold much, but my dresses and ribbons for my hair were there. I pointed out what she could pack before I returned to the pantry to grab the instructions I'd stolen from Tarron's box and the silver that Felix brought for me. From the kitchen, I packed a few pans and some measuring equipment. Since Felix didn't seem to know what a plin was, I didn't want to chance not being able to make the treatment for my mother properly.

"Evalina?" Calista called my name from my room just as Darius returned from outside.

"It's clear," he announced to the whole house, his deep voice easily filling the small space.

"We're ready," Felix replied from my mother's room. "Evalina?"

"Almost." I darted back to my own room and found Calista with the bag overflowing. "Yes?"

She lowered her voice as she stepped closer to me. "I didn't find any underwear. Where do you keep those?"

"Underwear?" I repeated slowly. The word was foreign to me, and I wracked my brain for any meaning it might hold, but nothing came to mind. Maybe a type of armour?

"Garments to wear under your clothes," Calista clarified.

That didn't clear anything up and the others were ready to go so I simply shook my head. "What you have is fine. Thank you for your help."

From my room, I ducked into my mother's room next door to see that Felix and his friend, Vaughan, had created a makeshift hammock for my mother from her bed sheets. She looked warm and cozy, tucked in the blankets and she gave me a weak smile as she caught sight of me at the door.

"Your friends are nice, Lina. They say we're going on a trip."

I probably should have explained things myself, but it seemed like Felix had done a good job of keeping her calm while also getting across that we needed to go. I'd worry about offering her a more complete explanation later, hopefully when her health had recovered to the point where I could be sure she understood what I told her.

My eyes met Felix's and a little zing of... something... travelled through my body, almost the same as when he touched me. "I'm ready."

With a nod, he and Vaughan lifted my mother up, looping a knotted end of the sheets over each of their shoulders so they could carry her between themselves, their hands still free.

"Let me take that," Felix offered, holding out his hand for the bag I held, but I shook my head.

"No, you're already doing so much."

"I got it." Darius' arm appeared from behind me and he snatched the bag from my grasp, already holding the one Calista had packed for me with his other hand. "Let's move."

"Stay close to me," Felix instructed as we all stepped out into the nighttime forest. All the other staff cottages were quiet, their inhabitants sleeping peacefully, unaware of the fugitives in their midst. The orange moon cast a warm glow over the forest, dancing between the branches of the trees and lighting our way. Felix and I led the small group, the others watching our backs as we weaved through the woods to the portal.

As we drew close, muffled sounds reached us and Felix put out a hand to stop me. Everyone else instantly stopped as well. Without any of them saying a word, Darius crept forward to investigate, but he soon returned, his shoulders relaxed.

"It's just the guards we tied up earlier. They're still restrained."

"That's a lucky break," Vaughan stated. "Let's take advantage of it."

We began to move forward again, coming into the clearing where the edges of the portal shimmered, much brighter than the last time I'd been there. Was that because I'd been through it before? Once I crossed through, I might never return again, and my heart panged once more at the thought of Keerla never knowing what happened to me. The guards' eyes glinted with fury as they thrashed against their bonds, the muffled sounds of their protests carrying through the clearing. Restrained as they were, they couldn't do anything to stop us as we approached, but they all got a good look at us. Tarron would know where I went and with whom, but at least we'd have a head start if he decided to give chase.

But even that small advantage seemed to disappear when a sharp voice sliced through the still night air behind us.

"Stop! Don't move or we'll fire."

Chapter Twenty-Two

~Felix~

We went from stealth to flight mode in a matter of seconds when the voice in the darkness ordered us to stop.

On my signal, get Evalina and the other fairies through the portal, Calista's voice said in my head. *I'll hold them off.*

The fuck you will, Vaughan growled back. *I'm not going without you.*

Get over yourself, Alpha, she shot back, only half-teasing. *We're not in your territory right now and I know what I'm doing.*

Ready to go when you say so, Luna, I interjected, making it clear that I would obey even if her mate wouldn't. *And since you're attached to me, Vaughan, you're coming too.*

Darius simply nodded his agreement. Since neither Evalina nor Jermyn could hear our conversation, I had no chance to warn them before Calista reached down and grabbed the small gun hooked around her calf. The bang when she fired it into the air reverberated through the nighttime fae forest, sounding even louder than usual. My ears rang as I grabbed Evalina with one hand, Darius nudging Jermyn forward as we raced towards the portal, passing through it with Calista covering us from behind.

To my relief, I could still see Evalina as we emerged back into the Vermilion pack territory, under the white moon of our own world. She might still be invisible to those who had never visited the fae world, but I'd never lose sight of her again.

"I'm going back for Callie," Vaughan stated as soon as we were through, starting to untie the makeshift gurney we'd constructed for Evalina's mother.

"Don't," I begged. "At least not yet. She's got it under control and you might screw up her plan. If she's not here in two minutes, I'll go back with you."

"You don't know her plan any more than I do," he grumbled, but he stopped his movements, his whole body twitching as he fought against his instincts.

Seconds dragged by, each one seeming unending until Calista raced through the portal, immediately dropping her bag on the ground and rooting around in it.

"Hold this," she instructed, holding up a piece of string at one end. She didn't address the order to anyone in particular, and since Evalina's hands were free, she stepped forward and took it while Calista continued her directions. "Hold it across the portal, nice and steady, then close your eyes. Darius, make sure none of the other fae watch either."

Evalina went to one side of the portal while Calista stood on the other, the string spanning the width of the entrance like a piece of caution tape. I couldn't see what good it would do if any of the fae soldiers tried to follow us, but I held my tongue, waiting to see what Calista had up her sleeve. As instructed, Evalina closed her eyes, covering them with her other hand as a precaution.

From her bag, Calista produced a container of salt, sprinkled the ground in front of the portal with it, and recited some words in a language I didn't recognize. Evalina seemed to, though, based on the way she startled in surprise when the words came out of Calista's mouth.

I only knew her incantation had finished when the bright light surrounding the portal began to dim. Soon, it disappeared completely.

"Alright, you can let go now but keep your eyes closed," Calista told Evalina. Once my mate dropped the end of the string in her hands, Calista rolled it back up and returned it to the bag along with the container of salt.

"You want to explain what all that was about?" Vaughan asked gruffly, but I could tell he was impressed, the same as I was. His gruffness came from residual concern over Calista's safety, nothing else.

"I disabled the portal," Calista explained. "If they want to come after us now, they'll have to find another entry point, and they'll need to be able to track us from there. It won't be quick, if they can manage it at all."

"Why didn't they follow you straight through?" Darius wondered.

"I spilled some of the salt on the other side. They had no choice but to stop and count the grains. I figured it would buy us the time we needed."

That also explained why she made sure Evalina and Jermyn didn't watch her sprinkle the salt in front of the portal either. It was quick thinking.

"We have the best Luna ever," I announced.

Calista shook her head while Vaughan echoed his agreement. "She's incredible, and I'm ready to take her home to the Crimsontooth pack now. Let's move out."

With my hand on Evalina's shoulder, I moved her away from the salt, and once we were out of sight of it, she opened her eyes. My hand dropped when she could see on her own, but I immediately missed the feel of her beneath my fingers.

As we walked, I gave Evalina a brief overview of what would happen next. "Our home is a couple of hours from here, but it's only a ten-minute walk back to the cars. We'll drive the rest of the way."

"Cars?"

Once she mentioned it, I realized that I didn't remember seeing any kind of vehicles in the fae world. Granted, I'd only seen a very small part of it, but technology in general seemed different. "They're a mode of transportation, a lot faster than walking. When you see them, you can tell me if you have another name for them."

She nodded before shooting a curious look at the dark forest surrounding us. "It smells different here."

The pine-scented forest, rich and earthy, definitely contrasted with the almost sickly-sweet fruit scent in her own world.

"A lot of things are different," I agreed. "Nothing will hurt you though, not as long as we're around."

We stayed quiet for the rest of the short walk, focused on watching the ground for hazards in the dark night. A hundred different things I wanted to say to her danced across my tongue, but too many of them were things we needed to discuss in private, not in front of a crowd.

When the pack house came into view, Vaughan took charge again. "I'll go update Alpha Marcus while you guys get packed up. Calista and I will take Evalina's mother and the fae man. Darius, you can go with Felix and Evalina. We'll send someone back tomorrow to collect the other car."

That worked for me.

Darius placed Evalina's bags next to my truck before taking the other end of Evalina's mother's hammock from Vaughan. Together, we got her set up comfortably in the SUV that Vaughan and Calista drove over in, and I put Evalina's bags in my truck before offering a hand to Evalina to help her up. Honestly, she might need more than a hand. The step into the raised pick-up truck sat almost at her waist.

Her wide eyes surveyed the vehicle with curiosity and a bit of apprehension. "What is it?"

So, they *didn't* have cars then. "We sit inside them and they'll move us pretty quickly. Do you have anything like this where you're from?"

Her hair swished over her shoulders as she shook her head, still looking uncertain.

"It'll take us back to where I live, where Tarron can't find you and you can prepare the treatment for your mother. After that, you can decide whether or not you want to go back."

Obviously, I hoped whatever she decided for the future would include me, but we'd take that one step at a time.

Evalina's thoughts were still on the large, unfamiliar vehicle in front of her. "Is it scary?"

A grin broke across my face at her innocent question. "I promise it's safe. You can sit next to me, and if you're scared, you can squeeze my hand."

I held my right hand out to her and she only hesitated a second before placing her tiny palm against mine. Again, the sparks of our bond travelled up my body from where our skin connected, and I had to bite my lip to stifle a groan. Sitting next to her in the car would be torture, and I couldn't wait.

Chapter Twenty-Three

~Evalina~

Felix's large body filled the seat next to mine in the 'car', and his big, strong hands helped me to use the strap to tie myself down. When I cast a wary look at him, his broad shoulders lifted in a shrug.

"We'll be moving pretty fast, so this is just a precaution in case there's a sudden change in speed. I promise it's safe."

He'd said those words outside too, and they affected me just as much the second time. Hearing him vow to keep me safe, the words rumbling from his muscular chest in his deep voice, I didn't doubt for a moment that he would do it. What I still didn't understand was *why*.

Why did this unusual man take such an interest in me, and why did I feel more drawn to him than I ever had to anyone before?

Why had I agreed to go with him to a world I knew nothing about? Why did I believe that he'd protect me?

Nothing about my surroundings reminded me of the familiar warmth of my kitchen or the quiet rustle of the Etta trees in the breeze, but rather than feeling lost, excitement sparked inside me every time Felix looked my way.

Why did it all feel so right?

Darius got into the car on the other side of me, and when he twisted his hand, the whole thing rumbled to life beneath us. Vibrations travelled up my legs and a warm breeze began to blow.

"It's alive?" I whispered, more confused than ever.

Felix chuckled. "No, it's a machine. Do you know what that means?"

I shook my head, letting out a small yelp as we began to move forward. Felix's large hand covered mine in support, and just like every time he touched me, my body tingled in response, warmth blooming where our skin connected and spreading outward. The gentle pressure of his hand helped to calm me as we moved faster, a bright light illuminating the way in front of us and red lights ahead showing the other car with my mother and Jermyn inside.

"You can sleep on the way if you need to," Felix added, his voice sounding even gruffer as he lowered its volume. "My shoulder makes a pretty good pillow. If you want to use it."

The idea of curling up against him appealed to me far more than it probably should have, but truthfully, I couldn't imagine going to sleep after everything that just happened. Adrenaline still pumped through my body, filling me with a nervous energy that wouldn't be dissipating anytime soon, not to mention the dozens of questions spinning around inside my head.

"Is Vaughan your king?" I blurted out, since I needed to start my questions somewhere. The others all seemed to defer to him, including Felix.

"Kind of," Felix replied. "We don't call him a king, but he's the one in charge and he was born into the position like a king. It's similar."

"What do you call him?"

"Alpha. And I'm his second-in-command, or Beta."

The words were new to me and I repeated them slowly, turning them over in my mouth to see how they felt. "Alpha. Beta." It didn't surprise me that Felix held such a high position given his strength and capability, but it made his interest in me even more difficult to understand. "And Calista is his queen?"

"Close enough," he agreed good-naturedly. "Her title is Luna."

"Luna." The unfamiliar words sounded almost magical to me.

"She's his mate," Felix added, his voice catching slightly on the last word, and I craned my neck to look up at him.

"What does that mean?"

He swallowed so hard that I could see his throat working. I'd never realized a neck could be masculine before, but everything about him seemed manly in a way I'd never experienced.

"You said you don't know much about werewolves?" he asked, answering my question with one of his own.

"Not much at all. I saw a drawing when I was young."

The way his chest rumbled when he laughed pulled at something deep in my stomach. "I used to read stories about fairies," he admitted. "I liked the pictures."

When I found that image in Tarron's box, I couldn't have ever imagined I would be sitting next to a real werewolf, and from the twinkle in Felix's eyes, I suspected he felt the same about me.

He cleared his throat before continuing. "Werewolves were created by the moon goddess, and as part of her blessing to us, she gave each of us a mate. They're our other half, the person who completes us perfectly. We recognize them on sight."

"Like love at first sight?" That concept, I'd heard of before.

"Kind of, but it's not just about attraction," Felix explained. "It's like your soul recognizes theirs. Being apart from your mate feels like missing a part of yourself, and being with them makes everything in the world feel right."

Blinking quickly a few times, I took that all in. It sounded... wonderful, actually. "That really is a blessing."

"It can be," he agreed. "But it's not always straightforward. For example, with Vaughan and Calista, he recognized her but she didn't know he was her mate because her werewolf side had been suppressed."

My brows drew together as I tried to understand what he meant, and Felix laughed.

"It's a long story. My point is that werewolves recognize their mates, but sometimes, they're mated to other species, and those species don't feel it in the same way. It can complicate things."

"It does sound complicated," I confessed. I wasn't sure I fully understood but I wanted to. I wanted to learn all about him and his species. "Do you have a mate?"

I found myself hoping the answer was no, though it really wasn't any business of mine.

Felix's jaw tightened, his gaze flicking away from mine for just a moment before returning with an intensity that sent a shiver down my spine.

"It's complicated."

Swallowing my disappointment, I nodded, glancing down at his hand still covering mine. I'd barely realized he still held it; it felt so natural there. Gently, I pulled it from his grasp and reached up to tuck my long hair behind my ears.

"What about the fae?" Felix asked, moving his arm to the back of the seat since I'd taken my hand back. "How do you decide who you spend your life with?"

I kept my gaze down, not wanting to think of Tarron's demands again. "It's by choice, usually."

"Usually?" He picked up on the word immediately.

"For the royal family and other rulers, it's often arranged," I explained with a shrug. "They will have a contrar, the person they are officially bound to, but often, they will also have an amorta, someone who is their own choice."

"Human kings used to have something like that. They called it a mistress. It was usually someone they were attracted to, and they were treated well, but the woman had no official power and their children couldn't inherit any official positions. Is it like that?"

"Yes, it sounds very similar." I was glad not to have to explain it further. "For common people like my parents, they take an amica. It's less formal."

"Fascinating." He said the word as if he truly meant it. "Where is your father now?"

"Dead." I'd found it easier to state the word bluntly. It stung a little less that way. "Your parents are mates?"

Felix nodded. "They were but my mother died a few years ago. I'm not sure my father will ever fully recover."

"I think if you truly love someone, you never do. You can move on and be happy again, but you're never exactly the same person you were before."

"I think you're right." Felix shifted in his seat, his body angling towards me even more than before. "That's why we'll do everything we can to help save your mother. You shouldn't have to lose her too."

He didn't even know my mother, but his words sounded so passionate, I couldn't doubt that he meant them sincerely.

"Thank you." I whispered the words as my head rolled back into the crook of his arm. Somehow, despite all my earlier energy, the humming of the car around us and Felix's comforting presence had made me relax more than I realized, and as soon as my eyes closed, I fell into a deep, profound sleep.

Chapter Twenty-Four

Contented.

No other word adequately described how I felt sitting in the truck with Evalina tucked into my side, fast asleep. Her soft breath warmed my arm, steady and reassuring. We still had problems to deal with, quite a lot of them, but having my mate there beside me, safe and secure, satisfied me on a level I didn't even know I had.

Kai felt it too. His deep serenity surrounded me, wrapping me up in a cocoon of peace unlike anything I'd ever experienced.

Did all mated wolves get to feel like this every day? No wonder Vaughan never wanted Calista out of his sight. I thought I understood it before but I didn't. I *couldn't*. I couldn't truly know it until I felt it for myself.

And she still didn't have a clue what she meant to me.

I almost told her when she asked if I had a mate. My instincts screamed at me to say the words, to claim her as mine, but my head pushed back against them. What if it was too soon? What if I scared her off? If someone told me I was meant to be with them when I didn't feel it for myself, it would honestly freak me out. She needed to reach that conclusion by herself, just like Calista had started to with Vaughan even before her wolf resurfaced.

It could happen.

It *would* happen.

I'd do everything I could to prove myself to her before I put the weight of our bond on her, and hopefully, at that point, it wouldn't seem like too much of a burden.

The Crimsontooth pack house made for a welcome sight after all the excitement of the last couple of days, and Evalina didn't even stir when I lifted her out of the truck and carried her into one of the guest room suites while Vaughan and Darius set up her mother in the room next to her.

She still wore her pretty dress, fit for a formal occasion. It didn't look like the most comfortable attire for sleeping but undressing her in any way without her permission felt wrong, so I simply tucked her into bed as she was.

Should I leave a note for when she wakes up, so she knows where she is? I asked Kai.

Why do you need a note? Just stay here with her.

I snorted softly. *Did you miss the part where I'm trying to avoid overstepping the boundaries of our current relationship as she understands it?*

Kai growled at me. *Then let **me** stay.*

That...

Actually, that wasn't a terrible idea. It would be easier for us to rest next to her, knowing she was safe and comfortable, and she might freak out less at the sight of Kai when she woke up than if she found a six-foot-tall man in her room.

Alright, but you have to respect her personal space.

Sure. Whatever you say.

He sounded far too smug about getting his way. *Why don't I believe you?*

After stripping off in the bathroom and leaving my clothes there so I'd have something to wear in the morning, I shifted to my wolf form and let Kai take control. He jumped up onto the bed and sniffed at Evalina, her caramel and apple scent even stronger and somehow even more appealing through his wolf nose, before he turned in a circle a couple of times and curled up towards the foot of the bed, taking up more than half the bed's length. It didn't take long for us to both give in to the exhaustion that had been creeping up on us for hours.

Warm, tingling shivers woke me. I had no idea how much time had passed, but when a soft hand brushed through Kai's fur, I sighed internally, feeling just as content as I had in the truck the night before.

She's been petting me for five minutes, Kai said, sounding ready to swoon. *You've been missing out.*

Let me see.

His eyes blinked open lazily, giving me my first glimpse of Evalina in the morning light. Somehow, during the night, she'd shifted down the bed until she curled in almost a semicircle around Kai's body. Her hand traced lazy circles through the fur on his side but her eyes remained closed.

Is she awake? I whispered in my head, though I didn't need to bother. She couldn't hear me anyway.

Not fully. She looks happy though.

She really did. A sweet half-smile skimmed over her lips with none of the tension I'd seen in her bearing during all our previous encounters. Maybe she felt the same contentment I did from the mate bond even if she didn't know why.

Should I wake her? Kai asked. *It's pretty late. I checked in with Atlas and the others are already up.*

Atlas was Vaughan's wolf, Kai's Alpha in the same way that Vaughan was mine. *Yeah, you probably should. Gently.*

Bending his neck, he leaned over and nuzzled the top of his head against Evalina's face. She let out a soft, sweet snuffle that was so cute, I could barely stand it. He repeated the action, and that time, her eyes fluttered open, and when she saw the wolf's face mere inches from hers, she did what any reasonable person would do.

She screamed.

Loudly.

Bolting backwards, she tumbled right off the bed and Kai howled in dismay, both from the noise and from the distress our mate was in.

His howl made her shriek again.

This really wasn't going well.

Bathroom. Now! I ordered him, and reluctantly, he bounded off the bed and into the adjoining room. Inside, I shifted back before calling out to Evalina.

"It's alright. It's me. It's Felix."

"Oh." She gasped in breaths of air and I could hear the rustle of sheets as she moved around in the bedroom while I quickly pulled on my clothes, keeping my ears tuned on her through the half-open bathroom door. "I'm sorry. I forgot where I was."

"It's alright," I repeated. "*I'm* sorry. I didn't mean to scare you."

"Where's my mother?" she asked.

"She's still sleeping in the next room." With my shirt over my head, I opened the door all the way. "You can go see her or you can have something to eat, or both. I can bring some food to her room so you can both eat together. Please, don't worry about the bed."

She'd already been halfway through making it, but when I told her to stop, she let her arms drop. Turning to me, her eyes started at my bare feet on the carpeted bedroom floor before slowly travelling up the length of my body until she looked me in the eyes, her cheeks tinted with a pretty pink blush by the time she reached my face. I couldn't stop the grin that tugged at my lips at the suggestion that she liked what she saw. "I'd... uh... I'd like to eat with her, please."

"Of course. We have cereal or toast or fruit or yogurt or eggs or sausages or bacon. Whatever you like, really."

Her lips tightened into an adorable pout. "I have no idea what most of that is."

"Right." She literally came from a different world; I had to remember that. "Never mind. I'll bring you a few things and you can decide when you see it."

Another door connected her room to the one next to it, and I left her at her mother's bedside before mind-linking to the kitchen to prepare some food while I went to have a quick shower and put on some clean clothes. For once, I actually hesitated in front of my closet, debating over what to wear since I wanted to look good for my mate. Leo would laugh if he could see me since usually, I was the one teasing him over the care he put into dressing.

Making a good impression mattered, though. Once she healed her mother, Evalina would need to decide whether to return to the fae realm or stay with me. It didn't give me a lot of time to convince her that with me was exactly where she was meant to be.

Chapter Twenty-Five

~**Evalina**~

My mother's eyes stayed closed while Felix let me into her room, but as soon as he disappeared out the door, her eyelids sprang open and she assessed me with a vigour I hadn't seen in her expression in months.

"You've been keeping things from me, Lina! Who is that man?"

Where did I even begin? I decided to start with the basics as I sat next to her on the bed, reaching out to place my palm on her forehead. Rather than being cool to the touch as it had been, a healthy warmth greeted my hand. "His name is Felix."

"He told me that much when he introduced himself to me last night. Where on earth did he come from? How did you meet him? Where are we now? I've never seen anything like this place. Your father would have loved this."

He really would have, but I could barely focus on that as I took in my mother. A rosier pallor brightened her skin and she seemed to have much more energy. She hadn't put so many words together in a long time and my heart quickened with hope. "You seem to be feeling better."

"Don't ignore my questions!" She fixed me with a pointed glare before her expression softened into a smile. "But, yes, I feel much better."

Why would that be the case? Had something in Etta been making her sick in the first place? Did simply taking her away from it make such a difference?

"He's a werewolf," I explained, not sure if she would even know the word. I hadn't until I saw it in Tarron's box, but my father clearly knew about them, and nothing in my mother's expression suggested confusion. Surprise, certainly, but not confusion. "He's from... well, here, apparently. This is his home. And I met him..."

I trailed off, not knowing how much information to share. If I told her I'd gone through the portal on my own to find a cure for her, she'd be furious, and I didn't need to upset her when she was making such good progress. I decided to stick to a half-truth instead.

"He came to Etta looking for a thief and Tarron captured him. I was sent to take him food in the pens."

I looked down as I picked up her wrist to check her pulse but really, I just didn't want her to figure out how much I'd left out.

It didn't work, since she immediately had suspicions. "How come he's not in the pens anymore?"

Thankfully, a knock at the door saved me from having to answer that question, and I called out, "Come in," expecting it to be Felix.

Nothing happened, and a moment later, the knock repeated.

Maybe he didn't hear me, so I got up and opened the door, finding not Felix at all but a young woman around my age with a tray on wheels full of delicious-smelling food. I stepped back out of the way as she pushed it through the door. Although not nearly as tall as Felix, she still towered over me, probably at least a foot taller than I was.

Once inside, she glanced around, her brow knit and her lips pursed. "Hello?"

"Hello." I came out from beside the door to stand right in front of her. "I'm Evalina. Did Felix send you?"

She continued to look around, looking straight through me and past my mother on the bed before shrugging and walking back out, leaving the tray with us.

"She can't see us," my mother reminded me, figuring it out before I did. "Only people who have been to our realm can see us in the terrestrial world."

"I totally forgot about that," I admitted. My father used to tell me stories of the mischief fae got up to in the terrestrial world, just for fun, since they couldn't be seen.

How I wished he could have been there to come with us on this adventure.

"Back to Felix," my mother prompted. "Why did he bring us here?"

I turned to the tray that had been left for us. The smell of the food was like nothing I'd ever experienced: savory, warm, and rich, and my stomach growled in appreciation. My last meal had been an awfully long time ago, and I couldn't even remember the last time someone else had cooked for me. "Maybe we should eat some of this food, it looks amazing."

"Evalina."

Sugarlumps. When my mother used my full name, she meant business.

Turning back to face her, I offered her a sheepish shrug. "Felix escaped from the pens. When Tarron found out, he blamed me and Jermyn and imprisoned us both. Felix came back with his friends and broke me out."

She absorbed all of that information remarkably calmly. "Prince Tarron won't be pleased that you were taken."

The thought sent an unpleasant pang of anxiety through me. If Tarron managed to track me down, what would he do? Would Felix and his pack be in danger because of me? Felix didn't seem worried but he didn't know Tarron as well as I did.

"No, he won't be, but I'm hoping that…"

"Good," she interrupted before I could finish. "He needs to learn that he can't always get his way."

Her words stunned me into silence, mostly because I'd never heard my mother whisper a word against any of the royal family. Not even after my father's punishment.

One side of her mouth crooked up in a wry smile. "We aren't in Etta anymore, are we? We can finally speak freely."

I offered my tentative agreement, still a little shocked. "I suppose so."

"I don't like the way he looks at you," she added bluntly.

"Felix?"

"No," she chided, shaking her head with a smile. "Tarron. The way Felix looks at you... well, that's something altogether different."

What did *that* mean? Before I could ask, the man himself reappeared, knocking softly on the door before letting himself in.

"Am I interrupting?" His eyes darted back and forth between my mother and me curiously. "Have you eaten? What can I do to help?"

"We haven't eaten yet," my mother answered smoothly, as if we hadn't just been talking about him behind his back. "The food isn't like anything we've ever seen before."

"Right." He shook his head, as if he were disappointed with himself for not anticipating that. "Let me show you what we've got."

He pushed the tray closer to the bed, explaining each of the dishes and sharing his favourites. His attention remained mostly on my mother, but every now and then, his eyes slid over to meet mine, a smile brightening his face and showing off a sweet dimple in his cheek. My stomach fluttered at the sight.

I felt something when he looked at me, that couldn't be denied, but I assumed it stemmed from his raw masculinity and how different he was to anyone else I'd ever met. Although, once I thought about it further, I realized I didn't feel the same thing when Vaughan or Darius looked at me and they were just as masculine and exotic as Felix.

Did this fluttering deep in my belly actually mean something? Had my mother seen something I missed?

Would I be crazy for hoping she might be right?

Chapter Twenty-Six

~Felix~

Both women gave me their rapt attention as I pointed out the various food items on the cart that the kitchen had sent up. Too late, I realized that I didn't know the first thing about fae dietary practices.

"Do you... uh, do you eat animals?"

Were they vegetarian? Vegan? What kind of animals did they have in the fae world? The longer I thought about it, the bigger the gaps in my knowledge seemed.

"The royal family does," Evalina's mother answered smoothly. "The rest of us don't get much of a chance to."

So, it came down to economics rather than morality? That seemed easier to handle. As a werewolf, I didn't know very many vegetarians.

"Lina and I both worked in the royal kitchens," she added, giving her daughter a warm smile. "We snuck a few tastes now and then."

My eyes darted over to Evalina, who seemed less at ease than her mother. Something appeared to be bothering her but it could be so many things, I didn't know where to start.

I decided to stick with something simple. "Lina? Is that what you prefer to be called?"

Her icy blue eyes met mine with much more uncertainty than they had earlier. "Most people close to me call me Lina, but I like the way you say my full name."

Her answer sent a small spark of warmth through me, and Kai crowed in joy in my head at the fact that she liked *anything* about me.

Thanks for the vote of confidence, I snorted back.

"I'll stick to Evalina then." Flashing her a grin, I turned back to the food. "Did I miss anything?"

"I do have one question," Evalina spoke up. "You said that you couldn't eat my food in Etta because you wouldn't be able to return to this world. Does it work the same way in reverse? If we eat here, will we be stuck?"

All of Kai's happiness evaporated along with my own when she referred to staying with us as being 'stuck', but I swallowed down my disappointment, determined not to let it show. "I'm actually not sure about that. Let me check."

Opening a link to Calista, I addressed my Luna in my head.

Quick question: can the fae still return to their world if they eat here?

She replied to me immediately, not leaving me hanging like her mate often did. *It shouldn't affect their ability to move between worlds. I'm not exactly sure why, but it only seems to affect beings from our world and not vice versa.*

Perfect, thanks.

To Evalina and her mother, I spoke out loud. "It's safe. You can eat here and still go back to your world, if that's what you want."

Evalina's brow furrowed into an adorably confused frown. "I thought you were going to check."

Ah, right. Mind-linking didn't occur in many species like it did for werewolves. I'd have to do my best to explain. "Werewolves have a telepathic link with the other members of their pack. I just asked someone inside my head and they answered me already. You're fine to eat."

Her eyes widened in surprise and, unless I was mistaken, a little bit of wonder as she and her mother exchanged a look. "Some fae have that ability but not many. It's very rare."

"I would love to hear more about your world; *all* about it, actually. But first, please eat."

Evalina filled up a plate for herself while I made one for her mother, insisting that she stay in bed even though she looked a hell of a lot better than she did the night before. Evalina took a seat on the bed next to her and they tried small bites of everything, exclaiming over the tastes and comparing our breakfast items to the things they ate at home. A natural grace infused each movement; the way her chin tilted in laughter, the delicate way her tongue darted out as she placed a piece of fruit onto it. Watching her left me feeling almost spellbound.

I could have happily watched her all day.

However, a soft knock on the door came before they'd finished, and Calista appeared from behind it, her blonde hair tied back and wearing a simple sweater and jeans. "How are you both doing today?" she asked the two women on the bed.

"We're well, thank you," Evalina answered for them both before making some introductions. "This is my mother, Maudi. Mama, this is Calista. She's the queen of this place."

The older woman immediately bowed her head while Calista shook hers in dismay. "No, no, I'm not a queen. Nothing like that."

"You kind of are," I countered with a grin.

Calista threw me a dirty look. "Is that what you've been telling them?"

To the fae, she gave a different explanation.

"The social structure here is much less formal. My mate and I are in charge, yes, but you don't have to treat us any differently."

Neither Evalina nor Maudi looked convinced, so I jumped in again, keeping my tone light. "What's up, Luna?"

Calista's lips pursed at the title but she ignored me, addressing the women instead. "I've been doing some research into using silver as a treatment since you mentioned you were going to try that."

Evalina nodded. "I'd like to get to work on it right away."

"Actually, I don't think you should." She paused for a moment to let that sink in before continuing. "The reading I've done suggests that metals behave differently between our world and the fae world. There, it might be a cure, but here, ingesting silver could be fatal."

Evalina's face scrunched up as she processed that. "But our physiology is different too, isn't it? Wouldn't that make a difference?"

"Possibly, but I don't think it's worth the risk. It might be better to have your mother checked by our doctors instead to see if they can determine an appropriate treatment in this world."

"I'm confused," I had to admit. "If she's healed here using our methods, how do we know she won't get sick again if they go back?"

I had to stick with saying '*if* they go back' because saying 'when' would have made my chest ache.

"Possibly," Calista repeated. "There's a lot we don't know."

"I'm feeling much better just from being here," Maudi interjected. "I'm not sure I even need a treatment anymore."

Evalina nodded emphatically. "I wondered if something in Etta had been making you sick to begin with since you've taken such a turn just from us leaving."

"There are a lot of factors at play here," Calista stated again. "And until we have more information, I think it's best that no one goes around drinking any silver. Why don't I accompany Maudi to the hospital once she's finished eating and Felix, you and Evalina can search the Crimsontooth territory for another portal to the fae world. Since you've both been there, you'll be able to spot the portals easily."

By that, I assumed she meant they would glow in the same way the other one did after I came back through it. More than that, I knew exactly what she was doing: orchestrating a little time alone for me and Evalina so I could get to know her better. I mouthed a silent 'thank you' to her while Evalina consulted with her mother.

"Are you sure you'll be okay without me?" Evalina asked, her small hands grasping her mother's in a gesture both protective and affectionate.

"I'll be just fine," Maudi insisted. "You've spent too much time looking after me already. Go and take a nice walk outside with your new friend."

The word 'friend' sounded almost sarcastic, and she smiled over at me in a knowing way that made me suspect she knew exactly how I felt about her daughter, though how she could have figured that out, I had no idea.

To my great relief, Evalina gave in, flashing me a sweet smile of her own. "I guess you're stuck with me, then."

Nothing in the world could have made me happier.

Chapter Twenty-Seven

~Evalina~

With the way the fluttering in my stomach kicked up at the idea of spending time with Felix, I knew I wouldn't be able to eat anything else. Luckily, I'd already eaten quite a lot. All the food of this world fascinated me, but the tart red berries that Felix called raspberries might have been my favourite. I already had a dozen ideas how I could incorporate them into some of my favourite desserts. Maybe I would have time to visit the kitchens before I left and ask the staff some questions about what they did with them.

"I'll go change into some fresh clothes," I announced, avoiding Felix's eyes as I realized I had been wearing the same thing for more than a full day. Both my dress and myself had felt a lot fresher when I put it on the previous morning. "Is there clean water somewhere that I can wash with?"

"Like... a shower?" Felix asked, his throat contracting heavily with the word.

Once again, I had no idea what he meant. "A what?"

"A show..." He started to repeat himself before shaking his head. "Never mind. I'll show you."

His large frame followed me back through the doorway into my room, and he went into the small, white and shiny room next to it, where he'd gone that morning to change back to himself after waking up as a wolf. I hadn't taken a look at the room yet, and my eyes widened as I stepped through the door behind him. It looked like some kind of laboratory.

"You'll find fresh water here," he said, pointing to a silver-coloured tube over a large basin. When he lifted a handle next to it, water immediately flowed out of the tube and I squeaked in surprise.

"Is it magic?" I breathed. We had nothing like it in Etta.

Felix chuckled, the sound rumbling in his broad chest. "No, just technology. The shower is here, it works the same way, but the water comes from higher up, so you can wash yourself under it."

He reached into the glass box that stood on one side of the room, lifting another handle and, as he promised, water fell from another silver-coloured tube high above my head.

"Like a waterfall," I murmured.

"Yes, kind of," he agreed, beaming with pride at my appreciation. Finally, he pointed at a chair with a hole in it and water sitting in a bowl beneath it. "And this is the toilet, for when you need to... relieve yourself."

He gestured vaguely towards his hips, and my cheeks immediately heated with the thought of what might be lying beneath his clothes in that area.

"I understand," I quickly assured him. "And then I use this?"

The chair had a silver handle on it, like the ones in the basin and the shower, so I tried to lift it as he'd done with the other ones, but nothing happened. A frown creased my lips as Felix chuckled again. "Press down on this one."

"Oh." I did as he said, and instantly, the water in the chair swirled around and disappeared before being replaced by fresh, clean water. "Are you *sure* this isn't magic?"

People in Etta spent hours gathering fresh water. To have it at my fingertips *felt* like magic.

"I'm sure," he promised. "What do you use instead of a toilet?"

I'd never really discussed bodily functions with anyone other than my mother, but he seemed genuinely curious and not embarrassed at all, so I did my best to follow suit. "We have fire pits."

His blue eyes went so wide, I almost giggled. "*Fire* pits?"

"Everything that goes into them burns."

"I suppose that makes sense," he said slowly. "But it sounds dangerous. I fell into the toilet once as a boy and I only got wet."

That time, I did giggle, glancing down at the chair. "How did you fall in?"

He answered me with a smirk. "I wasn't always this big."

My eyes dropped to his waist and the strong, thick thighs beneath it, my cheeks heating once again as my thoughts strayed in directions they really shouldn't be heading about a man I barely knew. Before he could notice my stare, I looked away. "Well, thank you. I think I have what I need. I'll get ready now. Where should I meet you?"

"I'll be just outside the door, in the hallway. Take your time."

Once he left, I peeled off my dress and hung it up on a hook on the wall to let it air out. With a bit of playing with the handles in the shower, I discovered that I could make the water cooler or hotter. "Amazing," I murmured under my breath before shrieking when I made it a little *too* cold. My nipples immediately pebbled as goosebumps sprouted along my skin.

"Evalina?" Felix's voice carried through the closed door. "Are you okay?"

"I'm fine," I called back, shivering until I managed to warm the water up again. When warm, steamy drops started to fall, I relaxed, sighing as the water slid down my skin. As my muscles started to loosen, my mind began to wander. How close had Felix been standing that he heard my cry? Was he still there now? How much distance separated him from my wet, naked body?

Why did it excite me to think he might be nearby?

As my hands slid across my slippery skin, washing away the dirt and grime of the pens and the trudge through the forest, my eyes closed and for just a moment, I let myself imagine they were Felix's hands instead. His hands were so big, one of them could easily cover my breast. My fingers slid across the nipple, still taut from the earlier blast of cold water, and I let out a soft moan as I imagined bigger, rougher fingers in their place.

I'd never had these kinds of fantasies before, not about a specific person. The thought of Tarron touching me turned my stomach, but with Felix, it felt different. I didn't know why or how, only that it did.

Shaking my head at myself, I forced myself to abandon those day-dreams and finish washing. Reluctantly, I turned off the water and found a cloth to dry myself before putting on a clean dress from the bag Calista packed for me the night before. My damp hair made a tight braid, and I added some colour to my eyes and cheeks from the small jars of herbs I'd brought with me.

The reflection in the glass on the wall showed a bright-eyed, eager woman, ready for an adventure.

Could that really be me?

With my mother on the mend and Tarron far away, my problems seemed like a distant memory. A whole new world awaited me outside the door and I couldn't wait to explore it.

Chapter Twenty-Eight

~Felix~

My jaw clenched tightly to keep it from dropping when Evalina walked out of her room, freshly changed and ready for the day. She wore another pretty dress, this one a pale yellow that reminded me of morning sunshine, and her long hair had been pulled back into a braid that fell over her shoulder and hung half-way to her waist. More than ever, she reminded me of the fairy in the story my mother used to read me, and the idea that I should be the lucky man who got to be the hero in *her* story filled me with both pride and a deep, profound desire unlike anything I'd ever known.

Keeping my distance until we got to know each other better was going to take all the self-control I had.

"Will you be warm enough?" I asked, my voice sounding gruffer than usual before I cleared my throat. "There's a bit of a chill in the air."

I wore a long-sleeve shirt and jeans that seemed a lot warmer than her dress, however pretty it might be.

"I'll be fine," she assured me. "This fabric is warmer than it looks and we won't be standing still. Let's go."

She seemed eager to get started, almost as eager as I felt, and I chose to take it as a compliment. "This way."

Side-by-side, we walked down the stairs and out the back door of the pack house. As she got her first glimpse of our territory, Evalina's lips parted, a soft sigh slipping through them that sent blood rushing straight to my groin. "It's beautiful here."

"It is."

My eyes remained trained solely on her as I said it, taking in the way her cool blue eyes sparkled in the morning light and the sun played with the red highlights in her hair, and when she glanced up and found me staring, a sweet blush crept up her cheeks.

I cleared my throat. "Your world is beautiful too, in a different way."

"It can be," she agreed. "I suppose I know more about the ugly things that balance it out. Here, everything looks beautiful."

Her eyes darted down to my chest with her final words before returning to my eyes, the blush in her cheeks deepening, and the seed of hope in my heart grew a little bigger. Was I fooling myself in hoping that she already felt *something* for me?

"We'll head west first, to the lake," I suggested. We were supposed to be looking for portals, and without having any direction about where to begin, we may as well begin with the most scenic spot in our territory. I had a feeling she'd like it.

Evalina followed my lead, her shorter legs rushing to keep up with mine until I remembered to slow my pace. "What are these trees? They're so tall!"

Her neck craned back as she gazed up at the towering pine trees above us.

"Those are ponderosa pines. I used to climb them as a boy."

"All the way up there?" Her mouth gaped as she leaned so far back to look, she looked ready to fall over.

"As far as I could get. We've also got some Douglas Fir trees, like those ones there." I pointed out the bushy evergreen trees in the distance. "And these with the yellow leaves, they're aspens. The leaves will be falling off soon."

I'd never cared all that much about trees before, but having Evalina hang on every word made me wish I knew more than I did.

Thankfully, a small patch of mushrooms distracted her, and she slipped away from me to inspect them more carefully, kneeling in the dirt in her shimmering, flowing skirt. "We have these! Or something very much like them, anyway. We eat them. Are these edible?"

"Mushrooms in general are, yes, but I'm not sure about those," I admitted, rubbing a sheepish hand over the back of my neck. "I never learned the difference."

Wide, round eyes stared up at me. "But what if you eat the wrong ones? Won't you get sick?"

"Yes, so I just don't eat any of them."

She considered that for a moment before nodding in understanding. "Your cooks know which ones to use, then. You don't gather them yourself."

"Actually, no one gathers them unless you count driving to the store in town to pick some up."

Apparently, there were too many unfamiliar words in that sentence for it to mean anything to her. She stared at me so blankly that I had to laugh.

"I'll tell you all about it eventually. For now, don't go eating anything unless it comes from our kitchen and you'll be fine."

Evalina stood up again, getting to her feet so gracefully, it almost seemed like magic. "I think our lives are quite different," she said quietly as she fell back into step beside me. From her tone, I couldn't tell if she meant that in a good way or not, but I knew what it meant to me.

"I think so too. It'll take us a long time to learn everything about each other, which is kind of exciting, don't you think?"

A sweet smile spread across her face as she glanced up at me again, but it vanished again a moment later as the lake came into view and an expression of awe replaced any other trace of emotion.

"Oh! Felix, this is..."

She trailed off, unable to find the word, and I looked out over the familiar vista, trying to see it for the first time again through her eyes.

With the trees falling away behind us, we could suddenly see the sky, wide and high and blue, with mountain peaks rising in the distance beyond the water and many more miles of forest. The fall colours had turned the trees heading up the foothills a mixture of yellows and oranges with the occasional red dotted through the ever-present evergreens. The blue of the lake sparkled only a few shades darker than Evalina's eyes and a few lazy, puffy, white clouds completed the tableau.

"Magical?" I suggested teasingly as I gave Evalina a gentle nudge, her lips still parted in wonder as she stared at the scene in front of her. I loved how she found such delight in things I took for granted, like the shower that morning, and I loved how knowledgeable she was about her own world and the things in it.

The view was nice, sure, but to me, she was the most awe-inspiring thing I had ever seen.

"It's magical," she agreed, breathlessly and unironically.

"Let's take a picture," I suggested, suddenly wanting to capture the moment to remember it. Years from then, we could look back and remember how we felt when everything between us was new and limitless.

Since I didn't expect her to know what I meant, I didn't wait for a response, pulling my phone from my pocket and setting it to selfie mode. Evalina gasped when she saw us reflected in it, but slowly, that incredible smile spread across her face again when she realized it showed her in real time, and I snapped a photo of both of us beaming with the glorious Montana wilderness behind us.

"You froze time," she whispered in awe as I showed her the static photo, and when she glanced up at me that time, her eyes full of such delight, I couldn't hold back any longer.

My lips found hers, pressing firm against them in a kiss that sent the sparks of our mate bond exploding through my body, a cascade of desire and fulfillment, promise and satisfaction, and everything in between. Her scent surrounded me, sweet and warm, as every nerve in my body ignited.

For two long beats, she did nothing.

My little fae mate stood there, her eyes still wide open, her limbs unmoving and her mouth frozen against mine while my heart pounded, afraid to take things further as I waited for her verdict on what I'd just done.

Luckily for me, something *truly* magical happened next.

Her slender arms reached up to wrap around my neck and she pulled me tighter, her lips pushing back against mine, and every problem or worry I'd ever had completely fell away. With her in my arms, the world seemed utterly right.

Chapter Twenty-Nine

~Evalina~

For as long as I could remember, something had been missing in my life. Not a big something, not like the hole in my heart after losing my father, but something small that left an empty space in the puzzle that made up *me*, leaving the picture incomplete.

As much as I loved my parents and enjoyed spending time in the kitchen experimenting and laughing with my friends, part of me always felt like I never truly belonged in Etta. For a long time, I attributed that feeling to Tarron's bullying. Once that stopped, I chalked it up to the fact that my time serving the royal family jaded me towards the entire ruling class.

I always thought the problem came back to me. Something about me simply didn't fit, and it wouldn't make a difference where I went since the problem came from within.

But in Felix's arms, with his lips moving against mine, the crisp, clean air around us and the gorgeous views of his world providing the most stunning backdrop for my first kiss, for the first time in my life, I felt like I was exactly where I was meant to be.

The feeling made me bold enough to keep kissing him, brave enough to pull him tighter towards me and demand more with my body if not my words, and by the time we finally broke apart, we were both gasping for air, my body on fire and my heart pounding.

Did he feel it the same way too?

His bright blue eyes gazed down at me with something close to wonder. "Evalina, I..."

Whatever he wanted to say fell away when a branch snapped in the woods behind us and we both spun around to find the noise's source.

A strange four-legged creature stood there, its hair a soft brown and its legs long and lean, and it seemed to hold my gaze for a moment or two before it turned and bounded away. As it disappeared back into the dense trees, something else caught my eye: a faint glowing in the distance, not the way we had come but further to the east.

"Felix, look, there..."

I pointed, not needing to say anything else. He saw it too and his lips tightened, looking much harder now that they were no longer pressed against mine. "A portal. So close to our pack house, and we never knew."

"It must not be used often, if at all," I pointed out. "You would know if it were, right? Like how you knew that Tarron was using ours?"

"Right." His slow nod spread into a warm smile. "Good point."

"And after travelling so fast in your car last night, we must be a long way from Etta. The portal probably leads to another kingdom. There are many in the fae world. I could go through and check."

I started to head towards the distant glow, but Felix immediately pulled me back, his arm wrapping around my waist and pulling me towards him as he sank onto a nearby rock, so that I somehow ended up in his lap, face-to-face. The hardness of his muscular body beneath me sent heat flooding through me even before I noticed the *other* hardness poking against me, one I had never felt before but knew instinctively what it meant.

"You're not rushing in there without a plan," he nearly growled into my ear, sending goosebumps prickling down my arms. "You might get hurt and I won't let that happen. You're too precious to me to let that happen."

No one had ever said anything like that to me before, and I felt the truth of his words deep in my core. The blood rushed through my body faster, my heart drumming a steady, insistent beat that seemed to settle right between my legs.

There was one thing I didn't understand. "Why?"

"Why what?"

"Why am I... 'precious' to you?"

I had to force the words out, feeling silly saying them even though they were exactly what he said.

Felix let out a soft exhale that tickled the side of my neck, sending another shiver of delight through my body. It felt like lightning had somehow gotten trapped inside me, like I might actually combust if he kept stimulating me in these ways.

"There's something between us," he said quietly, the words barely a whisper in the cool air. His handsome blue eyes pierced into mine, open and clear. "Don't you feel it? Did you feel it when we kissed?"

Of course I did, but I still didn't understand it, especially given the conversation we had the night before. "I thought you said that you have a mate."

Another exhale from him.

Another shiver for me.

"I do have a mate," he answered me slowly. "But she's not a werewolf. She doesn't know she's my mate and I'm hoping she'll figure it out for herself."

The idea of that lucky, clueless woman, more closely tied to him than I would ever be, settled into a heavy lump in my throat as I tried to sound supportive. "I hope that she does."

"Me too." He stared at me for a long moment, as if he expected me to say something else, but I didn't know what else *to* say. If he had a partner out there, even if she didn't know it, encouraging anything between us would be wrong, no matter how much I might want to.

When I didn't reply, he sighed again, the exhale stronger than before, and in one fluid motion, he stood back up, lifting me with him and placing me gently on the ground once he was upright, as if I weighed no more than a child.

"I think we should go through the portal, like you said, to see if you recognize what's on the other side. If you think Tarron might be able to reach it, we'll need to take precautions. I'll shift to my wolf first so if anyone's there, they won't see my face. I'll also be able to protect you better if anything goes wrong. You'll stay beside me at all times, and if I nudge your stomach with my nose, that means 'run back to the portal'. No questions, no hesitation. Got it?"

I nodded firmly. "I understand."

He and his friends had helped me so much already; assisting them in figuring out where the portal on their territory led seemed like the least I could do in return.

Together, we walked the short distance to the portal's glowing entrance. The shimmering light both beckoned and repelled me, calling me back to a world and a life I didn't know if I wanted anymore. But what place did I have in the terrestrial realm either? The feeling of belonging I'd experienced in Felix's arms seemed a distant memory after the discussion about his mate.

"Turn around and I'll get undressed," he instructed. I did as he said, but after a few seconds, I couldn't resist taking one little peek over my shoulder. His back faced me as he reached down to remove his pants, giving me a rather spectacular view of his firm, muscled ass.

I'd never found a man's backside particularly attractive before, but on Felix? It qualified as a work of art.

Quickly, I snapped my head back before he could catch me looking.

A few seconds later, a warm, furry head rubbed against my hand, and I looked down to find Felix's wolf beside me, his appearance starting to become familiar to me. The animal gave me a solemn nod, and side-by-side, we stepped through the portal back into the fae world.

CHAPTER THIRTY

~Felix~

You should have told her, Kai grumbled in my head as we looked around the wooded spot on the other side of the portal. It bore several similarities to Evalina's home, with its pink sky and spongy grass, but the vegetation had changed and it smelled different too. I had a strong feeling we were no longer in her kingdom.

I gave her as many clues as I could, I pointed out while Kai sniffed the air and Evalina walked to a nearby tree, examining its leaves carefully. *I really thought she'd figure it out.* I wanted to tell her, to see her eyes light up with understanding, but I still thought it would be better if she came to the conclusion on her own. The possibility of rejection when she didn't fully understand what the bond meant loomed heavy over me.

Kai had his own theory about why she hadn't picked up on my hints. *She's too modest. It won't occur to her that she's special unless we tell her so.*

I hated that he might have a point. She did seem to view herself as completely ordinary, even though to me she was anything but.

And now she thinks there's some other woman! Kai added with a growl of frustration. *How are you going to win her over when she thinks you're a cheating bastard?*

Alright, I hear you. I'll figure something out, I promise. For now, let's focus on finding what we need and getting home safely.

Vaughan would probably kill me for going through the portal with no backup, but my eagerness for answers won out over my worries about disobeying my Alpha. I needed to know how far away we were from Tarron and any potential threat to Evalina's safety. If we could gather that information with a quick look around, it didn't make sense to put it off. Better to know what we were dealing with and go from there.

Since I couldn't speak to Evalina while in my wolf form, I had to wait for her to voice her thoughts out loud, which she did after a couple of minutes of exploring the trees and plants around us. "This definitely isn't Etta but it's not too far away. Traders at our markets sell some of these fruits and flowers but I don't know the name of the territory we're in or what their relationship is with the royal family in Etta. Maybe if we can get a glimpse of a nearby town or building, it will tell us more."

Kai growled deep in his throat, issuing a warning that I agreed with. We didn't want to push our luck by straying too far from the portal. If we needed to, I wanted to be able to get back to Crimsontooth land immediately, where help would only be a mind-link away.

The growl didn't intimidate her like it should have. Instead, she shook her head at me almost affectionately. "I promise we won't go far and we'll be careful."

That didn't make me feel any better. Every step away from the portal felt like a gamble. If something went wrong or someone followed us back, I'd have to answer to Vaughan, and to myself.

Kai's second growl came out louder, loud enough that the ground around us seemed to vibrate. *That* definitely didn't happen in our own world.

Neither did what happened next.

Out of nowhere, a man appeared. One second, the space was clear, and the next, he stood there, pointed ears poking through long, dark hair that shimmered in the pink daylight. Pale fingers flexed at his sides as he studied us with quiet curiosity.

Evalina yelped in surprise as Kai immediately stepped in front of her. We were only a dozen or so yards from the portal, but the man stood between us and the glowing space that led to home and safety.

Much taller than Evalina, and possibly even taller than me, the man had to be an elf rather than a fairy. Normally, I would have found that pretty cool, since I'd never met an elf before, but at that particular moment, every nerve in my body stood on edge, waiting to see what he would do next.

"Good day. I don't believe I've seen you around here before."

With impeccable manners, he bowed to Evalina before stepping forward, his hand outstretched as if to shake hers. His delicate fingers were so pale, they almost looked translucent, especially with the white clothing he wore.

Kai snapped his jaws when the elf got close, and the stranger immediately stepped back, his eyes widening in alarm.

"My, that's an interesting... beast... you have there."

"My pet wolf," Evalina blurted out, speaking louder than she normally did out of nervousness. "He's not fond of strangers, please forgive him. He's harmless."

I'll show him 'harmless' if he tries to touch her again, Kai growled.

"I appear to have gotten a bit lost," she continued, sounding more natural the more she settled into the conversation. "Could you tell me where we are?"

"Where do you come from?" the man asked in reply, not answering her question.

Lie, I begged her in my head, but not hearing me, she told the truth.

"Etta."

The man let out a low whistle. "That's a long way for a young fairy to travel, all on her own."

Her hand reached down to stroke Kai's head. "I'm not on my own, as you can see, and I simply lost track of my path. Please, sir, could you tell me what land this is?"

That time, he answered her, but the answer didn't make me feel much better. "You're in Exteria. Normally, the dark canyon between us and the fairylands keeps people from 'losing track' and accidentally wandering in. Are you sure you didn't arrive another way?"

His glance over his shoulder at the portal made it clear that he knew for certain how we really got there. Lying about it wouldn't do us much good.

Evalina reached the same conclusion without me intervening. "My path may have involved some travelling through the terrestrial realm." Though I kept my eyes on the elf, I could picture Evalina's sheepish shrug as if she also stood in front of me. "Do you ever visit there yourself?"

His nose wrinkled as if he found the idea distasteful. "No, there's no reason for us to. The terrestrial world is of no interest to elves."

That was excellent news. First, it seemed the elves had no intention of using the portal, making its existence on our land moot, and second, even if Tarron figured out which portal would lead to Evalina and wanted to use it, he would have to cross a 'dark canyon' and enter the elves' territory first. It sounded like an awful lot of work.

The man remained polite but his tone grew firmer when he spoke again. "You should return to your 'path' now, little fairy, and be careful of crossing any other portals you may see. Not all kingdoms are so tolerant of strangers in their lands."

"I understand," she assured him. "Thank you for your hospitality, and good day, sir."

We both took a few steps towards the portal, me staying between the two of them, just in case, before the man spoke again.

"It's strange, I've never seen a tie of such strength between a fae and an animal. I'm guessing that your pet is more than he seems?"

"Tie?" Evalina repeated, obviously not sure what he meant.

"A link," he expanded. "A binding. I've seen it on rare occasions between fae, but never with another species."

My heart sped up within my wolf chest as I realized what he must be talking about: *our mate bond.* Could he actually see it? Did elves have that power?

Evalina's feet stopped moving entirely and I felt the stiffening of her body next to me. Already, my senses had become completely tuned in to her; how much stronger could it get once we accepted the bond?

"You can see something between us?" she clarified. "Something elemental?"

Elemental. That was a good word to describe it, actually. It went down to the deepest, most basic level.

"It's impossible to miss," the man replied. "I only hope for your sake that he's better looking in his humanoid form than he is as an animal."

Kai let out another deep growl that made the ground around us vibrate again, but the man only laughed. Her feet unstuck, Evalina strode the remaining few steps towards the portal while I hurried after her, suddenly a step behind.

We burst back onto the Crimsontooth territory where everything looked the same as when we left, but in truth, everything had shifted. I knew it before she opened her mouth, and her first words only confirmed it.

"*I* am your mate? Are you serious?"

Chapter Thirty-One

~Evalina~

Still in his wolf form, Felix couldn't answer me, and I took advantage of that fact, refusing to turn away and let him shift until I got out everything bubbling up inside me.

At first, I didn't understand what the elf meant when he said he saw a 'tie' between me and Felix. Elves were known for being hard-to-read and speaking in riddles, so when he spoke of a tie with Felix still in his animal form, I thought perhaps the word had a double meaning that I didn't know. But as he explained it further, calling it a 'binding' when Felix had previously spoken of a 'bond', things started to make more sense.

Elves could see things the rest of us couldn't, and since the one we spoke to could also teleport himself, he likely had all kinds of additional powers. Since they lived such long lives, elves often learned additional magic the older they got. I had no reason to disbelieve anything he said. Suddenly, everything Felix had said to me about his mate clicked into place and I wanted to kick myself for being so dense. I sat there, not five minutes earlier, feeling jealous of the 'clueless' woman who got to be his mate, not realizing that the idiot in question was actually me. He could have told me. Why *didn't* he tell me? Why bother with all this talk of me being 'precious' to him and pretending to help me out of the goodness of his heart?

Why not just be honest?

Was he actually just like Tarron after all?

Those were the thoughts spinning around my head as I paced back and forth, my eyes locked on Felix's wolf and my whole body tense.

"You've had multiple opportunities to tell me the truth about why you came to Etta and why you were so interested in helping me. Was this your plan all along? To lure me here and keep me as... as some kind of amorta? You want me to trade a life bound to Tarron for a life bound to you, just because some goddess told you so? Were you going to give me any choice in the matter?"

Everything that had happened since I first laid eyes on him took on a new meaning as I reviewed it through the lens of my new knowledge, and any excitement I'd felt at the prospect of finding a new life in this world felt tainted. "Tarron may be selfish and spoiled, but at least he never lied to me about what he wanted from me. He never tried to convince me he's something he's not. He never..."

I had no intention of stopping my rant, but to my surprise, Felix suddenly transformed back into his human form, despite it leaving him completely naked right in front of me. He stayed crouched down, his body bent to conceal his most private parts, but I could still clearly see his strong, broad, bare chest giving way to his defined, muscular abs and the thick, bent legs supporting him. When it came to appearance, at least, he and Tarron had *nothing* in common.

"What do you mean a life bound to Tarron?" He spoke the words quietly but in a tone deeper and firmer than I'd ever heard him use before. "What has he said to you? Has he claimed you're his mate too?"

Tarron could wait. I wanted to address *Felix's* deception. "What do you mean 'too'? *You* never told me!"

A grimace stretched across his handsome face. "I wasn't trying to deceive you, Evalina. I didn't want to put any pressure on you. The whole concept of mates is new to you, and I didn't think you'd be thrilled to have some random man you'd never seen before announce that you're meant to be his. I wanted you to get to know me first. Think about it, please, *really* think about it: if I had told you right at the start, what would you have done?"

Reluctantly, I pushed my indignation to one side and cast my mind back to seeing Felix for the first time in the pens. He asked for my help to escape and I gave it because I believed he would help me too, that we were making a deal.

What if he had said 'help me escape because you're linked to me through an invisible bond'?

If I were being honest, I had to admit I probably would have assumed he was crazy. "Right at the start might have been a little off-putting," I conceded. "But what about last night when you were telling me about mates? When I asked you if you had one? Why not tell me then?"

"You were in a different world surrounded by strangers, just escaped from prison yourself and worried about your mother's health. I didn't want to add to the stress and turmoil you must have been feeling."

His calm, reasoned logic made some sense, I supposed. "And today? Just now, when you kissed me?"

He shot me a sheepish grin, made all the more adorable by the naked, vulnerable state of him. "I kind of hoped you would put the clues together and figure it out on your own. My wolf says I'm an idiot for not realizing that someone as humble as you wouldn't make that assumption."

I tried to reach for the anger and frustration that I'd pushed aside earlier, but I could no longer find it. Felix might have deceived me, but in his explanation and his earnestness, it seemed clear there had been no malicious intent behind it.

Felix didn't demand or manipulate.

He offered. He waited.

Comparing him to Tarron was unfair.

"You could have told me," I said softly, letting the corners of my mouth lift slightly to show him that he had made his point. "I wouldn't have thought you were trying to manipulate me."

"I'm really not. The truth is: you *are* my mate, Evalina, but only if you want to be. I would never force you to accept something that didn't make you happy, and I know that even if you do accept me, there are decisions we'll need to make together about our future. But the one thing I want you to be perfectly clear about, no matter what happens next, is that I am so happy and grateful to find you and to have you as my mate. We might not know each other well yet but I'm already falling for you. You're amazing."

With those words, the happiness and excitement that had briefly been extinguished roared back to life, stronger and deeper than before. I thought back to every moment we'd spent together: the way he rescued and protected me in Etta, the tenderness in his eyes when he looked at me, and the fire in his kiss. From my first glimpse of him, I felt a connection to him. I felt safe with him. Could something that felt as natural as breathing really be a trick or a trap?

No, I didn't think so. He was telling the truth; this incredibly strong, handsome, kind, generous man had been chosen for me, and he was *happy* about it.

Put that way, what in the world did I have to complain about?

Chapter Thirty-Two

~**Felix**~

Trying to explain myself to Evalina felt like fighting for my life. When she accused me of being like Tarron, every nerve in my body bristled in response to the insult. I still didn't know what that guy wanted from her, but I knew what *I* wanted: to love and worship her every day for the rest of her life.

I sincerely doubted those were his intentions.

But despite my revulsion at the comparison, I could understand why she made it. She didn't really know me yet, and I *did* lie to her, no matter how well-intentioned it might have been.

With that in mind, I did my best to lay out my reasoning and hoped with all my might that my mate, the woman who, despite coming from a literal different world, was destined for me, would understand the truth of my heart even if she had to take a leap of faith to do it.

And to my great relief, after thinking over everything I said, she smiled. Actually *smiled* at me.

"I think you're kind of amazing too. But don't lie to me again, ever. Understood?"

She pointed her finger at me, her little feet planted firmly on the ground, and she looked so adorable as she tried to appear stern that it took all my self-control not to burst out laughing or pick her up and cradle her in my arms. The only thing that stopped me was that she wouldn't appreciate either of those things, at least not at that exact moment.

"I understand," I promised. "Now, let me put my clothes back on, and can you please tell me what you mean about Tarron? What does he want from you?"

With a sigh, Evalina sank down onto a tree trunk next to the portal, as if the prospect of talking about Tarron left her too weary to stand. With her back turned, I quickly pulled my clothes back on, and when I stepped back into her line of vision, she began talking.

"He wants me as his amorta. I have no idea why. He made my life miserable growing up and I'm a servant. I have nothing that would benefit him. It doesn't make any sense to me."

Taking a seat on the ground in front of her, I cast my mind back to our conversation about fae relationships and what 'amorta' meant. All that she'd said was that the ruler chose his amorta, and we compared it to a mistress. It would be a sexual relationship, then, that much seemed clear, and my blood boiled at the thought of him touching her. Had he already? She certainly didn't seem to have any fondness for him. Had he forced her? Bile rose in my throat at the thought, but I needed to know.

"Start at the beginning, please," I managed to force out in a calm tone that concealed my inner turmoil. "How long have you known him?"

Her shoulders lifted in a casual shrug. "All my life. As the crown prince, everyone in Etta knows who he is, but since my mother worked in the royal kitchen, I saw him up-close more than most people did. He ignored me when we were young, until he caught me one day in his room, looking through his possessions. I didn't take anything, I simply got curious while helping to clean and he found me there. After that, he went out of his way to make my life as difficult as possible. I would have sworn he hated me."

"What kind of possessions were you looking at?" Any detail might be important so I wanted to know as many of them as she remembered.

"He had this box beneath his bed, and inside it were scribblings on paper and some dried flowers, unusual things but not of any particular value. But one of the papers had a drawing on it, a drawing of a large man and a strange animal that I now know was a wolf. The man was a werewolf. It looked like you."

That certainly seemed significant but I didn't want to jump to any conclusions. "Did you have stories about werewolves and other beings from this world, the same as I grew up with stories of fairies and elves?"

Evalina shook her head. "No. I'd never heard of a werewolf before then, nor after. My father knew about them, apparently, but I only found that out later, after his death. It's interesting, actually: Tarron seems to have a fascination with this world. Aside from the things in his box, he went through the portal to get the silver, and he seemed almost nervous when he realized I knew he'd been using it. I don't think he wanted people to know, but I'm not sure why not."

That *was* interesting, but like her, I couldn't be sure what it all meant, especially without knowing the political situation in her world. But a prince curious about werewolves who took an unhealthy interest in my mate? That didn't seem like a coincidence to me, not at all.

Unable to sit still any longer, I stood back up and began pacing as I turned over everything I knew in my head. "So, he treated you badly once he found you snooping, but at some point, he changed his mind?"

Her pretty head bobbed in agreement. "A little over a year ago, he stopped persecuting me and began pursuing me instead. I've managed to fend him off while still giving him hope that I may change my mind. If I rejected him outright, I would have lost my job or worse."

Her having to lie to that arrogant bastard did nothing to ease the anger bubbling in the pit of my stomach, but I kept my focus on the narrative as much as possible. "Did anything in particular happen a year ago that might have led to this change?"

Her lips pursed as she gave my question some careful consideration. "I can't think of anything. It was around my birthday, I suppose, but that didn't involve him."

The hairs on the back of my neck began to prickle. "Your eighteenth birthday, by any chance?"

She hadn't told me her age yet, but I would have placed her around twenty, a few years younger than me. When she nodded in confirmation, my mouth pressed into a firm line.

"Eighteen is the age at which werewolves can recognize their mates. It's the age when our wolves come to us."

She followed each word carefully, but didn't catch my point. "What does that have to do with *my* eighteenth birthday?"

"I'm not entirely sure, but I think something about you must have changed on that day too, something related to being my mate, so that if I came upon you after that date, I would recognize you exactly as I ended up doing."

Now she got it. "And you think Tarron recognized this change? How?"

"I have no idea, but the elf saw the connection between us. Maybe Tarron sensed something too. Maybe it made you more desirable to him."

"That actually makes some sense," she admitted. "I could never understand why he suddenly found me attractive after torturing me for so long. My appearance didn't change *that* much."

It made sense to me too, but I still had a lot of unanswered questions. "We should go back to the pack house and tell the others what we've found. We can check on your mother too."

I offered my hand to her, helping her back to her feet, and when the sparks of our bond flared to life between us again, Evalina's gaze dropped to our joined hands. "Is that because you're my mate?"

"You can feel it?" I hadn't been sure she would, so when she nodded, my chest swelled with happiness. "We call it mate sparks. It happens between a mated pair whenever their skin connects."

"It feels... nice."

She flushed with those words, and once again, the desire to pull her into my arms nearly overwhelmed me.

First, we had to talk to Vaughan and Calista about the portal, the elf we met, and about Tarron's interest in werewolves. Then, I planned to take my mate somewhere private and truly get to know her, in every way she'd let me.

Now that she knew what she meant to me, I didn't want to hold back any longer.

Chapter Thirty-Three

~**Evalina**~

Felix held my hand as we returned to the large house where I'd spent the night, the 'pack house' as he called it. In basic terms, he explained werewolf packs to me and how the house was both the home of the pack's leadership team, like the royal residence in Etta, and an administrative building for managing pack business.

Most importantly, it was *his* home. I couldn't wait to get a chance to explore his private rooms and learn more about him through the things he chose to keep close to him. Everything about him fascinated me, and I didn't see that changing anytime soon.

First, though, we still had business to attend to, and when Felix suggested we first visit the medical facility where my mother had been meeting with the pack's healer, I jumped at the chance.

"Mama!" We found her sitting on a crisp, white bed, looking even better than she had first thing that morning. Calista stood next to her and gave me a warm smile as I walked in, stepping back as I approached my mother on the other side of the bed. "How do you feel?"

"I feel wonderful," she assured me. "Twenty years younger, actually. I think the air is good for me here."

"That's amazing." Grasping her hands in mine, I beamed up at her before turning to the woman scribbling some notes on a piece of paper. She seemed to be the one in charge. "What was wrong with her?"

The woman didn't answer me, didn't react at all, and it took Calista's gentle reminder for me to remember why. "She can't see you or hear you. She can't see your mother either, so this has been an interesting examination."

"Shit, I forgot about that," Felix groaned. "Were you able to act as a go-between?"

"For the most part," Calista confirmed. "They're going to run some blood tests to look for anything obvious that might have caused her illness, but the doctor has never dealt with fae blood before. It might help if they could take a sample from Evalina too, for comparison purposes."

"Yes, of course," I agreed without hesitation, though how they would compare our blood, I didn't fully understand. It must be some kind of werewolf magic. "Do you have a knife?"

"Whoa, whoa. No. Stop. No knives." Felix stepped in front of me, his handsome face lined with concern. "The doctor will use a small needle to pierce your skin, you don't need to cut yourself."

I glanced over at my mother for confirmation and she nodded, looking impressed. "Their magic is quite remarkable."

"No magic," Felix contradicted her with a smile. "Just technology. But please, for my sake, don't be so quick to volunteer to slice your veins open, okay?"

His protectiveness might have bothered me coming from someone else, but from him, it felt sincere, as if the thought of me in any kind of pain literally hurt him. Did the bond between us do that? Or did it just come down to him?

"I'll be the one taking the sample, since I can see you," Calista explained.

"Are you trained to do that?" Felix wondered.

Her lips quirked into a wry smile. "As a hunter, I learned all kinds of skills. Evalina, you just need to hold out your arm, like this."

I followed her lead, and the Luna inserted a small, sharp needle into my arm, drawing some of my green blood into a small container through a translucent tube. It might not have been magic, but it seemed pretty close to it.

"Can the doctor see the blood?" Felix asked.

"No, I can't," the woman herself answered. "But the machines register it. It's fascinating."

That was a good word to describe a lot of what had happened in the past few days.

"I'll go run these tests now and see what I can find out," the doctor continued, taking the container from Calista. "You don't need to wait here. I can contact you when I have some news."

She left the room and Felix turned to Calista. "Where's Vaughan? We have some information to share."

"In his office. I'll ask Darius to come and meet us and he can take Maudi back to her room, since he's the only other one who can see her."

The other werewolf who'd helped us escape met us at the staircase in the pack house, and though I didn't like leaving her alone, my mother insisted she would be fine. Following Felix and Calista down a long hallway, I found myself in a large room with a stone fireplace and large, clear windows looking out over the surrounding forest. Vaughan sat at a big desk, full of papers and more machines I had never seen before. Calista went to sit next to him behind the desk while Felix and I sat in two large, comfortable chairs in front of it.

"Did you find a portal?" Vaughan asked, getting straight to the point.

"We did." Felix told him about our trip to the fae realm and our encounter with the elf, including the way that the elf recognized the connection between Felix and me.

The Alpha's face turned stony as Felix talked and I could sense his displeasure long before he spoke. "And you thought it would be a good idea to venture into an unknown world where, for all we know, you're now a wanted fugitive, all on your own?"

"It worked out, didn't it?" Felix asked with a shrug, his tone not entirely serious.

Vaughan raised his eyes to the ceiling in exasperation. "One of these days, Felix, your curiosity will get the better of you."

"Let's focus on the elf," Calista suggested, putting a calming hand on her mate's arm. She seemed so confident and utterly sure of her place, while I'd never once known the Etta queen to take part in discussions of strategy or diplomacy. "From what I know of them, they're less emotional than fairies, more ruled by logic. Evalina, would you agree with that?"

I nodded slowly. "I don't know any personally, but that matches with the stories we've been told. They say that if you get into trouble with an elf, appeal to their reason rather than their mercy because they might not have any."

"Why is that important?" Vaughan asked, his deep brown eyes moving between me and Calista. "Do we need to be worried about them using the portal?"

"I don't think so, but I *am* worried about how much information you gave them." She sent a sympathetic grimace my way, obviously not wanting to scold me but stating the facts as she saw them. "He now knows there's a fairy from Etta, in the company of a wolf, who came through the portal on their land. If the people looking for her reach out to the elves, what incentive do they have not to share that information?"

"You think they'd betray us?" Felix asked through gritted teeth.

"I think they wouldn't see it as a betrayal," Calista countered. "They might simply share the facts as they know them, and what the fairies might do with that information is hard to say."

Guilt flooded through me as I realized that my actions might have inadvertently placed the whole pack in danger when they were only trying to help me. "I'm sorry," I whispered to Felix.

He shook his head, reaching over to take my hand and giving it a gentle squeeze. "Don't apologize. I'm just as much to blame."

"What do you know about the relationship between this elf kingdom and your own?" Vaughan asked me. As much as I respected him, it also slightly terrified me when he turned his piercing gaze on me. He radiated authority in a natural way Tarron never could. "Are they allies?"

"As far as I'm aware, Etta has no allies." I glanced around the room, wondering if any of them thought me disloyal for so easily giving up the secrets of my home, but no trace of disapproval registered on any of their expressions. "We used to when I was younger but Tarron has made many enemies. He considers himself better than his position as prince of a minor kingdom, believes he should hold a place at the table with the high princes, and hasn't been shy about making his views known. His father the king spends most of his time mollifying the people Tarron has offended."

The royal family probably would have been shocked to hear my assessment of their situation, but they forgot servants had ears. They spoke freely in front of the serving staff who carried the gossip back to the kitchens where I heard all about Tarron's arguments with his parents and the troubles he caused for them.

"So, he can't call on their loyalty to track you down," Vaughan mused. "But it doesn't mean he can't make them an offer that would appeal to their sense of logic. He doesn't sound like the kind of guy to live and let live."

That was putting it mildly. Felix shifted in his seat, his whole body coiled with tension. "What do we do now?"

The Alpha didn't hesitate. "Establish a barrier around the portal that will alert us immediately if anyone comes through it. We'll feel the intrusion on our territory, but I want to know for sure that it came from that portal."

"Should I disable the portal, like I did with the one on the Vermillion pack territory?" Calista asked.

"Not yet. If these elves respond to reason, maybe we can get to them before Tarron does and make them an offer that would help to protect us in the long term."

"You want to negotiate?" Felix asked, sounding intrigued with the idea.

"I'd like to think about it," Vaughan agreed.

"What should I do?" I piped up. After causing more trouble, I wanted to be helpful.

However, Vaughan shook his head. "You've been through quite a lot, and I'm not sure either of you are thinking strategically right now." He shot a meaningful look at Felix next to me. "Why don't you take a break and get some rest, and I'll send for you when I need you?"

Felix opened his mouth, looking ready to protest, but when his eyes met mine, something warm flashed within them. His mouth closed and he sat back in his chair. "If those are your orders, Alpha."

For the first time since we got there, Vaughan almost smiled. "I had a feeling you wouldn't mind. Go. I'll let you know when you're needed."

Without another word, Felix got to his feet, offered his hand to me and pulled me up with him. Once we were back in the hallway, he turned to me, his eyes dancing with anticipation.

"How would you like to come and see my rooms?"

Chapter Thirty-Four

~Felix~

I'd be lying if I said I hadn't tidied up a little more than usual after my shower that morning, hoping there might be a chance of bringing Evalina to my room later. Even so, I didn't know if I really believed it would happen. Now that we actually stood in front of the door to my suite, my nerves kicked in, as if what lay beyond the threshold might make or break her decision to accept our bond or not, and I found myself frozen to the spot as all the potential outcomes, good and bad, flashed before my eyes.

"Is something wrong?"

Evalina's sweet voice beside me pulled me out of my temporary trance, and I shot her the most confident smile I could manage. "Not at all. Come on in."

Throwing the door open wide, I let her go in first before closing the door behind us, all the while keeping my eyes glued to her, hanging on every clue she might give me about how she felt about what she saw.

Like the Alpha's suite, my rooms consisted primarily of the large bedroom we walked into, with its king-sized bed at one end and a sitting area at the other, two arm chairs and a small table with a wonderful view of the forest and a glimpse of the lake we'd visited earlier that morning. Two doors led off the main room, one to a large walk-in closet and the other to my private bathroom.

Honestly, I didn't spend a lot of time in the suite other than sleeping. My waking hours were spent downstairs in the public areas of the pack house or outside on pack business. I ate in the communal dining room and hung out with the other guys in the bar or games room, or in my office. Like Vaughan, I didn't date much within the pack since we both agreed that a bad breakup could cause issues that we didn't need. I'd never had a serious girlfriend since it didn't make sense to get involved with anyone who wasn't my mate. Thanks to my frequent diplomatic trips outside the pack, I'd had sex, but, long story short, I'd never had a woman in this room before.

"It's very... nice," Evalina finally said, completing a 360-degree turn in the centre of the room to take it all in. "It looks like the room I stayed in last night."

She sounded almost disappointed in that fact, and my stomach dropped. "You don't like it? I don't have to stay here. As long as I'm close to the pack house, I can live anywhere. There are cottages nearby, or houses in the town, or..."

"I don't want you to move, Felix." She nearly giggled, and the sound of my name on her sweet lips sent a wave of desire through me that I didn't see coming. My hand reached out to grip the edge of my dresser so my knees didn't buckle. "I only meant that there's not a lot of your personality in here."

I blew out a breath, trying to regain my equilibrium. "If that's what you're interested in, my office is the place to go. That's where I have all my books and personal items. This room is where I sleep and not much more."

*Do you **want** her to leave this room right now?* Kai growled in my head. *It sure sounds that way to me.*

That's not what I meant, I was just...

I didn't get to finish that thought before Evalina walked over to my closet. Throwing the door open wide, she walked in and inhaled deeply. My cock swelled instantly at the sound.

"I like this room. It smells like you."

Swallowing down my lust as best as I could, I took a couple of slow steps towards her. "What do I smell like to you?"

"What?" Her head tilted to the side curiously, making her look like a little bird inspecting something new.

"Mates have a scent that's particular to their other half. You smell like apples and caramel to me. It's... delicious."

The last word came out as almost a growl as I inhaled the same way she did a moment earlier. Evalina's cheeks instantly flushed with a pink that travelled all the way to the tips of her pointed ears, and a new scent hit my nose: the clear smell of her arousal.

Fucking hell, Kai muttered in my head, mirroring my thoughts almost exactly. *I didn't know anything could smell that good.*

You and me both.

The back of my hand swiped across my mouth, just in case I had started to drool. It certainly felt possible.

"Pullaberries," Evalina blurted out, her eyes wide and her body shifting slightly, as if she'd pressed her legs closer together. "You smell like pullaberries."

"I... don't know what those are." From her expression, I couldn't tell if she liked the smell or not.

"They're a small fruit that grows on the edge of our kingdom. We don't get them very often. People say they're an acquired taste, but I loved them from the first time I tried them. My mother got some to use in the royal family's dinner once when I was a child, and they smelled so good, I had to try one. That one was so good, I had another. I stuffed them all in my mouth before she realized it. She had to lie and tell the royal family that one of the bulpas ate them."

I had no idea what a bulpa was either, but at that moment, I didn't particularly care. All I heard was that I smelled good to her, and I took another step closer.

"Are you saying that I'm an acquired taste?" My eyebrow lifted in a teasing arch, and as I hoped, she blushed even deeper.

"I liked the taste of our kiss," she admitted softly, so softly I might not have heard her if not for my werewolf hearing.

"I liked it too. I want to taste you again, Evalina. I want to taste *all* of you."

Another deep inhale revealed that her arousal had grown even stronger, and no amount of squeezing her thighs together could hide it from me.

"I don't... I'm not... I..."

She stumbled over her words before taking a calming breath and trying again.

"I haven't been intimate with a man before. I don't know what to do."

"That's okay." Knowing for certain that Tarron hadn't forced her into anything came as a relief, but aside from that, it didn't matter to me one way or the other if she had experience with other men. As long as it had been her choice, and as long as she felt comfortable with me now, I would be thrilled no matter what. "Would you like to learn with me?"

Her icy blue eyes gazed up at me, open and vulnerable and so trusting, it stole the breath from my lungs. "I would."

Kai howled for joy in my head while I clenched my fists, fighting against the urge to take her in my arms immediately. One more thing still needed to be said first.

"If you change your mind at any time, just say so. We can stop and I won't be upset or angry with you, I promise. I want you, but I want you to be happy far more. Do you understand?"

She nodded slowly, her eyes never leaving mine. "I do, and I believe you, Felix. That's why I want you too."

Those words broke any semblance of self-control I had left, and in the next second, she was in my arms. Lifting her from the ground, I cradled her to my chest, bringing her face to mine and letting her make the next move. Her lips pressed against mine, tentative but completely of her own free will, and with that sweet little gesture, I knew I was hers from now on, no matter what happened next.

Chapter Thirty-Five

~**Evalina**~

Perhaps I should have been afraid, or at least reluctant. A modest fairy in my position should *not* have kissed a werewolf so willingly, and definitely not as if her life depended on it, as if I needed the air from *his* lungs to survive.

As I told Felix, I had no experience with men. Between working in the kitchens and caring for my mother, my free time had been limited, and I hadn't met anyone who made finding the time for romance worthwhile. Besides Tarron, no one had shown me any outward signs of interest. During those uncomfortable minutes lying beneath Tarron's mattress while he bedded the woman brought to meet him, I'd felt nothing but disgust at the idea of being the one in her place.

Yet when Felix walked towards his bed, holding me in his arms, my feelings couldn't have been further from the revulsion I'd felt that day. My body buzzed with anticipation, with desire, and with that warm, tingling feeling that he called the 'sparks' of our mate bond.

He promised to teach me what to do and I had no doubt that he would fulfill that promise in ways that benefitted us both.

"You're so delicate," he murmured as he lay me down onto the soft mattress. The sheets smelled like him, just like the clothes in his dressing room did, and I closed my eyes to inhale the sweet scent that surrounded me when he lay down next to me, his body pressed tight to mine. "I'm worried I'll hurt you."

With his strength and size, not to mention the literal animal he could shift into, he certainly *could* hurt me if he wanted to, but I had no such concerns. "You won't. I'm stronger than I look, Felix. I won't break."

My words didn't do much to reassure him.

"Do you..." He trailed off, searching for the right words. "Do you understand the mechanics of mating?"

His formal phrasing drew a giggle from me, my body shaking with amusement at his discomfort. "You mean: do I know how a man and woman fuck?"

Felix's blue eyes grew almost comically wide before a dazzling grin lit up his face. "Well, shit. I didn't know you knew that word."

"I don't use it often," I had to admit. "But fae men are no different in their crudeness than those in the terrestrial realm. I hear the way the male servants speak."

"It sounds strange coming out of your sweet mouth." His gaze dropped to my lips, sending another sharp zing of desire through me. "But I like that you can speak freely with me."

"I'll save it for you, then." His gaze turned even more heated, and in a rush, I answered the question he asked before we got sidetracked. "And yes, I know the basics, I've just never done it before."

"Okay. Good."

His head dropped down, his lips pressing against mine again, and my body reacted instantly. He didn't have to tell me to lean into him, to wrap my arms around him and pull him closer. It simply felt right, and when his tongue pressed against my lips, prodding until they opened for him, and connected with *my* tongue, the smoldering heat inside me caught fire.

My hips tilted forward, seeking his body out of instinct, and when he pressed back into me, the hard length of his cock impossible to miss, the deep, throbbing ache inside me I'd barely been aware of became all I could think about. His cock felt almost impossibly big against my thigh, and I supposed if it were proportional to the rest of him, it would be bigger than anything I had ever seen in Etta.

Maybe I *should* have been worried that he might hurt me, sheerly because of his size, but at that moment, I only wanted to ease the aching need inside me.

I only wanted *him*.

"I'm going to make you come first," he whispered as our lips separated a few inches, enough for me to gasp in a few breaths. "Have you ever orgasmed before?"

Since I couldn't be certain, I suspected the answer was probably no, and I shook my head accordingly, my breath too thin to be able to speak.

A deep, animal-like growl rumbled in his chest. "I'm going to use my mouth. I want... I *need* to taste you. You smell so fucking good."

His words didn't fully make sense to me, since he'd already been using his mouth to kiss me, but I nodded in agreement anyway. If something existed that he might suggest and I would refuse, I couldn't imagine what it would be.

To my surprise, though, instead of kissing me again, he moved away from me, further down the bed, and when I tried to sit up to see what he was doing, he held out a hand to me.

"Lie down. Relax."

Still confused, I obeyed, resting my head back against the soft pillow that smelled of him, and shivered when his hands slipped beneath the skirt of my dress and began lifting the fabric up.

Part of me wanted to press my legs together and pull the dress back down, suddenly shy at the idea of being so exposed to him, but the other, braver part wanted to spread my legs wider and beckon him closer to the drumming beat at my core that grew even stronger and more insistent the nearer he got.

Felix drew in a deep breath, exhaling it in another low rumble. "Evalina."

My name sounded as if it pained him to say it, but he couldn't help himself. His hands trailed up my bare legs, over my knees and higher up my thighs. My heart beat even faster. The pulse between my legs quickened, and when his fingers brushed against the soft hair no man had ever touched before, he let out another groan.

"You're not wearing any underwear."

Calista used that word too but I still didn't know what it meant. "What is that?"

His deep chuckle vibrated against my skin as he pressed his lips to my inner thigh. "I'll show you in a minute. But first..."

Without another word, his tongue connected with the tender skin between my legs and I gasped in surprise, the sensation new and un-expected, especially with the sparks that lit up every place he touched. He licked me lazily, exploring me slowly, *tasting* me just as he said he would, and when his tongue dipped inside me, into the hole that ached to be filled, I let out a moan that I had never made before. It echoed in the stillness of the room, and I would have been embarrassed if Felix hadn't answered it with a groan of his own and an even deeper thrust of his tongue inside me.

Almost without realizing it, my hips began to rock against his face, trying their best to pull him in deeper. His strong hands pushed my legs further apart, his head burying deeper while I panted, the throbbing pressure inside me building almost to the point of pain.

His tongue left my hole and I almost cried out in disappointment, but when it connected with my clit instead, my hips bucked forward, my whole body jolting in undiluted pleasure.

"Felix!" I gasped out his name, my hands grabbing onto the pillow beneath my head as my back arched, my body now out of my control. His tongue didn't stop, circling around my clit and running over it, the sparks adding to the intensity until I truly didn't think I could take any more. My legs began to tremble, the need in me growing tighter and stronger until, in an exhilarating release, it crested and broke.

Pleasure flooded my body, unlike anything I'd ever felt before, and Felix hummed in satisfaction from his spot between my legs. I glanced down to see him smiling up at me.

"That's lesson number one, and it's the most important one: you should feel that every time we're together. If you don't, tell me, and I'll make it right."

Somehow, I suspected I wouldn't ever need to tell him. He seemed to know my body just as well as I did, and maybe even better.

"What's lesson number two?" I managed to stutter out as my breathing slowly returned to normal.

A wolfish grin spread across his face. "I thought you'd never ask."

Chapter Thirty-Six

~**Felix**~

Nothing had ever fulfilled me the way bringing my mate to orgasm did.

Overall, I enjoyed my life a great deal: good friends, good food, a pack I'd willingly die for and an Alpha I could serve without reservation. Nothing had seemed to be missing, but nestled between Evalina's legs, I finally saw the truth.

I'd only been half alive before her.

Her happiness was my happiness. Her successes were mine and her problems too. She was my other half, and every minute spent in her presence tied me closer and deeper to her.

But at that particular moment, my only focus was making her feel as good as possible.

"Lesson number two?" I pressed another kiss against her inner thigh, my mouth inches from her delicious pussy. "There are multiple ways we can make each other feel good. That time, I only used my mouth, but this time, I'm going to get my fingers involved."

My cock throbbed as I inhaled her sweet scent again, desperate to play its part, but I pressed my hips into the mattress instead, stifling my groan at the friction. As small as Evalina was, I would have to go slow to make sure I didn't cause her any more pain than absolutely necessary. Getting her as relaxed and wet as possible would help, and using my fingers to stretch her out a bit first seemed like a good idea.

Not to mention I simply couldn't wait to feel her on my hand.

I wanted to know how every part of her felt on every part of me. I wanted the knowledge so firmly entrenched in my memory that I could summon it whenever I needed a reminder of just how blessed I was or simply to make me smile.

My tongue found her clit again and Evalina gasped, her body still sensitive from her orgasm, and her thighs clenched together out of instinct. Gently, I pushed them apart, keeping the pressure of my mouth light and teasing until she relaxed and began to subtly angle her hips towards me again, silently asking for more.

Keeping my mouth where it would distract her most, my index finger began to trace around her opening, giving her plenty of warning and plenty of time to change her mind if she wanted to. She didn't; in fact, her hips pushed further towards me, as if she could draw me in through sheer force of will.

Slowly, I slid my finger into her, groaning against her clit as the warm, wet walls of her pussy closed around me, and Evalina let out a soft moan.

"Sugarlumps."

Instantly, both my hand and my mouth stilled, and I raised my head to look at her. "What?"

Her eyes gazed down at me from beneath her half-closed lids, a look close to pain on her pretty face. "Please, don't stop."

I had no intention of it, but first, I needed to clarify what I thought I heard. "What did you say before that?"

An enticing red blush began to creep up her cheeks. "Nothing. It was nothing."

She couldn't lie to save her life, and seeing her flustered like this made me almost giddy. I couldn't have stopped the grin that spread across my face even if I wanted to. "It didn't sound like nothing."

With a groan, Evalina slapped her palms against the mattress. "It's a fae curse word, kind of. One that we're allowed to say as children."

She was too adorable for words. "Sugarlumps?"

Her cheeks flamed crimson but her gaze turned defiant. "Do you want me to say something else instead?"

"I want you to say whatever you feel like saying. I want you to moan and cry out my name, and anything else that comes into your head. But 'sugarlumps' might just be the cutest damn thing I've ever heard."

Her eyes narrowed as my grin widened, but I could see her fighting back her own amusement. "Go back to what you were doing before," she ordered.

"Gladly."

My head dipped again, my lips wrapping around her clit as I sucked it gently into my mouth, and my finger pressed deeper inside her. That time, she *did* cry out, a sound of pure pleasure with no words, and it stirred me on further, as if I needed any additional encouragement.

Her body yielded to me, her legs spreading wider on their own as I fingered her slowly, curling my finger and rubbing it along her walls until I found the spot that brought the loudest gasp she'd made yet. I added a second finger, still not as wide as my cock but closer, letting her adjust to the feel of it before I started to pump them into her and her hips rocked against me, understanding the basic rhythm of sex that stayed the same no matter what species we belonged to, werewolf or fae.

Her second orgasm hit her faster, her cry of surprise accompanying the clench of her pussy around my hand.

"Good girl."

I sat up and licked my fingers clean, unwilling to let even a drop of her arousal go to waste, as she watched me from beneath her sated, heavy eyelids. With her eyes on me, I got to my feet and pulled off my shirt before unbuttoning my jeans and kicking them off.

"For the record, this is underwear."

I pointed down at my black boxer-briefs barely containing my stiff cock, and Evalina's head raised from the pillow, her eyes widening as her eyes slowly raked over me, head to toe.

"You... you want me to wear that?" she asked in a light, breathy tone.

"Well, not exactly like this. Yours would be smaller and prettier and... fuck." My cock twitched so hard at the thought of her in lacy lingerie that I winced. "Never mind. Not important right now."

With that, I pulled the briefs down and threw them to the side, standing before her fully naked and harder than I had ever been in my entire life.

Evalina's rosy cheeks paled. "Oh." Her lips stayed parted after the word, her eyes glued to my cock. "That's... you're... oh."

"The goddess wouldn't have paired us together if we weren't perfectly matched," I told her, interpreting her reaction as concern about her own safety. "We'll figure it out. Would you like to take your dress off?"

I still hadn't seen her completely naked and I desperately wanted to feel her skin against mine, everywhere, but I left the choice up to her and what she would be comfortable with this first time. Thankfully, she seemed to feel the same as I did, sitting up and reaching behind her to unlace the strings holding the bodice in place. Once loose, I could easily lift it off her, and her full beauty hit me like a lead weight settling over my chest, knocking the air out of me until I could barely breathe.

"You're perfect," I whispered, taking in her soft skin, her curves and all her delicate lines.

"So are you." Appreciation coloured her expression as she continued to examine me. We could hardly have been more different, or any better suited for each other.

"I'm going to wear a condom," I told her as I stepped over to the bedside table and pulled one from my drawer. After hearing Vaughan's story about needing to mind-link the doctor to bring him one when things between him and Calista heated up, I invested in a box for myself. Better to be prepared, I figured, and I couldn't be happier that I'd decided to follow through on it.

The drawer also held a bottle of lube, used for solitary purposes before, but I coated the latex with it to help ease the way for Evalina's first time. Anything I could do to make it easier for her, I would do.

"What does that do?" she asked, eyeing my sheathed cock curiously. Apprehension still lingered in her eyes, but desire superseded it.

"It will stop you from getting pregnant when we mate," I explained plainly. "I assume you're not on any kind of birth control?"

The confused tilt of her eyebrows answered me without words. "What does that mean?"

"I'll explain later. Right now, I'd really like to get to lesson number three."

"Which is?"

Her trusting, hopeful smile sent another wave of need through me so strong that I'd be lucky if I didn't come before I even got inside her.

"How we can make each other feel incredible at the exact same time."

Chapter Thirty-Seven

~Evalina~

A shiver of anticipation ran down my spine as Felix climbed back onto the bed, naked other than the odd, translucent covering he placed over his cock.

It took me a second to realize that *only* anticipation caused my shiver. Not fear. Not even a little bit.

I never imagined I would feel so comfortable being naked with a man for the first time, but somehow, with Felix, it felt right. He made me laugh even while his tongue stirred my body into a frenzy. He teased me until I forgot to be nervous, until I issued him an order, scarcely believing my boldness. Under his affectionate, heated gaze, I felt wanted, certainly, but I also felt *understood*, and I already knew that feeling would linger long after the heat of our passion faded.

He promised we were made to fit together, and even though the size of him seemed to directly contradict that statement, I trusted him, and I opened my legs for him willingly, even eagerly, as his hard, firm body settled between them.

"We'll go slow," he promised, his breath catching as he slid the rounded head of his cock through the wetness still coating me. I groaned as it grazed over my clit, still tender from his previous attention. It didn't take much for the aching inside me to start up again, as if he hadn't just satisfied it. "Tell me if it hurts, okay? I won't know unless you tell me."

My eyes locked on him, I nodded, and he leaned forward, his hands on either side of me as his large frame hovered above me. I had to crane my neck up to keep looking at his face, using his raw masculine beauty to distract from the pressure between my legs as he began to slowly push his hips forward.

His fingers had felt incredible inside me, but I quickly realized they hadn't fully prepared me for the size of his cock. My body tensed as he began to fill me and Felix immediately stopped.

"I need you to relax," he coaxed, his voice low and encouraging. One hand reached between us to stroke across my clit again, distracting me from any other sensation. "It'll feel better if you're not so tight."

"I'll try."

From beneath him, I watched him swallow, the muscles in his throat as strong and beautiful as the rest of him.

"No, *I'll* try," he muttered before he pulled out of me, sliding down my body so that one hand remained on my clit and his mouth went to the peaked nipple of my breast.

"Oh... fuck." I breathed out the word, the only one that seemed to fit the situation properly, and Felix growled in approval. He literally *growled*, the sound far more animal than man, and desire flooded my body. His tongue, his fingers, the rumble of his chest... everything combined to whip the drumbeat of need inside me to a fevered pitch.

My legs spread wider and Felix responded immediately, his body completely tuned into mine. The head of his cock pushed into me again, and though it still strained my limits, I breathed through it, moaning as he pushed in further.

"That's perfect," he whispered from above me, his fingers still on my clit. "You're doing so well."

The praise heated my cheeks and sent another rush of pleasure through me, more emotional than physical. "I'm okay. You can go deeper."

Felix hissed a breath in through his teeth as he followed my instructions. "You feel so good. Even through the condom, I can feel the sparks. Do you feel them?"

I hadn't noticed, too distracted by the fullness, but when I focused my attention there, pleasure tingled deep inside me, deeper still as he gently pulled back before pushing in again. "I feel it. I feel *you*, and it's so good, Felix. So good."

"Fuck." His arms trembled above me from the effort he must have been making to hold himself in check. "I don't know if I should go any further."

Although I already felt almost impossibly full, I knew he couldn't be all the way in yet. "I want you to, as much as you can. I'll tell you if it hurts, I promise."

Exhaling, he pressed his hips forward, deeper, slowly, as if expecting resistance, but none came. My body continued to stretch, aching a little but not hurting, until he finally stilled completely.

"I don't believe it. You're taking all of me, Evalina. How...?"

He trailed off, the disbelief in his voice letting me know that despite his earlier words about us fitting together perfectly, he hadn't truly expected it to happen. Basic spatial reasoning suggested he shouldn't have fit, and yet, he did. I could feel the full length of him inside me, every blessed inch filling me in a way I never imagined but had somehow always needed.

"It must be magic," I whispered, my hands gripping onto his forearms. "Some fairies are blessed with more than one kind. Maybe this is another gift."

"Because you were made for me." His reverent whisper heated my blood even further, and when he began to move again, pulling out and thrusting back in firmly, his movements still slow but deliberate, I let my eyes close, giving in to the feel of him around me, against me, *inside* me. Nothing existed for me in that moment except Felix, the rhythm of our bodies, and a desperate desire to share this pleasure with him.

He thrust and I moaned. My legs wrapped around him and he stuttered out my name. My hands went to his chest above me, to the hard muscles of his stomach and the warmth of his skin. He bent down to place a kiss on my forehead as his hips rolled against me. My body met his as his pace grew faster and harder, his earlier fears about hurting me forgotten. Pleasure built inside me again, but unlike before, it fed off his groans and every jagged breath. It revelled in each brush of our skin against each other, in the sparks that I knew travelled beneath his skin the same way they did under mine. Knowing that he felt all of it too, in his own way but equal to me, made it even better, and when I came for a third time, his name leaving my lips on a sharp gasp, his movements turned erratic, his hard cock pulsing inside me as he let out a soft sigh into the air above me.

My mate.

I didn't know the word before I met him, but no other word did him justice.

The reason we had been matched remained a mystery, but the fact that we *were* matched could no longer be in any doubt. He was mine and I was his, at least for that moment, and I wanted to bask in that certainty as long as possible.

Because what we were going to do about it once we left that room, we still needed to figure out.

Chapter Thirty-Eight

~**Felix**~

Evalina went into the bathroom to clean up while I pulled my clothes back on in my room. She swore she didn't feel sore at all, which must have been part of the same magic that helped her accommodate me in the first place. I offered to clean her up myself but she got adorably shy at the suggestion, even after everything we'd just done together.

As much as I would have liked to stay in bed with her all day and teach her many, many more lessons, as much as my body craved her again even though we just finished, the rest of the world didn't stop because I found my mate. At least there were no possessed sasquatches roaming our territory like when Vaughan and Calista were trying to solidify their bond. I'd have to take that as a win.

When I grabbed my phone off the floor where it had fallen when I tossed my clothes aside, I saw a message from Savannah.

Why did I have to hear from my brother that you found your mate?! He won't give me any details, says it's 'complicated'. Spill the beans, Felix. Now!

Finding *her* mate didn't seem to have changed Sav at all, and thank the goddess for that. I wouldn't want her any other way.

See for yourself.

I attached the photo of me and Evalina that we took that morning in front of the lake, knowing it would only be a tease and she would still have a million more questions, but the response that came through a moment later wasn't at all what I expected.

> You've got the dopey-in-love look down, but how about you send me a picture of your mate instead?

> Very funny. I know she's short, but she's not **that** short.

> What the hell are you talking about? There's no one in that photo but you.

My brow furrowed, I scrolled back up, double checking that I had sent her the right photo. Evalina's sweet, smiling face looked back at me

> What are **you** talking about? She's right beside me.

> There is no one beside you in that picture. Jasper agrees, so don't try to gaslight me.

With a groan, I realized what the problem had to be. Neither Sav nor Jasper had ever been to the fae realm, so they wouldn't be able to see Evalina. It hadn't occurred to me that it would apply to pictures too, but apparently, it did.

> Shit. My mate is a fairy, which means she's invisible to most people. I thought you'd be able to see her in the photo but I guess I was wrong.

The phone rang a second later.

"Invisible?!"

Savannah didn't even let me say hello before she screeched in my ear.

"How can you have an invisible mate?"

"The same way you had a rogue one? This is what Vaughan meant when he said it's complicated."

"Hang on." I could picture Savannah taking a deep breath, trying to compose herself. "Are you seriously saying you can't see your mate?"

"I can see her *now* because I've been to the fae realm, but when she first appeared, I couldn't. I could only smell her. Kai could sense the bond, but we couldn't see anything. I thought I was losing it."

"I can imagine." She exhaled, the line crackling in my ear. "And no one else can see her?"

"Vaughan, Calista and Darius came with me, so they can see her too, but no one else."

The more I explained it to her, the more I had to actually consider the implications of Evalina's invisibility in the long term. It would make it difficult for her to interact with others on her own, and I wanted her to have as much independence as she wanted. Selfishly, I also wanted to be able to show her off.

"So... if you kissed her in front of anyone else, it would look like you were making out with the air?"

The absurd statement shattered my somber reflections on impact and a burst of laughter left my mouth right as Evalina opened the bathroom door. The corners of her mouth lifted into a smile at the sound of my laughter, as if my happiness made her happy too. It probably did, since it worked that way for me.

"Yeah, I guess it would. Calista's doing some research into all things fairy-related to see what our options are, but we've got other things to worry about in the meantime. We found out there's a portal to the fae realm in our territory and Evalina's former prince might try to come here and track her down."

Sav let out another breath as she processed all of that. "Never a dull moment, is there?"

"You're one to talk, Beta of the Ravenstone pack."

Her laugh rang with both amusement and pride. "Actually, I'd love to pick your brain on some Beta-related stuff soon, but you've obviously got your hands full right now. Besides, my mate is naked and waiting for me and looking like he might explode if I make him wait any longer."

"Too much information, Sav," I warned while Jasper tried to stifle a laugh in the background. "Go enjoy yourself. I'm happy for you."

"I'm happy for you too. I'd love to meet this woman soon, assuming I'll be able to see her."

"We'll try to figure that out," I promised, saying goodbye before we both hung up. I lowered the phone from my ear and Evalina stepped over to me, looking even more radiantly beautiful than before. A post-orgasmic haze looked damn good on her.

"What were you doing with that?" she asked, pointing to the phone in my hand.

"It's a communication device. It lets me speak to anyone anywhere in the world, if they consent to it. I was talking to Vaughan's sister. She lives in another pack several hundred miles away."

I offered the phone to her and she took it tentatively, turning it over in her hand as if she could figure out all its secrets by examining its exterior. "You used it earlier to make the portrait of us."

"It does a lot of things. It's incredibly useful. I'll get one for you, if you like."

That same smile as before pulled on her lips. "I would be interested in learning more about it, but perhaps we should wait. Like you said, we have other things to worry about first."

Indeed. "We should get something to eat and check in with Vaughan. He said he'd contact me when he needed me and he hasn't so far, but he might have been trying to give us some time alone. It doesn't mean..."

My sentence cut off part-way through as a different sound echoed in my head, one that I knew very well. The wail of the siren pierced my consciousness, ringing loudly for a couple of seconds before fading to a dull roar in the back of my mind.

Someone had crossed into our territory, uninvited.

Report.

Vaughan's voice growled through the mind-link shared with me, Darius, and the border patrol teams.

We don't see anything, the guards at the main crossing point stated. *It's quiet here.*

Here too, said the men patrolling the western ridge.

Team after team, the same answer came: no one had seen anything. The alert didn't seem to originate from any of the borders but rather from right in the heart of our territory.

And if no one saw the intruders, maybe that meant they *couldn't* be seen, at least not by anyone who hadn't already seen their kind before.

Chapter Thirty-Nine

~Evalina~

Though Felix didn't say a word, I felt the shift in him immediately. His eyes went unfocused and his breathing quickened, and I reached out to place my hand on his strong, solid arm. "What's wrong? What happened?"

His voice, usually so steady, had a tight edge to it. "Someone's on our land. Might have come through the portal."

My chest tightened again, just as it had in Vaughan's office when I realized I might have inadvertently exposed these people to danger. "The elves? Tarron?"

Even saying the prince's name made me shudder. The more time I spent with Felix, the more repulsive Tarron became.

Felix strode to the door so quickly, I almost had to run to keep up with his longer legs. Fear fuelled each of my steps. "I'm not sure. No one has seen anything yet."

Because they *couldn't* see anything; he didn't need to say it for me to understand what he meant.

Wordlessly, I followed him down the stairs and back to Vaughan's office where the Alpha already had a small group of men assembled. They stood in groups of two or three, chatting with each other while keeping an eye on Vaughan's movements, a buzz of anticipation filling the air. Darius gave me a curt nod but the others didn't glance my way, not seeing anyone in the space next to Felix.

"We need to get out there since we're the only ones who can see anything," Vaughan told Felix as soon as we arrived. "We'll divide the

"

house guard into three and you, me and Darius will each lead one of the groups."

"What about me?" I interjected. "I can see them too."

Felix grimaced, his hand sliding into mine and squeezing it gently. "It's too dangerous. You'll stay here where it's safe."

The other men in the room exchanged confused glances, unsure who he was talking to or why his hand gripped the empty air.

"You'll cover more space with four sets of eyes than three," I argued back. "If I have your men with me, why wouldn't I be safe?"

"Because it's you they want, and because none of our men can see or hear you. It doesn't make sense to send you out there when you wouldn't be able to tell them even if you spotted something and they wouldn't know if you were taken."

My brow furrowed with frustration and Vaughan winced, probably hearing how the dismissal in Felix's words sounded to me. Still, he backed up his Beta. "He's right, Evalina. Until we know for sure who it is and what they're looking for, it's not worth the risk to send you out there. The house has the best protection in the territory and Calista will stay here with you."

Accepting the word of his Alpha as final, Felix released my hand and strode over to the desk where Vaughan already had a map of the territory laid out. "We'll move out in circles, crossing over at the edges to make sure we don't miss anything. I'll take my group towards the portal we went through earlier."

The men spoke amongst themselves in a shorthand language that suggested they'd done this kind of thing before while I slowly backed away towards the door. If I could get away with them all distracted, maybe I could...

I didn't even get to finish that thought before I bumped into a solid form behind me. Spinning around, I found the Luna blocking the doorway.

"He means well," Calista promised, obviously having overheard the exchange and choosing to ignore the fact that I'd been attempting to sneak away. She leaned towards me with a smile that felt both sympathetic and conspiratorial. "Werewolves have a protective instinct towards their mate that makes them act a little crazy sometimes."

I glanced back at Felix and Vaughan, both completely focused on their task. "It doesn't bother you?"

"I choose my battles, and this isn't one of the ones to waste your energy on. They won't let you go and I need your help anyway."

I'd been ready to argue but her final words stopped me. "Help with what?" I asked instead.

"Understanding the fae world. Would you mind?"

She gestured down the hall behind her and I threw another glance over my shoulder at Felix. He looked up, catching my eye, and when he saw Calista standing behind me, he gave us both a grateful nod.

My heart softened at his show of appreciation. Perhaps I shouldn't take his refusal to let me help too personally. After all, everything else he'd done to that point suggested he valued my input, but safety came first. We still had a lot to learn about each other and I could extend him the benefit of the doubt, at least for now.

"Let's go," I agreed, and Calista led me to the room next door, a room similar to Vaughan's office but with a decidedly less masculine air. The walls were painted in a light grey colour rather than dark, with furniture to match. "Is this room yours?"

"It's my office, yes. I'm still getting settled, but as Luna, I have responsibilities within the pack." She stepped around to the seat behind the desk, gesturing for me to take the chair in front of it.

My elbows perched on the edge of her desk, scattered with papers just as her mate's was. "Are there responsibilities for the Beta's mate too?"

"Not officially," Calista replied, her blue eyes scanning me curiously. "But I'm sure Felix would help you find a use for your talents. Have you decided to stay?"

"I haven't decided anything yet. I was just curious."

I couldn't tell her about the things that happened up in his room or the feelings our intimacy had stirred up. I'd never talked about those kinds of things with anyone, and we had more immediate problems anyway.

"What do you want my help with?"

From the pile of documents, Calista pulled out several pieces of paper that formed a kind of puzzle. When she pieced them together, I found myself staring at a map of my own world, or so I had to assume based on the 'Etta' written in large letters in one of the small pieces of land. I'd never seen a full map of the whole world before and my fingers ran tentatively over the lines on the page as if it might feel like home.

My eyes raised to hers again, both confused and impressed. "Where did you get this?"

"A hunter friend of mine bought it off a collector. He wasn't sure if it was real, but I think it might be based on the things you said. Look, here's Etta, and there's a deep canyon separating it from elvish territory, just like the elf told you. The portal on our land must lead into this space here."

Her fingers skimmed over the lines of the map as I tried to take it all in.

"Do you know anything about these other neighbouring territories?"

I read the names of the lands, but though some of them were familiar from talk among the kitchen staff, I had very few useful details to share. Still, I dug into my memory for any tidbits I could find. "The craftsmen in Pylcher make the most beautiful musical instruments. We had a travelling band come through last summer. Nithika has fruits late into the winter, we trade for them with our canned berries. Adowar is Etta's chief rival, we're warned not to wander too close to the border with them."

A frustrated sigh blew through my lips.

"I'm sorry, I wish I knew something more useful."

"That *is* useful," Calista assured me. "The fact that you recognize these names as real places suggests the map is accurate. That's good for us to know."

Encouraged by her words, I searched my memory once more for anything else that might be of use. "My father had a rough map with some of the portals marked on it, but I didn't bring it with me. I wish I'd known it would be useful. I don't think there's any way to go back and get it."

"Not an easy way," Calista agreed. "Do you remember any of it?"

Closing my eyes, I tried to conjure the image as I'd seen it. "I found the portal that I went through, and there was another one in Etta, on the opposite side of the territory. That would be over here."

I pointed at the spot on the map, and Calista quickly marked it with an X. "Since the elvish territory is west of Etta in your world but we're east of the Vermillion pack in ours, that suggests things are opposite. We might be able to find that portal west of the Vermillion pack in our world if we need it."

We continued to pore over the map together as the minutes ticked by, no sounds in the room but the rustling of paper and our quiet conversation while we did our best to distract ourselves from the threat lurking outside the pack house walls and the danger it might pose to our mates who had gone out to find it.

Chapter Forty

~Felix~

"Does it get any easier?" I asked Vaughan as we headed outside to shift and begin the search for the intruders.

"Does what get easier?"

"The terror that something might happen to your mate?"

The thought of fae warriors coming to take Evalina away tied knots into my stomach that threatened to push out everything I'd eaten that day. I'd never felt that way about heading into dangerous situations or defending the pack before because I never had quite so much at stake.

"Ah. That." Vaughan gave me a wry smile as he tossed his clothes to the side. "No. It doesn't get any fucking easier. At least it hasn't yet, and I honestly don't know if it ever will."

"Great. Thanks. I feel much better now."

He shot me one more smirk before shifting into his wolf and I quickly followed suit.

Darius, Vaughan, and I each led our assigned groups in a different direction from the pack house to search for intruders. We'd make wide arcs, everyone keeping alert for any unusual scents or strange movements among the trees, while the three of us who had been to the fae realm kept our eyes peeled for anyone who shouldn't be there.

Could Tarron really have tracked Evalina down already? Even if he had, could he have reached our land so quickly? I knew from Evalina that they didn't have cars, but I didn't know what other methods of transportation they might use. The elf from that morning had materialized out of thin air, but I doubted Tarron could do the same. He hadn't done it when I chased him back to his own world that first night, and that would have been a perfect time to use the ability if he possessed it.

But if not Tarron, who would it be? The elf we spoke to said they had no interest in visiting our world and he had no apparent reason to lie.

I had to be missing something but I had no idea what it might be, and the cool forest air did little to ease the heat of my rising worry.

Since we only knew of one portal on our territory, heading towards it seemed like the best place to start. We advanced quickly, the paws of the wolves behind me barely making a sound as they moved across the packed dirt of the forest floor. Every ear strained for any unexpected sound, every nose trained on the ground, searching for unfamiliar scents.

I smelled it first, maybe because I was in the lead, or maybe because of my visit to the fae realm. A floral scent floated on the crisp autumn air, its sweetness unnatural and foreign in the earthy forest. Not werewolf and not human either.

I think we're close to something, I warned the others by mind-link. *Be on guard and listen for my orders.*

The collective tension in our group sharpened, the air charged with anticipation. As we drew closer to the portal, the scent grew stronger, backing up my suspicion that the two must be linked, but I still couldn't see anything. Maybe they'd come through the portal but had moved away from us, away from the pack house? Maybe they'd already returned to their territory but the scent still lingered? Maybe...

I didn't get a chance to finish that thought before the air seemed to ripple around us. The trees shifted, and my fur bristled as their forms sharpened into focus. I blinked, my eyes struggling to make sense of what I saw, until I realized they were fae, camouflaged against the trees until they chose to reveal themselves.

A dozen of them, at least, taller than Tarron, who didn't seem to be among them.

Elves.

A deep growl rumbled from my chest as I pulled up short, a warning sign to them to get off our land immediately.

What is it? one of the other men with me asked in my head as they all came to a stop behind me. *Do you see something?*

A dozen men are surrounding us. They don't seem to be armed.

"That's the one, right in the front there."

The man Evalina and I spoke to a few hours earlier appeared to my left, just as suddenly as he'd materialized that morning, and a jolt of fury shot through me as I recognized the elf's smug face.

"He's the one the prince wants."

What the fuck? Kai growled, echoing my own thoughts. The prince? Did he mean Tarron? Wanted *me?* And the elves came to find me for him? Why?

Close in around me, I ordered my men. *I need to shift.*

They immediately obeyed, and with a circle formed, I shifted in the centre of it.

"What do you want?"

I addressed the elves, who all stared at me curiously, apparently not having seen a wolf shift into a man before.

"Ah, you do speak. That will be easier," the same man spoke again. "Your presence is requested in the court of Etta. Something about you kidnapping some of their subjects. The details aren't important."

My fists clenched at his arrogance, my wolf snarling inside me. Those 'details' were sure as fuck important to me. "I didn't kidnap anyone and you have no authority here. Get off our land."

Vaughan? Darius? I've got them by the lake. Come this way, now. I sent the message out by mind-link as quickly as I could before the elf replied.

"Your unauthorized visit to Exteria gives us permission to visit you. It's an ancient agreement."

Shit. Going through that portal with Evalina really hadn't been the best idea, but since I couldn't change the past, I focused on the present instead.

"Well, you've had your visit, so you can go back home now. We won't bother you again and you can stay on your side."

"Certainly. Come with us and we'll be on our way."

"I'm not going anywhere with you," I growled.

"The prince of Etta insists that you do."

"And you do his dirty work for him?"

The elf bristled but didn't yield. "We'll make an exception to our normal neutrality when circumstances call for it."

Almost there, Vaughan's voice sounded inside my head. *Thirty seconds.*

Around me, the circle of wolves pawed at the ground, coiled to strike. If I could stall until the others arrived, the extra wolves would be enough to launch a proper attack even if most of them couldn't see what they were meant to be attacking. We could drive the elves back and have Calista disable the portal like she did with the other one.

"What circumstances?" I asked, simply to buy myself time. I didn't really care what deal he and Tarron had come to.

"It doesn't concern you," the elf replied before his eyes scanned my naked body with distaste. "You really should have some clothes on, but I suppose it can't be helped."

"Sorry I don't meet the dress code. I guess I'll have to take a rain check."

The sound of Vaughan's approaching steps, along with his men, reached my ears at the same time the elf heard them, and he gave a swift nod to the others. "Let's go."

I was about to give him a sarcastic send-off when he suddenly appeared right next to me, inside the circle of wolves. Without a word, he placed a hand on my shoulder and the air around me compressed, my lungs straining as the world twisted and fell away.

Everything seemed to close in around me, the very molecules of the air pressing down on my skin until it felt like I might implode, until, just as suddenly, the pressure eased. The ground lurched beneath me and only the steady hand of the elf, surprisingly strong, kept me upright.

"One werewolf, as requested," the man next to me said as I squeezed my eyes shut, trying not to throw up. I'd never felt so disoriented before. "Try not to lose him again."

With my eyes closed, I didn't see the man who spoke in reply, but I recognized Tarron's voice immediately. My blood boiled at the sound.

"We won't. Trust me: this time, I'm getting exactly what I want."

Chapter Forty-One

~Evalina~

Calista and I were still exploring the map of my world when she trailed off mid-sentence and her eyes glazed over. I'd noticed that happened when the werewolves communicated telepathically, so I waited anxiously to see what news she received.

"That was Vaughan," she announced when her eyes cleared, focusing back on me with a trepidation that quickened my pulse. "Felix has disappeared."

The words hit me like a blow, and I clutched the edge of the desk to keep myself upright. "What does that mean? They can't find him?"

"I'm not entirely sure. He said he literally disappeared." Her lips pressed together into a frown, as dissatisfied with that answer as I was. "Vaughan's on his way here right now, he'll tell us more."

Each second we had to wait felt like an eternity. I wanted to jump out of my skin, to do something, *anything*, rather than sitting there and waiting, but without knowing the details, I had no idea where to start.

Finally, Vaughan burst through the door, his expression grimmer than I'd ever seen. A loose pair of pants covered his lower half and he wore nothing else, as if there hadn't been time to put anything more on. "They took him. I got there just in time to see them vanish."

"Who took him? Where?" Somehow, I ended up standing right in front of him though I couldn't even remember getting to my feet.

"Those damn fairies. Elves? I don't know." He raked his hand through his hair, his fingers tangling in the curls as he did. "He linked me and said he'd found the intruders. I was on my way to him and I saw a tall, thin man talking to him. One second, they were right there, and the next, they disappeared into thin air. The others with them scattered back into the trees. I chased them back to the portal and they all went through."

"What were they talking about?" Calista asked.

"I was too far away to catch what they were saying, and the wolves with Felix could only hear his side of it. Apparently, he said something about kidnapping, circumstances, and a dress code. It doesn't make any sense without the other half of the conversation."

Calista's eyes moved to me, full of just as much concern as Vaughan had. "Do you have any idea what he might have been talking about?"

I wished I did, but the words didn't make any sense to me. "I don't even know what a 'dress code' is."

"How did they disappear?" Vaughan asked me.

His intense stare could have cowed me, but concern for Felix overrode any other considerations. "Some elves can transport themselves instantly, but it takes centuries to master. It's likely the same man we met earlier."

"And he could take Felix with him?" Calista's voice tightened with concern.

"Yes. The most skilled can move other people or objects with them."

"Where would he take him?" Vaughan growled. "And why?"

Those questions, I had no answers for, but Calista stepped in.

"After our conversation this morning, I reached out to some hunter acquaintances of mine. The one who sent me the map gave me some information about elves as well. He said they'll generally mind their own business unless there's an incentive for them to intervene. I don't know what they would want with Felix, but we know that the prince from Evalina's kingdom wasn't happy that he escaped. Maybe he offered the elves something in exchange for bringing Felix back, which would mean that we would need to look for him in Etta rather than Exteria."

Vaughan slammed his palm against the top of the desk in frustration. "I don't care about fae politics; I just want my Beta. Talk to me like I'm five: what do we need to do to get him back?"

Respecting her mate's impatience, Calista wasted no time in laying out our options. "The way I see it, we have two potential moves. We can't use the portal on the Vermillion pack land because I disabled it, but Evalina thinks there's another portal into Etta, and she has a rough idea where it leads. Using the map, we can try to locate it in our world and cross back to find Felix."

Vaughan nodded as he considered that. "And the other strategy?"

"We could try negotiating with the elves through the portal here, but if they're aligned with Tarron, it's a gamble. We'll need an incentive big enough that they want to help us instead."

"There are risks both ways," he mused. "And I don't like the idea of putting all our eggs in one basket."

I didn't know what eggs and baskets had to do with anything, but Calista seemed to understand him. "You want to try both?"

"Yes, but I want to go along with both teams." His grimace made it clear that he hated the idea of sending any of his team into danger without him.

He was exactly what a leader should be. Unlike Tarron.

I straightened my spine, determination hardening my voice. "I'll go to Etta. I know the land and the residence. I've worked there most of my life. You should meet with the elves. Protocol and status are important to them and they might be insulted if anyone less than the Alpha attempted to negotiate with them."

"That makes sense," Calista agreed before Vaughan could say anything. "I'll go with Evalina and we'll take Leo and some of the warriors. Darius and his lieutenants can go with you."

Vaughan's jaw tightened, his displeasure at the idea of being separated from his mate visible in every tense muscle. "If there is *any* sign of trouble, you get out of there. We'll find another way of getting to him. We don't even know for sure that's where he is."

I didn't respond to that, but the more I thought about it, the more convinced I became that Tarron must be behind it, even if I still had no idea what he wanted with either Felix or me. The prince might be a poor excuse of a man next to my werewolf mate but he had power in Etta.

Leaving Felix to Tarron's whims was out of the question.

"I promise we'll be careful," Calista said, and the two of them shared a fierce kiss that had me blushing to the tips of my ears before Vaughan pulled away.

"Get your team together and go," he instructed, his eyes returning to me with grim determination. "Good luck."

"And to you."

We were all going to need it.

Chapter Forty-Two

~Felix~

Gradually, the spinning in my head slowed, and I forced my eyes open against the pink-tinged light to get a look at my surroundings.

Tarron stood in front of me, dressed in fine, elegant clothes, looking regal and unnervingly beautiful, his fae features finely etched in perfect proportions. I wouldn't have blamed Evalina if she found him attractive, but she'd made it clear she didn't. In fact, after learning about the way he treated her, first bullying her and later trying to force her to be his mistress, it took all my self-control not to lunge at him on sight.

The only reason I forced myself to remain still was the fact that I was severely outnumbered. Even if I shifted back to my wolf, armed men lined the walls of the large, square room we were in, their sharp eyes tracking my every move. No furniture filled the space, nothing to indicate anyone lived there. It felt more like the training rooms our men used, some kind of barracks, and the presence of the armed men backed up that theory.

Two guards, bulkier than the lean prince, stood in front of a tall wooden door on one side of the room. On the other side, streams of light filtered through the windows, casting pink streaks across the polished floor.

My chances didn't look good if I attacked the prince. There would be nowhere to run afterwards. A week ago, I might have tried anyway, but now, my safety meant more to me.

It meant getting back to Evalina, and I would do whatever it took for that to happen.

"What the hell do you want with me?" I growled at Tarron, letting my wolf come right to the surface so that my voice rumbled with Kai's power as well as my own.

A few of the men at the side of the room shuffled nervously.

Tarron didn't even glance my way, his attention fixed on the elf as if I were beneath notice. "You'll find your payment with my clerk in the residence. He's expecting you."

That supported my theory that we were not in the official residence at the moment. Though it still didn't tell me exactly where we were, the more information I could gather about my situation, the better.

The elf bristled at the dismissal in Tarron's tone. "I won't surrender the werewolf to you until I receive what you promised. You will deliver it to me personally."

My ears pricked at the edge of frustration in the elf's voice. A crack in their alliance, perhaps? Sowing discord between them didn't seem likely to hurt my cause, so I inserted myself into the conversation. "Tough to find good mercenaries these days, isn't it?" I shot Tarron a smirk, gesturing towards the elf with mock disappointment.

As I hoped, the elf stiffened even more. "I am *not* a mercenary."

"No? You brought me here and he's giving you a payment in return. Sounds pretty mercenary to me."

"Stay out of this," Tarron instructed with a glare in my direction. "It doesn't concern you."

"It concerns me a great deal if I'm the subject of the transaction between you. What's the going rate for my capture? If I escape from you again and turn myself back in, can I collect it?"

"I doubt you'd be interested in this type of payment," Tarron sneered.

"I don't have all day," the elf next to me snapped at him. "The payment, Your Highness, or I take this man back where I found him."

That works for me, Kai grumbled in my head.

"Is it clothes?" I asked before Tarron could say anything. "I could really use some clothes right about now."

I gestured down at my naked body while a few of the men by the wall tried not to snicker.

"Or maybe it's pullaberries? I've heard they're rather good. I'd like to take some back with me."

"Someone shut him up," Tarron ordered his men in exasperation. "And bring the clerk to me, though it would be faster if you went to him yourself."

He addressed those last words to the elf next to me, and I leaned over to speak to him in a stage whisper, loud enough for Tarron to hear. "Who does he think he is, speaking to you that way? He really does see you as the help."

"Shut him up *now*!" Tarron bellowed in frustration, and four men quickly approached me, producing an item whose dull gleam made my stomach sink.

Silver chains. *Fuck.*

Evalina told me silver wasn't common in her world, but Tarron had obviously found a stash of it somewhere. If they got those chains on me, my chances of getting free by myself would fall dramatically, so if I wanted to make a move, I would have to do it before that silver got anywhere near me.

"Consider whether working with this jackass is really worth it," I said in parting to the elf before shifting into my wolf form and bolting out of the way of the chains. Tarron cowered behind his guards, immediately putting several bodies between me and himself, but he wasn't my target. As much as I wanted to take him on, escape mattered more.

Shouts echoed off the stone walls as I darted towards the door in an attempt to draw more of the guards in that direction. It worked; they all ran to block off my exit from the room, leaving the windows unguarded.

The impact would be brutal but I didn't see any other choice. With a howl, I changed course and ran towards the window, leaping towards it with as much force as I could, claws out to help shatter the glass.

Except the windows weren't made of glass.

The unyielding surface, slightly flexible but not breakable, threw me back, slamming me to the floor with a jarring thud. The prince's soldiers rushed to surround me, shouting orders to each other.

Get up, I urged Kai, but he couldn't move fast enough. Silver chains wrapped around our ankles, a searing pain biting into our skin and sapping our strength in seconds.

A moment later, Tarron's smug face appeared over me again. "If you're quite finished embarrassing yourself, my men will take you to your new cell. I promise that you won't be breaking out of this one."

The growl I tried to give him didn't sound much stronger than a dog's under the silver's influence.

I should have ripped his throat out when I had the chance.

With all my remaining strength, I shifted back to my human form and gasped out the question he still hadn't answered. "What do you... want... with me?"

Tarron's smile turned even more sinister as he bent down over me. "Evalina's the one I want," he hissed, his breath hot and moist against my ear. "And with you as my bait, I finally have something she can't refuse."

Chapter Forty-Three

~**Evalina**~

Calista put a team together while I ran upstairs to let my mother know what was happening, dread settling further into my stomach with each step. Propped up in her bed, she jumped in surprise when I burst through the door, and with no time to waste, I blurted out the essential details.

"Tarron has Felix. I'm going back to Etta to help him. The staff will keep bringing you food and I'll return as soon as I can."

I made it halfway back out the door before she called after me, her voice sharper than usual. "Evalina, wait!"

Reluctantly, I turned back. "Yes?"

"I don't think you should go back." Getting to her feet, she stepped closer to me. Her eyes scanned my face, concern clear in the lines of her brow. "If Tarron finds you, it won't end well. Don't forget what happened to your father."

A lump filled my throat but I did my best to swallow it down. "I won't let him find me. I'll have Calista and the other werewolves there for backup."

"It's not worth the risk," she insisted, her hands wringing together. "They can go without you."

"I can't let them go in blind. They need someone who knows the territory."

She refused to back down. "You can tell them what they need to know before they go in."

"But what if they run into a situation we're not anticipating? They won't know who can be trusted. I have to go. I promise I'll be careful."

"Please, don't." Her eyes brimmed with tears. "If he catches you, he won't let you go."

The ache in my chest deepened, my heart torn between wanting to comfort her and needing to get to Felix. "Mama…"

She shook her head, not letting me finish. "I know you've tried to shield me from his behaviour towards you, but I've seen enough. He watches you. He makes excuses to go to the kitchen to see you. And this illness of mine… now that simply coming here has healed me, I don't think it's a coincidence."

My mind flashed back to Tarron offering to cure my mother if I became his amorta. Would he really go to such lengths to get me to agree?

"I don't know exactly what he wants from you," she continued, "but I know it can't be good. Felix is a nice man and I'm sorry he got caught up in this but you can't throw your life away to save his."

"He's my mate."

Without warning, the words leapt from my lips, startling us both. I hadn't meant to tell her like this, but I didn't know how else to make her understand why I needed to go, no matter the danger.

Confusion mingled with the concern in her eyes. "What does that mean?"

Taking a deep breath, I tried to remember everything Felix had said and put it into words she would understand. "All werewolves have a person that they're fated to be with. Usually, it's another werewolf, but for Felix, it's me. I don't know why. I don't understand all the ins and outs of it, but I feel it, Mama. I feel it here."

My hand rested on my chest, over my heart.

"He wants me to be his. He wants me to stay here with him and for us to have a life together. And even though it's fast and crazy, I want it too. You know that I never fit in back in Etta. Maybe this is why. Maybe I was always meant to come here and find him. He's my future, and if

Tarron has him, if he's in trouble, I have to go and help him. He would do it for me, no matter the risk. He already has."

My mother took a long moment to process all of that before she slowly nodded. Her voice wavered, caught between happiness and fear. "I knew there was something in the way he looked at you, but I didn't imagine it would be all of that. I understand, Lina. I still don't like the thought of you going there, but I understand."

I wrapped my arms around her for a strong, quick embrace. "I'll be careful, and I'll be back home to you soon."

I'd already made it halfway down the stairs before I realized I called this place 'home' and my mother didn't bother to correct me.

A man named Leo came with me and Calista for the long drive in another car. Though just as big and imposing as the other men, an air of calm, considered competence surrounded him. Using maps of both our worlds, a notebook, and measuring tools, Leo charted the best route to take us to where the portal should be. Although he couldn't hear or see me, he took the time to explain his thought process to me anyway and I liked him immediately.

I liked all of the werewolves I'd met so far.

A second car behind us carried another four men, some of the pack's finest warriors, Leo promised me. Any more than that and we risked attracting too much attention. With my knowledge of the landscape and their combat skills, we would do the best we could.

Calista kept in touch with Vaughan through her phone until he and his group were ready to cross through the portal. I noted the way her lips pulled down into a concerned frown as she put the phone away and I reached out to place a supportive hand on her arm.

"I'm sorry to cause you all so much trouble. I hope no one else gets hurt."

She patted my hand with hers while shaking her head. "It's not your fault. Besides, as Felix's mate, you're part of the pack now. They protect their own, no matter what." Her head shook again, this time with a bit of a smile on her face. "I mean, *we* protect our own. I sometimes forget that I'm a werewolf too."

Startled, I blinked over at her. "What?"

I vaguely remembered that Felix had said something about Calista's werewolf side being suppressed, but so much new information had been thrown at me since then, I couldn't remember any of the details.

My quizzical look made her smile widen. "It's a long story. I promise I'll tell you the whole thing when all of this is over."

Hopefully, we would have that time together, and it wouldn't be too far away.

The smooth road beneath us gave way to a dirt track that jolted us with every bump as we drove deeper into the forest. The white-peaked mountains Felix and I saw across the lake that morning loomed much closer when Calista finally came to a stop.

"This should be the spot. Since Evalina and I are the only ones who can see the portal and no one else can see *her*, we'll have to all stick together. Leo, can you lead the search to make sure we don't miss anything but also don't double back on ourselves?"

His chest puffed out with pride at being given the lead. "Of course, Luna."

Two of the men with us shifted to their wolf forms, in case we came upon any *other* wild animals in the wilderness, and we set out due north. Leo had brought us to the centre of the radius he thought the portal should be in, so if we made it two miles and didn't find it, we'd rotate to the west and come back towards the vehicle.

None of us spoke as we walked, Calista and I scanning the forest for any sign of the portal while the others watched for hidden dangers. Every rustle of leaves or snap of a twig could mean trouble, and each second we spent was one more that Felix might be in greater danger. The dread in the pit of my stomach urged me to run rather than walk, but we had to pace ourselves. We might be in for a long search.

Thankfully, it only took about twenty minutes before I noticed the smell of Etta berries in the air. They were faint, but distinct, since I hadn't smelled them anywhere else since arriving in this world.

"This way," I urged the others, and Calista passed that message on while letting me take the lead. The sweet, tangy scent of my home world pulled me forward, cutting through the earthy terrestrial forest air.

Sure enough, the soft glow of the portal filtered through the trees another couple of minutes later, and Calista paused to give us all final instructions.

"Because you're with Evalina and me, you'll be able to pass through the portal. Once we're through, you'll be able to see her. It's her land, so we'll follow her lead. An order from her is an order from me unless I say otherwise. Don't go off on your own, and whatever you do, don't eat anything. Understood?"

The men all gave their agreement and Calista gave me an encouraging nod.

Determination flared in my chest as I faced the portal back to Etta. "Let's go and bring Felix home."

Chapter Forty-Four

~Felix~

Tarron hadn't been kidding when he said my new cell would be harder to break out of than the previous one. Not that the other one had been particularly easy either; without Evalina's help, I never would have found a way out on my own. But this time, he had me brought into his own bedroom, a spacious, vaulted space with display cabinets lining each wall and a massive bed with intricately carved posts that took up most of the centre of the room. Next to it sat a cage lined with silver, where the fae guards who grunted and groaned the whole way dumped me when we finally reached our destination. The faint, acrid tang of the silver burned my nose the moment I hit the floor of the cage.

The men stood guard over me until Tarron returned, no sign of the elf with him. They must have gotten the payment issue sorted out, unfortunately. Entering the room with his head held high, he dismissed the guards so only the two of us remained. Others would be stationed outside the door, I was sure, and the view of the treetops out the window told me we were at least one story up. Escaping out the window wouldn't be an option, especially if they were filled with that weird fae rubber like the one I bounced off earlier.

First, though, I had to get out of this cage and past Tarron. It seemed like he literally wasn't going to let me out of his sight.

My stomach growled as I tried to sit up, the silver chains still wrapped around my limbs. The cage had enough space for me to sit but not to stand and they hadn't provided me with any clothes or a cushion to sit on, nor was there anywhere for me to relieve myself when I needed to.

"Your hospitality could use some work," I grumbled.

Tarron took a seat at a piece of furniture that looked like a cross between a desk and an easel. Documents were displayed on the top and boxes of items filled the drawers that I got a glimpse of when he opened one of the doors, pulled something out, and closed it again.

"You won't be staying here for long. You'll survive, at least as long as I need you to."

He didn't even glance at me as he spoke, his tone as cold as the silver in my chains. That chilled me far more than any words spoken in anger would have.

"What do you want with Evalina?" I demanded. My voice cracked on her name despite my effort to control it.

Tarron raised an unimpressed eyebrow in my direction. "I'm doing you a favour by not gagging you. Don't make me change my mind."

"What's the point of dragging me to your room if you're not going to talk, Tarrass?"

Even with the distance between us, I saw his nostrils flare as I mangled his name. *Good*, Kai encouraged me, his voice weaker than usual in my head thanks to the silver, but still there. *He's more likely to let things slip when he's angry. Keep needling him.*

"No one ever said werewolves were so annoying," he muttered as he returned to the papers in front of him.

"Who told you anything about us?"

When he didn't answer, I kept going.

"In our world, we have fairy tales. Literally. They don't all have fairies in them. Sometimes they're kings or queens. Or witches, or trolls, or mermaids. Anything not human, really. Usually, the fairies are really small. Like, fit-in-the-palm-of-your-hand tiny. I wonder if that's a reference to the size of your dick."

His palm slammed down on the top of his desk. If he were capable of growling, he would have done it then. "Stop. Talking."

"I would if you would keep up your end of the conversation. It's not polite to ignore someone when they ask you a question. I just want to get to know you."

"You want to know who you're dealing with?" His lips curled into a snarl as he left the desk and went to one of the display cabinets against the wall on the far side of the room and flung open the door. From inside, he pulled out a couple of items, the force in his movements stronger than necessary, betraying his agitation. "This is the last werewolf I met."

The items clattered onto the floor in front of me and my empty stomach heaved. Two large, white fangs stood out against the dark floor. A paw, preserved like a rabbit's paw, still had its claws extended. It took a moment to realize what the third item was, but when I did, I had to swallow down my nausea. What looked like a withered, thin scrap of paper was actually a dried piece of skin, displaying the wolf's mate mark.

I swallowed hard, forcing my expression to stay neutral. No way was I giving him the satisfaction of seeing my disgust. What kind of psychopath went around collecting pieces of other species? When that psychopath had already expressed a strong interest in my mate, it concerned me even more. "What did she do to you?"

"I thought she'd be the one to help me," he said, stooping down to collect the items again and return them to their case. They'd served their purpose. "Unfortunately, I miscalculated. This time, there won't be any mistakes."

"Help you do what?"

"Fulfill my destiny," was the only answer he gave me, the words dripping with self-importance but ultimately cryptic and unhelpful. "Now, I suggest you shut your mouth unless you want Evalina to end up in another one of my cases."

He could have threatened my life until he was blue in the face and I wouldn't have cared but the second he uttered Evalina's name, I pressed my lips together. He seemed certain she would come for me, but I hoped he was wrong. The portal to their land had been disabled, the elves through the portal on our pack land were obviously bastards, and even if they found another way in, Vaughan would be smarter than to allow Evalina to come back anyway. If *someone* tried to rescue me, it wouldn't be her. It couldn't be.

In the meantime, I'd have to do my best to figure out how to get the hell out of there before I ended up as one more trophy on his wall.

Chapter Forty-Five

~**Evalina**~

Though Etta had been my home all my life, it felt foreign as I crossed through the portal back into the fae world. The pale pink sky seemed muted after the terrestrial blue, and the overpowering scent of Etta berries from the nearby forest made my stomach churn.

The werewolf men cast curious glances my way as they got their first look at me, perhaps surprised to see that I did in fact exist, while Calista surveyed the rocky expanse ahead. "Where do we start?"

The portal had brought us into a desolate area at the far edge of Etta's territory. Uneven, jagged ground and a lack of fresh water and plants made it unsuitable for habitation and there were no signs of life anywhere. That meant we didn't have to worry about randomly running into people going about their day, but it also meant that we could be spotted from a distance if anyone happened to be nearby, or if the dragons that lived to the south happened to pass overhead.

"The only prison I know of is the pens, so we'll go there first. If he's not there, we'll go to the residence and find Tarron. We should move quickly until we reach the forest and have some cover."

Silently, Calista, Leo and the others followed me as I made for the trees that marked the start of Etta's forest. The distant call of a dragon spurred us into a sprint, my heart pounding as I struggled to match their longer-legged pace.

Thankfully, we reached the forest without incident, and after taking a moment to catch my breath, we started through the trees, slower and more carefully than before, everyone's eyes and ears trained for any sign of danger. The trail led us close to the territory's main town but we made a wide circle of it, staying in the trees and ducking out of sight whenever anyone came close. Once, a group of women passed only a few feet away as we all huddled behind a large bush. Thankfully, fairies didn't possess the same sensitive noses that werewolves did, and they walked right by with no idea we were there.

Nearly two hours passed before the rounded dome of the pens appeared in the distance. My heart ached with the thought of what Tarron might have done to Felix in that time, but I pushed my worry down. I couldn't change anything that had happened, only what might happen next, and we were getting close. I had to stay focused.

"There's the prison," I whispered to Calista as we all huddled behind the trunk of a wide heffa tree, pointing to the circular structure she'd helped me to escape from before. "And it looks like there are extra guards. That must mean he's in there."

Peering around the trunk, I spotted five royal guards, my heart thudding a little harder with each one I counted. I'd never seen so many at the pens before, so whoever they held inside, they were taking it seriously. It *had* to be Felix.

Calista frowned as her eyes glazed over in that strange werewolf method of communication. "He's not answering my mind-link. This close, he should hear me."

"Maybe the magical protection around the cells is interfering?" I suggested, refusing to accept the possibility that he might be too injured to answer, or worse.

"That's possible," Leo agreed, giving me a sympathetic nod, and I couldn't tell if he really believed that or if he just wanted to make me feel better. "So, what's the plan? How are we getting him out?"

"We'll need to get through the guards, the locks and the magical barrier. The first one, we should be able to figure out, the second, I can take care of, but I don't know how we get past the magic," I admitted. "I don't have that ability."

Rather than looking defeated, Leo pulled his phone out of his pocket. He tapped on it a few times, holding the strange, glowing object up in the air and bringing it back down while I watched in fascinated confusion.

"As I suspected," he finally announced. "The magic's giving off a signal similar to electricity. If I jam it, it might disrupt the barrier."

Not a word of that made sense to me, but Calista nodded at my side. "Should we do that first?"

On that point, I could offer an opinion. "If one of the guards is controlling the magic, they'll feel when it's disrupted. It would alert them that something's going on."

"Okay, guards first then. Here's what we're going to do about them."

She laid out a strategy for us to attack and take out all the guards at once while I listened in open-mouthed awe.

"How did you learn all of that?" I asked when the others left to take up the positions she'd assigned them. Her knowledge seemed almost magical to me.

A smile broke through her serious demeanour. "I spent a long time training on how to hunt different supernatural creatures. The situation might be different here but the tactics still work. And speaking of supernatural beings..."

She reached into her pocket, pulled out a couple of small paper rectangles and held them out to me.

"This is sugar. If you're cornered, rip it open and drop it. Any fae nearby will be compelled to count the grains. Just make sure you don't look at it or it will affect you too."

I tucked the packets carefully into the pouch attached to my dress and turned back towards the pens. I couldn't see any of the other werewolves anymore, but after another minute, Calista confirmed to me that they were all in place.

"We're ready to move when you are."

I gave her a firm nod. "Let's go."

She gave the order through their telepathic link and the men sprang into action. From nowhere, two wolves appeared, bursting out of the trees and running towards the guards at full speed. Shouts of surprise filled the air as the guards did their best to take a defensive position, bows aimed at the intruders. A few arrows flew but the wolves managed to avoid them. The animals retreated into the woods, drawing the guards into an ambush where the werewolves still in human form struck them down with swift, precise blows.

The whole thing took no more than a couple of minutes.

"That was amazing," I whispered to Calista but she only allowed herself a small smile of satisfaction before gesturing towards the pens.

"Let's see if he's in there."

The distant calls of harpies sent a shiver down my spine as Calista and I crept closer to the pens. We peered into the darkness of each cell, calling Felix's name, but no reply came and my heart thudded more heavily with each silent second that passed. There had to be *someone* in the cells or there wouldn't have been so many guards. Whoever it was must be too injured to reply.

Leo approached just as Calista and I finished our search. "Go ahead and try to disable the magic so Evalina can open the doors," she instructed him.

Using his phone, Leo pressed on the screen a few times again until I felt the protective layer disappear, allowing my own magic to access the lock system. Since I didn't know which cell he might be in, I had to open them all, and I could feel my power waning the more I used it. I'd never tried to undo so many locks all at once.

The cells creaked open, but as I stepped forward, a wave of dizziness crashed over me. My knees buckled, and I hit the ground hard.

"Evalina?"

Calista sounded far away as she called to me and I did my best to reassure her. "I'm okay. Find Felix. I'll be right there."

Shaking my head, I tried to regain my balance but the world continued to spin around me. I thought I heard shouting but everything had become muffled. My arms trembled beneath my weight when I tried to push myself up and I collapsed again, my face smashing straight into the hard ground. The last thing I saw before darkness swallowed me was a pair of pointed shoes stepping into view, shoes that I knew didn't belong to any werewolf.

CHAPTER FORTY-SIX

~Felix~

My stomach rumbled as I sat in Tarron's cage, time dragging by in excruciating silence. Hours must have passed, but I ignored the ache of hunger gnawing at my insides. No one had offered me food, and even if they did, I couldn't eat it. Being stuck in the fae world forever while my mate waited for me back in my pack sounded like the worst kind of torture I could imagine. Death by starvation would be preferable, and I wasn't dying quite yet anyway.

Tarron still hunched over his desk, his quill scratching against a piece of parchment, his face a mask of cold concentration. I studied him from my cage, hoping for a clue to his plans, but the distance and my growing exhaustion kept everything maddeningly out of reach. I also hadn't gotten any closer to figuring out a way to break out of the cage. Even touching the bars burned my fingers, and the silver chains around my limbs continued to weaken me. I definitely wouldn't be bursting out through sheer force.

I would need some help and a bit of luck, and with Tarron sitting there keeping guard over me, neither seemed likely.

A sharp knock at the door jolted me upright, hope flickering despite my growing despair. If Tarron got called away and assigned someone else to watch me, I could try to work my charm on that person instead. There had to be some way to talk myself out of this.

However, the man didn't ask Tarron to leave. He bowed low to his prince, keeping his head down while he delivered his message. "We have her, Your Highness. She went to the pens and collapsed, just as you predicted."

"Excellent. Her companions?"

"Captured, as you requested."

"Good. Bring her here."

"Yes, Your Highness."

The man bowed even lower before retreating from the room, and I couldn't keep silent any longer. "Who's 'she'?"

"Who do you think?" came his smug reply.

Cold panic crawled through my veins but I tried to stay calm. He had to be bluffing. There was no way he had Evalina. She wouldn't have come here. She couldn't have.

"I knew she worked some kind of magic to break you out of the prison before," he continued, unable to resist an opportunity to gloat. "I don't know exactly what her power is, but I placed a spell of my own on the pens. As soon as anyone tried to use magic on it, their power would be sapped. My men were standing guard as a decoy so any potential rescuers would think you were inside. It all worked out exactly as I planned."

Common sense told me to stay quiet but my heart compelled me to speak. "She wouldn't have come alone. She probably has an army of werewolves with her."

"Only six of them, actually," he sneered. "I have plans for them too, don't worry.

That couldn't be right. My Alpha wouldn't allow my mate to walk into a trap without a backup plan. Tarron had to be missing something, assuming *anything* he said was true.

I got my first confirmation that he wasn't completely bluffing ten minutes later, when two men walked into the room with a nearly unconscious Evalina held between them. The growl that burst out of me made the crystals in the chandelier vibrate.

"What did you do to her?"

At the sound of my voice, Evalina's head jerked weakly, only to slump back down, her body hanging like a broken doll in the guards' grasp.

Tarron ignored me, speaking to the guards instead. "Put her down over there."

He gestured towards his bed, drawing another deep growl from my throat. Even in Kai's weakened state, he could still make his displeasure known.

Still wearing the dress she'd put on at the pack house that morning, what felt like days ago rather than hours, Evalina was placed on the bed in front of me. Her head lolled to the side to face me, and when her eyes cracked open just a sliver, I smiled at her, doing my best to reassure her even in the middle of the undesirable predicament we found ourselves in.

"Fancy meeting you here."

Her lips twitched, but her eyebrows drew together in concern as she opened her eyes more fully. Her voice came out weakened and rough. "Are you alright?"

How could *she* be worried about *me*? Sure, I was naked and chained in silver in a cage, but she was the one Tarron wanted, for reasons I still didn't understand. "I'm fine, my little fairy. You shouldn't have come."

"I had to. You were taken because of me."

She tried to sit up, but her arms failed her and she fell back onto the bed with a frustrated grunt. At least the mattress softened her landing, but when Tarron walked over, having dismissed the guards with further instructions, any small comfort I took in that died.

"Chew on this," he instructed, holding out a glossy, emerald-green leaf that gleamed faintly in the dim light. "It will counteract the effects of the spell."

"She's not taking anything from you," I growled, even as I knew there might be no other choice.

Tarron snorted, his amusement only fueling my anger. "I won't harm her. If I wanted to kill her, I've had thousands of chances over the years. That's never been what I wanted."

As much as his words worried and disgusted me, I saw his point. Obviously, he had something else in mind for her, so the remedy he offered her was probably harmless. When Evalina looked to me for guidance, I gave her a nod confirming that I believed it would be safe.

After chewing on the plant for thirty seconds, she sat up fully, her strength returning as quickly as the prince had promised.

"Where are the others?" she demanded of her prince, glancing around the room as if looking for other cages. "Calista and the men, where are they?"

Oh, fuck. Tarron had Calista too? Vaughan was not going to be happy about that. Where the hell was he?

"They're being held in the pens, but they're all safe. I have no interest in keeping them here. As long as the two of you cooperate with me, no one has to get hurt."

That sounded pretty unlikely. He was laying a trap, and I needed to figure it out before we walked right into it.

"Cooperate with you?" I snarled. "What the hell do you want, Tarron?"

Tarron, for once, didn't brush off the question. Instead, he sat next to Evalina with a calm confidence that set my teeth on edge.

"Let me tell you exactly what's going to happen next."

Chapter Forty-Seven

~**Evalina**~

With my strength returned, I had to fight the urge to throw myself at Tarron and wring his scrawny fae neck. He sat back with infuriating ease, his smirk radiating the confidence of someone utterly convinced we couldn't touch him, ignoring the expression on Felix's handsome face that bordered on murderous.

I had to bide my time. As long as Calista and the others were being held, simply killing Tarron wouldn't be enough. Even if we could escape, the others couldn't without our help. We needed to see the bigger picture, and Felix and I needed to be able to work together. So, I bit my tongue and let Tarron speak.

"Evalina is going to be my amorta." He glanced at me as he spoke, a slight smirk in his expression that had bile gathering in the back of my throat, but he directed the words at Felix. "She'll agree to it willingly, and when she does, your friends will walk free. Simple as that."

"There's nothing simple about it," Felix snarled at him, muscles straining against the chains looped over his limbs. His eyes held none of the tenderness or mischievousness I usually saw in them, but although his expression remained firm, I could tell the chains hurt him from the way his usually strong shoulders hunched.

My hands clenched in my lap as I forced myself to remain still and not call on my magic to open the lock of Felix's cage. The right moment would come, but not yet.

"She isn't yours and never will be," Felix added, practically spitting the words.

"Because she's your mate? That doesn't matter."

A shudder rippled through my body at Tarron's cold, clinical declaration. How did he know Felix and I were mates? How did he know about mates at all? Felix let out a low growl, but Tarron held up a hand to stop him, amending his statement.

"Well, if we're being precise about things, it matters a great deal, but it doesn't change the fact that she will be mine."

"Why?" I interjected. Since they were speaking about *my* future, I deserved to be part of the conversation. "You don't even like me. You despised me for years."

Tarron's lavender eyes turned to me, still aloof and unbothered. "It has nothing to do with 'liking' you. I need what your body will give me."

My stomach twisted in revulsion and the cage rattled violently as Felix hurled himself against the bars, the sharp clang echoing through the room like a battle cry. The whole structure pitched forward but the door didn't give, and Felix hissed as his naked skin connected with the metal bars. Instinctively, I leaned towards him, wanting to soothe his pain, but Tarron's hand on my shoulder stopped me.

"You'll only hurt yourself if you keep doing that," Tarron informed Felix in a tone full of disdain. "And you're upsetting Evalina."

The first statement made no impression on my mate but at the thought of causing me any kind of distress, he went still. His glare could have cut through glass. "Get your hand off her."

To my surprise, Tarron actually released me, but the condescending expression on his face remained.

"What do you need my body for?" I asked. Something in the way he phrased it made me suspect it came down to more than simple lust. Tarron never lacked companionship in his bed, I knew that from the gossip in the servants' hall and firsthand from the time I spent hiding beneath the very bed I now sat on. The memory of how he groaned my name during that encounter sent another chill through me. Why had he been thinking of me then? What did it all mean?

Thankfully, Tarron seemed inclined to talk, even if he didn't get immediately to the point. "I've studied the legends of our world my whole life, and by extension, the terrestrial world as well. All kinds of magic exist, the kinds we are born with and the kinds which are claimed. The elves who can transport themselves across space, for instance; that's a magic they give themselves."

So far, I understood him. "And there's a magic you want to claim?"

His eyes gleamed with excitement. "Yes. It's an ancient spell, forgotten by most of the world, but I've found it. It will give me powers beyond any other fae prince."

That ambition fit in with what I knew of him and his delusions of grandeur. "What would you do with such power?"

"There'd be nothing I *couldn't* do. Everyone who ignored me because Etta is a small, insignificant kingdom would soon regret it. They'll all kneel before me."

His expression turned dreamy, as if he could see the scene playing out before him, and I suppressed a shudder. He'd truly lost touch with reality, making him even more dangerous than I'd realized.

"Sounds like you're compensating for something. The size of your dick, maybe?" Felix muttered.

Jolted back down to earth, Tarron fixed an icy stare on him. "I can assure you there's nothing unimpressive about it, as Evalina will soon discover."

If it were possible for Felix to break through the bars with sheer fury, he would have been free in an instant.

"What does this magic have to do with me?" I pressed, trying to continue with his explanation. If we knew exactly what he wanted, we might be better equipped to stop him.

"The werewolf mate bond is a unique power, deeply rooted in primal magic. To fulfill the spell, I need to corrupt that magic. Make it mine."

He answered each question without actually saying much at all. "Corrupt it how?"

"The spell requires many special ingredients. Producing one of them requires a werewolf mate bond."

At the word 'ingredient', my eyes darted around the room at his cases of objects. Was this why he gathered so many specimens?

"Get to the fucking point," Felix growled. "What's the ingredient?"

"The heart of a child."

My breath hitched, and Felix froze, his face contorted with a rage so intense it seemed to darken the room. "That's barbaric," I gasped.

Felix's blue eyes glittered with ice as he glared at Tarron through the bars. "What child?"

"My child," he replied as calmly as if he were discussing the Etta berry harvest. "Born of a woman with a mate bond tying her to someone else."

My hand flew to my mouth, as if that might stop the nausea bubbling inside me. *This* was why he wanted me? To breed me, to have his child, and then to kill that child to make himself stronger?

The man in front of me was no fairy. He was pure evil.

Felix remained still, his eyes still fixed on the prince. "The other wolf?"

I didn't know what he meant, but apparently Tarron did. "It didn't work with the child she bore, apparently because she didn't give her agreement. It was a footnote that I missed. That's why Evalina must be my amorta willingly. It will be her choice."

As if he hadn't just said the most disturbing, disgusting things I had ever heard another person utter, Tarron turned to me with a look of steely determination.

"And you *will* choose it. I thought you would accept me to save your mother, but you resisted even after I made her sick. This time, there's no other option. If you refuse me, your friends in the pens will die, and this beast?"

He gestured at Felix with a cruel smile, his tone dripping with venom.

"I'll introduce him to every agonizing torture spell I've ever mastered. And I've mastered quite a few."

My stomach crawled into my throat, a sickening mix of terror and revulsion clawing at me as his words echoed in my ears.

I'd wanted answers, but now that I had them, I almost wished I hadn't asked.

CHAPTER FORTY-EIGHT

~Felix~

I'd seen some messed-up shit in the past few months, everything from a spirit causing chaos to a mad scientist trying to play goddess, but Tarron's plan set a new bar for cruelty.

Or maybe it just felt that way since my mate lay at the heart of his twisted scheme.

At least we finally knew what he wanted. I had to believe he'd told us everything since I couldn't imagine anything worse. True, we didn't know yet what kind of powers the spell would give him if he succeeded, but that didn't matter because no way in hell would I let him get that far. Not wanting him to mistake my rage for fear, I spoke forcefully enough that my voice didn't tremble. "Joke's on you, Tarron. Pain gets me excited. Bring it on."

The fae prince remained unmoved. "In that case, you're going to enjoy yourself very much here."

"Felix." The way Evalina said my name, choked with worry, hit me like a punch to the gut. Her icy blue eyes were desperate when I met their gaze. What I wouldn't give to speak to her privately and figure out a plan between us. If we could mind-link, that would be even better, but without that ability, we'd have to do our best to communicate non-verbally.

It's okay, I tried to tell her with the nod of my head. *I'll think of something. Just don't agree to anything.*

When she looked away, I couldn't be sure she got the message. We really hadn't known each other very long yet so maybe we weren't entirely on the same page.

"Let's be clear about this," she said, addressing Tarron with a firmer tone than I would have expected after all the horrific garbage he just spouted. "If I agree, you'll let the other werewolves go *immediately*, including Felix."

Tarron shook his pretty-boy head. "No. The werewolves in the pens will be released, I promise you that. This one, however…"

He gestured at me as if I were no more than a dog in his cage.

"He stays until you're pregnant. I'm not naïve, Evalina. If I let him go, you'll both run. The only way to ensure your compliance is to keep him close."

"No." Evalina's eyes clouded with fear but she stood her ground. "If he stays that long, he'll never be able to leave."

Good point; eventually, I'd have to eat something, and once I did, I would be stuck in the fae realm forever. That would be a problem if we were actually intending to go along with this jackass' plan. Since we weren't, I could ignore my empty stomach for a little longer.

Whether or not Tarron knew about the effects of fae food on terrestrial beings, he didn't seem concerned. His shoulders lifted in an indifferent shrug. "Those are my terms."

"I don't know much about magic," I interjected. "But where I come from, forced consent isn't consent at all. You say she has to do this 'willingly'. Look at her: not a single part of her wants you."

Anger flashed across the prince's face, letting me know I was getting to him, but if that would help us, I couldn't be sure. "She'll be willing enough if she wants you to live. She'll say yes every time I ask her if she wants to continue or she'll watch you suffer."

"You make it sound like I'm going to be in the room with you," I scoffed, still trying to goad him, but when he held my gaze impassively, my stomach twisted. "You can't be serious."

"Why not? She'll see the consequences of her choices in real time. It's far more efficient."

Kai's growling in my head grew so loud, I could barely hear myself think. *I'm going to tear this fucker limb from limb. Get us out of here NOW.*

You don't think I'm trying? If you have any suggestions on how to do that, I'm all ears.

"And after I have a baby, you'll let both me and Felix go?" Evalina asked, not even flinching at the sadistic nature of what Tarron just said. Maybe the spell he cast on her hadn't fully worn off yet because she couldn't be in her right mind to even think about accepting that.

But her eyes slid over to me, only for a second or two, and in them, I could read her silent message to me, loud and clear.

I have a plan. Trust me, no matter how crazy it seems.

Every cell in my body screamed to protect her, but locked in that cage and chained in silver that ached and drained my energy more with each passing second, I really didn't have many options. I would have to let her take the lead, no matter how much it killed me. If she had a way out of this, I had to trust her.

That was what it meant to be mates.

"After you give me the child, you and your 'mate' won't matter anymore." Tarron sneered the word 'mate' as if it tasted bitter on his tongue.

"That's not an answer," Evalina pointed out. "Will you let us both go? Yes or no?"

She's so strong, Kai marvelled through his fury, and I had to agree. Everything about her impressed me as she refused to back down against her psychopath prince.

Tarron's jaw clenched but he nodded. "Once I have what I want, you'll be free to go."

Surely, her plan couldn't be to go through with this. The thought clawed at my mind and knotted my empty stomach. There had to be something I was missing, some piece of information she had that I didn't, and she was only going through the motions of this negotiation to convince him that she might actually give in. That seemed much more likely than her actually being willing to concede to him.

Are you saying you wouldn't agree to it if the situations were reversed and you had no other choice? Kai asked inside my head.

I'm not answering that.

His snort let me know that he knew the answer as well as I did: if the shoe was on the other foot, I would agree to pretty much anything to spare her pain.

Hopefully, the goddess had chosen me a mate a hell of a lot smarter than that.

Chapter Forty-Nine

~**Evalina**~

The tiny packets of sugar that Calista gave me felt like they were made of stone against my side as I sat on the bed next to Tarron. Like I tried to assure Felix in the glance we exchanged, I had a plan. It might not be perfect, but it would have to do.

I had the sugar and I had the admission Tarron made earlier that he still didn't know what kind of magic I possessed. He knew I did *something* to help Felix escape before but he didn't know exactly what I did.

So, my plan was simple: distract Tarron with the sugar, free Felix from the cage with my magic, decide what to do with Tarron while he couldn't fight back, and get as far away as possible. We could disable both the portals, the one we used to get back into Etta and the one on Felix's pack's land, and that should limit any immediate threat of a backlash against the werewolves from the fae world.

Hopefully, I hadn't missed anything.

Before any of that, though, I needed to get Tarron to release Calista and the others, and for that reason, I went through the motions of negotiating my agreement with him. Only once, when he mentioned keeping Felix for weeks or even months, did true fear grip me. If Felix had to eat, forcing him to stay in the fae realm forever, of course I would stay with him, but I didn't want to. I was ready to start a new life with Felix in *his* world. The way his pack worked together, everyone valued and accepted, felt like a warm embrace compared to the way my whole life in Etta, *everyone's* lives, revolved around the royal family.

Returning home and seeing Tarron again had only made the contrast starker, reinforcing what I'd already begun to feel: there was nothing left for me in Etta.

After reassuring myself that it couldn't come to that, I returned to my negotiation. Tarron needed to believe I would agree even though I had no intention of it. No matter how much I wanted to spare Felix pain, no matter how much I'd give up to keep him safe, his intense stare through the bars of the cage told me that he would rather die than watch me give in to Tarron.

Which meant the time had come to put my plan into action.

"To be clear: if I agree to stay willingly, you'll release the other werewolves immediately, and prove it. Once you have what you want, you'll release both me and Felix. Felix won't be harmed as long as I stick to the agreement. Is that all correct?"

Panic flared in Felix's eyes, but I shot him a warning look, silently pleading for him to stay quiet. Tarron needed to believe I meant it. He needed to trust me and let his guard down if the rest of it was going to work.

"That's correct." The prince's glittering eyes held my gaze coolly, assessing me as if he could read my sincerity in my expression. "And if you don't agree, they all die."

"Yeah, we got that part," Felix muttered, his voice hoarse and strained, though still laced with sarcasm. His shoulders slumped more with each passing minute. Despite his bravado, the silver clearly weakened him. I had to get him out of there soon.

"Alright." I gave a firm nod, trying to convince myself I was making the right move as much as attempting to make my reluctance believable for Tarron. "I'll do it."

"No." The word came out of Felix in a strangled gasp of pain and my heart clenched. Did he know I was bluffing or not? I honestly couldn't tell.

Tarron, however, smiled in triumph. "That wasn't so difficult, was it?" He spared a condescending smirk in Felix's direction before getting to his feet. "We'll begin immediately."

The growl that rumbled from Felix shook the bed beneath me and I stood too. "You'll free the others first. You promised."

"Of course."

With a wave of his hand, a shimmering veil of light appeared in front of us. It looked similar to the see-through glimmer of the portal, but through it, I could see the pens and the guards standing in front of it. They didn't seem to be able to see us, but they moved and spoke to each other normally.

What kind of magic was this? I'd never seen anything like it.

Felix leaned closer, examining the strange portal as I did the same. "You've got a video chat? I guess you're not quite as backwards as I thought."

He tried to sound as sarcastic and easygoing as usual but his voice trembled, in fear or in anger, or maybe in both, and it undercut the humour in his words. He didn't fool anyone.

"They can't see me," Tarron explained, his tone dripping with smug satisfaction. 'But they'll hear me when I speak. I've picked up all kinds of magic, as I told you."

I couldn't argue with that, not with the proof right in front of me.

Pressing the fingers of his left hand to his temple, Tarron spoke in a stern, commanding tone. "This is Prince Tarron. Release the prisoners. They are free to go."

The men in the portal immediately straightened to attention, and once Tarron finished speaking, they hurried to the doors of the cells.

Incredible.

As we watched, the doors were opened and Calista, Leo and the others walked out into the open, blinking against the brightness of the sun after their time in the dark pens.

Tarron spoke again, his words directed at the werewolves. "You will leave our world immediately. If you refuse to go, your lives are forfeit."

To back up his point, the guards all pointed their weapons at the werewolves. Calista looked around, trying to find Tarron, but when she came up blank, she spoke to the air instead. "We're not leaving without Evalina and Felix," she said, her voice sharp with defiance. "Release them, and we'll leave in peace."

"You're not in any position to negotiate," Tarron sneered. "If you don't leave now, you won't be leaving alive."

I shot a worried glance towards Felix but his eyes were glazed over, letting me know that he must be trying to communicate with Calista through their telepathic link. I didn't know how far it would work, especially in his weakened state, but when his eyes cleared, he gave me a quick nod.

"Fine," Calista said through gritted teeth, tension coiled in her voice but confirming what I'd just gathered from Felix's nod. He must have gotten through to her, at least enough to tell her to take the chance and go. "But we won't forget this insult. You came onto our land and abducted one of our pack members."

"After you came onto *my* land and took *three* of my subjects," Tarron reminded her. "I'd say we're even."

With another wave of his hand, the portal disappeared, vanishing into thin air as if it had never been there at all.

"Wait!" I cried. "I want to see them leave. I want to know they're safe."

"You asked for proof that I released them, and you have it. Whether or not they take advantage of the reprieve they've been given isn't up to me."

Unfortunately, he had a point, and I had nothing left to offer to force him to give me any other concessions. I would just have to trust that Calista and the others could take care of themselves.

The time had come to put the second and most important part of my plan into motion, but as my hand moved towards my pouch and the sugar packets held inside it, Tarron moved towards me and grabbed both my hands, pulling me flush to his body.

"Now that the details are settled, we can begin. I've waited a very long time for this, Evalina."

Before I could respond, he seized my chin and crushed his hungry lips against mine.

Chapter Fifty

~Felix~

The moment Tarron kissed Evalina, pain stabbed my chest, accompanied by a primal, savage instinct: the need to rip that bastard away from my mate. Stopping the raw, all-consuming rage wasn't an option. I couldn't have even if I wanted to. Every cell of my body urged me to burst through the bars of the cage and tear that fucking fairy limb from limb.

Unfortunately, that didn't happen.

Instead, I half-shifted into Kai's wolf form. My legs remained human, silver chains biting into my skin, but I managed to hurl myself into the cage with enough force to send it crashing onto its side. A deep ache spread through my body, the impact compounding the searing burn of the silver bars and chains, draining my strength further.

"Idiot," Tarron huffed, glaring at me as he got up. I whimpered in pain, still stuck in a half wolf-half human hybrid form. The taunting didn't bother me. He could call me all the names he wanted as long as he left Evalina alone.

With a strength that surprised me given his size, he lifted the cage back to its upright position and I rolled with a hard thump back onto the floor. With the silver from the bars no longer touching me, I managed to shift fully back to my human form.

Thanks," I croaked, forcing a grin to keep his attention on me for as long as possible. "You might want to bolt this thing down next time. Seems a little unstable."

Behind him, Evalina's hand darted to her pouch, her anxious gaze flicking between Tarron and her trembling fingers. Whatever she had in mind, she needed a few more seconds, so I kept talking as a distraction.

"You know, gold bars would match the room better than silver. Just saying."

"Do you ever stop talking?" Tarron muttered, his voice icy. "Keep it up and I'll gag you with those silver chains."

I'd never had silver inside my mouth before but I couldn't imagine it would feel good. The mere idea of it made me wince, bringing something close to a smile to his face.

"Now, where were we?"

He turned back to Evalina, ready to resume whatever pathetic attempt at seduction he had in mind, but she was ready for him.

With a sweet smile, she held up a small square of paper, her calm composure masking her intent. "I think you were about to help with this."

She tossed the paper over her shoulder, and tiny specks of something went flying into the air behind her. *Sugar*, I realized. *Of course.* She must have been thinking ahead when she came here, or Calista thought of it, and now that the others were free, she could make her move.

I *knew* she had a plan. Pride surged through my veins, replenishing some of the energy that the silver had taken.

Evalina kept her gaze on me, avoiding the trap she'd just sprung. Tarron, however, had been staring directly at it. He had no choice but to hurry forward and begin counting the grains that had scattered across the smooth, glossy surface of the floor.

With him out of the way, Evalina closed her eyes and the lock on my cage began to whir, whatever mechanism held it together bending to her will until it clicked open and she rushed forward to open the cage door for me. Sparks flew across my skin as she grabbed hold of my arm and pulled me out. "Are you alright?"

"I'm fine, thanks to you." Stumbling to my feet, I pressed a quick kiss to her mouth, hoping to erase the memory of Tarron's lips in that spot by replacing it with one of my own. My limbs cramped in protest at suddenly being called back into use, but I didn't waver.

It felt so good to hold her and see her safe, and I wanted to savour the moment and enjoy it, but we weren't in the clear just yet. We couldn't rest until we got back to our world.

We couldn't rest until Tarron paid for what he'd done and what he'd been about to do.

Evalina must have been thinking the same because she dropped to her knees to begin to untie the chains from my feet. With each link of the chain removed from my skin, my strength returned even more.

As soon as they were all gone, I would shift properly and rip Tarron's throat out with my teeth.

Not if I beat you to it, Kai growled.

For the first time since I got free, my eyes went to the fairy prince, on his knees as he gathered the grains of sugar, but as soon as I focused on him, my brow furrowed into a deep frown. *What the hell?* Tarron's hands blurred, moving with supernatural speed as he scooped up the scattered granules. He'd be done in seconds.

"Look out!" I warned Evalina as she pulled the last of the chain from my ankles and I reached back to grab the cage I had just been in. If Tarron could lift it, so could I, and even though the silver burned into my skin, I raised it off the ground and tossed it at Tarron right as he finished counting the sugar and got back to his feet.

Silver flashed in the sparkling lights of the room as the cage flew through the air, but the crash that should have followed when it collided with the prince and knocked him to the floor never came.

Tarron raised a hand, halting the cage mid-air. It hovered for a moment before he flung it aside with a furious snarl.

Evalina gasped, leaping back to her feet and pressing her body close to mine. "How did he do that? How can he be done already?"

Tarron answered her before I could say anything. "You already used that little trick with the sugar on me."

I did, back at the Vermilion pack when we caught him stealing silver. That was why I'd been so sure it would work this time, why we'd *all* been sure of it.

Tarron, however, offered a different explanation. "When I returned, I found a way to counteract it so I wouldn't be caught out again. There are spells for *everything*."

Well, shit.

He might have been one step ahead of us, but we weren't out of options yet. I was free of the cage and free of the chains, which meant nothing stood between me and the man who wanted to use my mate for his plans of world domination, or whatever the hell he thought he might achieve. Without magic of my own, I had only one weapon: brute, unrelenting force.

In the time it took him to blink, I pounced, leaping forward and shifting to my wolf in mid-air. My growl rumbled the walls of the room and I got close enough that my exhaled breath blew back his black hair.

Before I could land the death blow, however, an invisible force froze me mid-pounce.

I couldn't move forward any further, held in place just as the cage had been. Tarron's cold, lavender eyes stared into mine with steely fury, his hand raised as it had been to stop the cage, as I struggled against the invisible restraint.

With his other hand, he summoned the silver chain Evalina had just removed from me. It crashed into my back before winding tightly around my neck. My body shifted back to its human form even though I hadn't instructed it to do so, and my claws and fangs disappeared, leaving me defenseless.

"Felix!" Evalina's cry of terror stabbed at my heart but I could do nothing as the silver singed the skin of my throat, cutting off my air and I went flying backwards, slamming into one of the cabinets that lined the walls of the room. The ends of the chain looped over the doorknobs of the cabinet behind me, tying me in place even as the chain loosened enough that I could breathe. Shallow, painful breaths, to be sure, but at least air went in and out.

"So, that's your power," Tarron said to Evalina, straightening his clothing as if I had been a minor inconvenience that he'd now dealt with. "You can manipulate locks. I should have guessed."

She didn't try to deny it. "Don't hurt him," she begged, her eyes wide with horror as she looked over at me. Although I could breathe, I couldn't seem to speak. "You promised you wouldn't hurt him."

"And you promised to give yourself to me willingly," he reminded her coldly. "Trying to trap me with your tricks broke the bargain first. Do you want to try again, or shall I kill him now?"

"Don't..." I gasped, but even that one word burned my throat so much, no other words followed.

Evalina's icy blue eyes brimmed with desperate, silent questions across the space between us. *Don't what? Don't let him kill you? Don't give in to him?*

All of the above. Don't let this happen, I wanted to scream to anyone who would listen.

Sensing his victory, Tarron stepped closer to Evalina again. His hand went to her stomach, resting there with a territorial possessiveness that would have made me growl if I were capable of making the sound.

"Are you willing?" he prompted, seeming to relish the defeated hopelessness on her face. "Say yes and he lives."

Her eyes never left me, but as their questions turned to an apology, my stomach twisted violently. *No! Don't do it. I'd rather die for you, I'll do anything...*

I thrashed against the chain with all my might, but it barely rattled. One of the drawers at my waist slid open with the movement, bumping into my hand, and I looked down to find neatly labelled samples of minerals, the kind of display a museum might have.

Through the haze of panic and pain, a single label caught my eye like a beacon.

Tarron wasn't the only one who had studied other species and the things that would affect them. My supernatural hobby of tracking other creatures and chatting with hunters and enthusiasts online had taught me a great deal, and Tarron wouldn't have counted on that. He might know I was a werewolf but he didn't know anything about me as a person, and he definitely didn't realize that I knew exactly what the mineral in that drawer could do.

He didn't realize Evalina and I weren't out of tricks just yet.

Chapter Fifty-One

~**Evalina**~

All my bravado deserted me in the face of Tarron's overwhelming magical power. Before, whether with my mother's illness or when Tarron imprisoned me, I always found a way to avoid his offer if I kept calm and waited for the right moment to act. Now, however, I didn't have the luxury of patience. The silver chain wrapped around Felix's neck, choking and burning him, could kill him if I didn't give in, and I had already played all the cards at my disposal.

Sugar wouldn't help and my magic counted for nothing against Tarron's powerful spells. To save Felix, I only had one choice, no matter how much my body and soul cried out against it.

"Yes," I whispered, my throat tightening around the word like a noose. "Don't hurt him and I'll do whatever you want."

I wouldn't bear him a child and let him cut that child to pieces for his evil ends. I wouldn't accept my fate peacefully, day after day. I would fight and find a way to free both Felix and myself, long before Tarron could achieve his goal, but for all of that, I needed time. At that moment, time was the one thing I didn't have, and so I had to give in, just this once.

A strangled cry came from the side of the room where the chain bound Felix to one of Tarron's cabinets, but I didn't look in his direction again. I couldn't bear to see the horror and dismay I knew I would find in his eyes.

At least I'd already shared something real with Felix. At least Tarron wouldn't take that first from me. With all my might, I tried to find some bright side to what I just agreed to.

The smug, triumphant grin that spread across Tarron's face turned my stomach. It churned at the idea of his lips against mine again, and I turned my head as he leaned down, hoping to avoid it. Unfortunately, he just pressed his lips against my neck instead, and it took all my self-control not to shove him away.

"Not... not in front of him," I pleaded when Tarron's hands went to the laces of my dress. Letting him touch me would be awful enough, but having Felix watch it? My stomach twisted again at the idea. I still couldn't bring myself to look over at him. "I promise I'll comply but let's go somewhere else."

Tarron's 'tsk'-ing sound reminded me of a mother scolding a misbehaving child. "I don't make the same mistake twice, Evalina. You've seen that with the sugar. Just a moment ago, you promised to do as I asked and then you tried to trap me. Do you think I'm stupid enough to fall for that again?"

He didn't want me to answer that. If I started telling him what I actually thought of him, Felix was as good as dead.

Tarron pushed the fabric of my dress off my shoulders, just enough to expose them, and his fingers traced along the line of my collarbone.

"It's strange," he said, his voice sounding far-away, as if he were talking to himself and not to me. "I never found you the least bit alluring until I realized fate had destined you for someone else. That you were the one who would help me get everything I've ever wanted. Since then, I've thought of this moment so often and what you will give me. The build-up, the...*foreplay*... has been almost unbearable. I don't think I've ever wanted a woman as much as I want you."

Each word repulsed me more than the last, bile rising higher in my throat with every syllable. Did that explain why he called out my name when he had sex that time I hid under the bed? He got off on the thought of the power he would gain from the heart of our child?

How could anyone be so vile?

Felix's chain rattled in the background and my eyes closed, trying to block out the sound along with the knowledge that he witnessed all of this. I hated myself for causing him pain, but I didn't know what else to do. I had to keep him safe until we could figure out what to do next.

Tarron's hands went to my waist, lifting me off the ground and walking the few steps over to the bed to deposit me there. He didn't make any move to pull my dress further down but went to the hem of my skirt instead, lifting it up to my knees. Felix's growl thundered through the air around us, despite his weakness, but the sound only made Tarron smile as his clammy hands went to my ankles and pulled them apart.

"It might make the spell even stronger with the werewolf here in the room," he guessed, his eyes bright with a manic sort of excitement. "The betrayal of the bond is even stronger. I think it might…"

Whatever he meant to say next never left his lips. A heavy black chain looped around his neck, and Felix appeared behind him, thunderous fury etched into his face

How he got free, I had no idea, but I scampered out of the way of Tarron's flailing arms as he fought to free himself from the chain.

Was it the same chain that bound Felix before? It looked darker, not silver anymore, and Felix's strength seemed to have fully returned.

Tarron thrashed violently, refusing to give up without a fight. Raising that damned hand of his, he used his magic to push Felix back. My mate stumbled and fell to the ground, not hard enough to hurt him but enough to ease the tension on Tarron's throat. The prince's magic didn't seem as forceful as before, but it still gave him the edge.

We needed to neutralize his power, and as I stared at his hand, an idea came to me.

Leaping forward, I grabbed the chain around Tarron's neck, intending to wrap it around his hand. Pain seared through my palms the moment I touched the metal.

"Ouch!" I cried, dropping it out of instinct.

"It's iron," Felix called out as he pulled himself back to his feet. "Don't touch it."

I glanced down at the dark metal and up to Tarron's face. He was clearly struggling with it too, but doing his best to pull it off his body. We couldn't let that happen.

"His hand," I shouted to Felix, my voice thick with desperation. "Wrap it around his hand."

Tarron reached for me with that very hand, but before he could do anything, Felix grabbed his arm from behind, yanking a length of the chain from Tarron's neck and wrapping it around his wrist instead. "Now what?"

Now, I would try to use *my* magic. Up until then, I had only ever worked with locks, but the chain could be considered a kind of lock. Focusing on it, I imagined the links reforming themselves into a tight knot around his hand, and Felix leaned forward curiously as the metal began to obey. Soon, the iron formed a ring around his wrist, separating his hand from the rest of his body and dampening the power that flowed within him in the same way the silver weakened Felix.

"Release it," Tarron snarled at me, all traces of his earlier excitement gone as his eyes blazed in anger. "Do it now and I'll give him a swift death. If you don't, he'll be tortured until..."

Once again, his words were cut off.

From the corner of my eye, I could see a flash of fur as Felix shifted to his wolf form once more. Sharp teeth clamped down on Tarron's other arm, the one not wrapped in iron, and the wolf pulled the fae prince off the bed.

I couldn't stop my gasp as Tarron fell to the floor and Felix pounced. Tarron deserved no mercy, and Felix showed him none. Claws ripped jagged holes in his clothes, down to his flesh, and the sharp fangs of the wolf clamped down on the prince's neck.

Tarron's screams filled the room but I kept my gaze steady as Felix tore out a chunk of his throat, green blood spilling onto the shiny floor as Tarron's cries turned to gurgles. The man who had loomed like a dark shadow over my life as long as I could remember twitched on the floor, his body suffering its final throes before, finally, falling unnaturally still.

Perhaps I should have felt some kind of pity for the man, but after everything he'd done, everything he wanted to do, I only felt relief.

Felix shifted back to his human self again, his naked skin now stained and spattered with blood. With determination, he strode towards another of the cabinets along the room's walls, this one containing an assortment of swords. After examining them, he chose one and carried it back to the body of my former prince.

With a grim nod, he drove the sword into Tarron's chest and began to slice at his flesh. It took me a moment to realize what he was doing. *His heart.* Felix cut out Tarron's heart, pulling the organ from his body when he had made a big enough hole in his chest.

He looked up at me, not surprised to see me watching. "Magic resides in the heart, so if we want to ensure he can't come back, we need to destroy it. Do you know if cutting it into pieces will be enough?"

I had never destroyed a heart, but I remembered my father telling me a story of a wicked fae king whose heart had been divided into seven pieces and when they were reassembled and put back into his skeletal remains, the king arose from the dead. "I don't think so. It needs to be hidden somewhere that no one will ever find it."

"Any ideas?"

I thought about it for another moment before leaning down to peer beneath the bed I sat on. Tarron's box sat there, where it had been for years.

"I think I know just the place."

Chapter Fifty-Two

~Felix~

Holding Tarron's still-throbbing heart in my hand, I hardly dared to breathe, torn between disbelief at what we'd just done and relief that we'd actually managed to do it.

It wouldn't have been possible if I hadn't read about alchemy in my studies of other supernatural beings and magic. The process of changing base metals into more valuable ones usually focused on turning lead into gold, but some of the information I read suggested that metals could be changed in either direction by anyone in possession of the mineral known as alchemite. That mineral could only be found in the fae realm, had inherent magic in it, and was exceedingly rare. When I read about it, I filed the information away in the back of my mind as something interesting but unlikely to come up in day-to-day life.

I'd just been proven wrong.

On my own, I never would have recognized the deep purple stone. I'd never seen alchemite before, but thanks to Tarron's meticulous categorization and labeling, the word stared back at me from the cabinet drawer, and I knew it would be my best chance of escape. I rattled the silver chain deliberately, masking the sharp crack as I smashed open the drawer and seized the small, smooth stone.

Iron, I pleaded with the stone, hoping it would read my mind as the stories suggested it would. *Change the silver to iron.*

The stone's cool surface pulsed faintly in my grip, and when the chains stopped burning against my skin, I felt stronger almost instantly.

It actually worked, Kai breathed in surprise.

You doubted me? I teased, quickly unwrapping the chain from my body. Instead of weakening me, the iron would now work against the fairy prince who had Evalina on his bed.

My Evalina.

I saw red as my full strength returned, and I charged forward with no real plan other than to make him pay. Iron wouldn't kill the fae but it did hurt them, the same way silver hurt me. Thankfully, Evalina figured out that we needed to isolate the power in his hand to render his magic ineffective. The idiot even kept an iron sword amongst his collection, and I chose that one to carve his heart from his chest. I would take advantage of any opportunity to make him suffer more, but most importantly, we needed to get rid of his damn heart before anything else went wrong.

As if fate itself had overheard my mate say she had an idea, the bedroom door slammed open with a crash, cutting off whatever she intended to say next. Jumping in surprise, we both turned to see a furious-looking man march into the room followed by a group of Etta soldiers. The man took in the whole scene: Evalina on the bed, the skirt of her dress still up around her knees, Tarron's lifeless, mutilated body on the floor, the thumping heart in my hand and the bloodied iron sword held in the other.

His eyes grew wider with each passing second, his face turning a deep shade of red. "What. Have. You. Done?"

Each word snapped out of him, each one a statement of its own, and Evalina instinctively bowed her head.

"Your Majesty, we can explain."

Well, that cleared a few things up. The man in front of me had to be the fae king, and considering I'd just slaughtered his son, I couldn't imagine he'd be too happy to meet me. Evalina was right, though; we *could* explain why it had been necessary. I just didn't know exactly where to start.

"You can *explain* why you murdered your prince?" the king thundered. All the soldiers' eyes were fixed on me and the heart in my hands, making me wish, not for the first time, that I wasn't completely naked for all of this.

Thankfully, someone else strode in the door a moment later, a familiar face that towered above the fae men, and I breathed a deep sigh of relief.

"Hey, Vaughan."

Darius and a few other warriors followed behind him, evening out the odds in my favour even better. My Alpha examined the room, making almost exactly the same circle that the king's had, his eyes just as wide but with a lot less anger on his face.

"So, funny story..." I tried to joke, but when the king's eyes narrowed to thin slits, I gulped the rest of the words down.

Not the time, apparently.

"Prince Tarron was a monster, Your Majesty," Evalina stepped in, her voice steady despite the storm of emotions swirling in her eyes. "I'm sorry to say it so bluntly, but it's true. He threatened to force me to have a child with him so he could use that child's heart in a spell to give him more power. He performed other spells and killed at least one other werewolf in pursuit of this. He visited the terrestrial lands many times to steal materials for his experiments, and I'm fairly certain he made my mother sick too. Those are the crimes that I know of, but I'm sure there are more. We acted in self-defense."

"There are definitely more," Vaughan confirmed, stepping forward to place himself slightly ahead of the king, a clear sign that he was on our side. "As I told you downstairs, he blackmailed the elves into bringing Felix here. Seems like he unleashed some kind of illness on them too and promised the antidote if they would help him. At least the guy's consistent. Well, *was* consistent, anyway."

His gaze dropped to the heart in my hand, frowning as he noticed its steady rhythm.

"Is that... still beating?"

"Yup. And I'm pretty sure if it goes back in his body, it'll revive him. The guy was into some truly messed-up shit."

The king let out a long breath as he processed everything we'd just said. When he spoke again, his voice sounded calmer but still not at all friendly. "After my conversation with Alpha Vaughan, I understand that my son may have gotten a little carried away. You can be assured he'll be punished for it. Return his heart to his body and we'll take care of it. You're free to go."

Evalina let out a squeak of disagreement, but she didn't need to worry. We were on the same page; no way was I putting that heart anywhere near his body again, and I told the king so. "I'm sorry, but that's not happening. He threatened my mate and tried to assault her. He killed another werewolf after stealing her from her mate and raping her. I'm sure there are other atrocities we can't even begin to guess at. Death is the only suitable punishment."

"You killed my father for less."

The words from Evalina were quiet but firm, and all eyes in the room went to her. My mate stood from the bed, drawing herself up to her full height, her chin raised. She might not be tall, but at that moment, she looked as fierce as anyone I'd ever seen.

She had mentioned her father's death before, but she never said it had been a punishment. My heart panged at the pain I could see in her eyes even as she stared boldly at her king.

"Your men searched our house and found materials that they said could only have been gathered by visiting the terrestrial realm. Since that was forbidden, you sentenced him to death. Why should Tarron receive a lighter punishment than that? He visited the terrestrial realm and so much more."

The king's guards shuffled restlessly behind him at that news, and the king's jaw clenched. "It wasn't only that he possessed them. He intended to use them to cause harm to our world. Tarron told me about the spell books he found..."

He trailed off, but we all understood the implication. Tarron must have denounced Evalina's father, resulting in his death, and given how he had also poisoned her mother, I had to suspect the entire thing had been a set-up to make Evalina as vulnerable as possible. He wanted to leave her with no options other than to give in to him. How she resisted as long as she did only confirmed her strength of will.

That new information tempted me to put his heart back in his chest just so I could cut it out again.

"Your son brought this on himself," Vaughan said, matching the king's calm, firm tone but adding an edge of warning. "He brought Felix here against his will. He messed with our world and he paid the price."

"He fucked around and found out," I added helpfully, though I couldn't be sure they used that expression in the fairy world.

The king's expression remained tight. "Be that as it may, it is my right, as his king, to determine his punishment. As long as that heart beats, he's not dead."

"Only as long as you can get to it," Evalina announced before dropping to her knees. For a second, I thought she'd collapsed, but instead, she reached beneath the bed she'd just been sitting on and pulled out a metal box. Holding her hand over the lock, a faint glow emanated from her fingers before it clicked open. She held it up to me. "Put the heart in here."

Though I had no idea what she had in mind, I followed her instructions immediately, dumping the heart into the box along with the few other items already inside. Evalina slammed the lid shut and held her hand over the lock again. Smoke drifted out of the lock, accompanied by a burning, bitter scent, and she raised her head in triumph.

"It's locked inside and the lock is destroyed. No one will ever touch it again. The prince of Etta is dead, Your Majesty, and I won't waste a single second feeling sorry about it."

Chapter Fifty-Three

~**Evalina**~

Relief settled like a warm blanket over me as I clutched the locked box, my trembling hands barely steadying its weight, but no one else seemed to share my sense of triumph.

"Is that going to be enough to keep it safe?" Vaughan asked warily, his eyes roaming the box in my hands. "What if someone breaks it open?"

"She just melted the lock," Felix replied, immediately backing me up. "And I don't know what it's made of, but it looks solid."

The werewolf Alpha remained skeptical. "Shouldn't we burn the heart? Locking it up doesn't feel permanent enough."

"No offense, Vaughan, but you don't know much about magic. We could toss it into a volcano and it'd still beat. With the kind of dark stuff he was into, it's probably indestructible. Evalina has the right idea and as an added precaution, we'll take it back with us and put it where no one will ever find it. I'm sure Calista will have some ideas."

"No one is taking my son's heart anywhere," the king insisted, his voice sharpening with indignation each time someone ignored him, but Vaughan still paid him no attention. Instead, his eyes scanned the room, as if only realizing when Felix mentioned the Luna that she wasn't with us.

"Where *is* Callie?"

"Tarron let her and the others go," Felix assured him. "I was able to link with her through whatever communication link he had set up. I told her to take the others back through the portal and not worry about us."

I figured he said something like that to her, but the way the king's soldiers exchanged glances at Felix's words made my stomach twist. Obviously, they knew something we didn't.

"What?" I demanded. "They *were* let go, weren't they?"

One of the men near the king cleared his throat. "The prince's men dealt with that. I'm not privy to their orders, but just before we entered the house, I heard the forest horns blowing. It struck me as odd since I didn't know any reason for them to be used today, but this might explain it."

Those words meant nothing to me, and Felix and Vaughan looked equally confused. "What horns?" Vaughan barked out.

Even the king looked uneasy but he answered Vaughan all the same. "The horns wake the dragons that live near the border. I didn't order them blown, but if someone did, it must have been Tarron."

My stomach clenched, the air around me suddenly feeling too thin. "No."

Vaughan's eyes snapped to me, panic lurking just beneath the surface. "What does that mean?"

Swallowing down my fear, I did my best to explain. "Dragons live near the portal in the plain. If Tarron gave the order, he must have done it when Calista and the others were heading to the portal. There's nowhere to hide on the plain and the dragons wouldn't be happy about the noise."

I left it there but I didn't need to say anything else. Vaughan understood the implications perfectly and his eyes fell to Tarron's cooling body on the floor, murderous anger in his expression. If the prince weren't already dead, he would have been when Vaughan got through with him. "You're telling me that this son of a bitch unleashed *dragons* on my pack? On my *mate?*"

When no one answered him, he strode right up to the king. Vaughan stood almost two feet taller than the Etta royal, and he used every inch of that to his advantage.

"Take me to them. *Right. Now.*"

The glass of the cabinets in the room shook with the deep thunder of his growl.

"Will the dragons kill them?" Felix whispered to me as the king sputtered to find an answer to Vaughan's demand.

"Not right away, but they might take them to eat later."

Those were the stories parents told their children to make sure they did what they were told. If we didn't, the dragons would take us back to their nests and keep us there until they got hungry. The idea that Calista and the others might actually live that nightmare because of *me* sank like a lead weight in my stomach.

The king seemed to have agreed to take Vaughan to the plain, under threat of bodily harm from the furious werewolf, and everyone began to vacate the room. Since no one mentioned the box with Tarron's heart, I kept it close to my chest.

"I still don't have any clothes, so I'm gonna shift back now," Felix announced as Vaughan pushed the king out of the room. "I'm right behind you, Alpha."

He returned to his wolf form as the king's guard and the other werewolves followed close behind their leaders, with Felix and me bringing up the rear.

Amid the chaos, a familiar face caught my eye near the servant's entrance. I couldn't ignore her.

"I'll be there in just a second," I whispered to Felix before darting to the servant's entrance where Keerla stood, her eyes wide.

"You're alive!" were her first words as I reached her, and she wrapped her arms around me, hugging me tight despite the box still clutched in my hands. "I heard so many things, I couldn't be sure what was true."

"I'm not sure I understand it all myself," I admitted. "But Tarron is gone. He can't hurt anyone anymore."

Rather than looking shocked, Keerla almost appeared... disappointed. "I guess the poisoned dinner I was preparing for him won't be needed then."

"Keerla!" I gasped, torn between admiration and horror. Should I be flattered that she would risk so much for me or terrified by how close she'd come to danger? "You would have been caught."

She shrugged, putting on a brave face. "Probably, but you would have been free. I wouldn't have let him win, Lina."

With all the magic Tarron had worked on himself, I couldn't be certain poison would have worked, but I wouldn't tell her that. She'd been willing to fight for me and that meant everything. I might not have a big pack like Felix did, but in Keerla, I had the best friend I could ask for.

"Come with me," I blurted out. "To the terrestrial realm. My mother's there and she's doing so much better. We're going to stay and I know they'd be happy to have you too. We can start over, both of us."

Her smile held just as much affection in it as mine did, but I saw the refusal in her eyes even before she said the words. "It sounds like a wonderful adventure, but my life is here. My family, my friends, Pavla..."

She trailed off on the male servant's name, and my brows shot up. "Did something happen with you and Pavla?"

Biting her lip did nothing to stop her grin. "We've been plotting together since you left, and he's actually kind of wonderful. He's asked me to be his amica."

Remembering the way his eyes always tracked her movement, respectful and protective, the joy I felt for my friend mingled with the sadness of leaving her behind, a bittersweet taste lingering on my tongue. "I'm so happy for you. Where is he now?"

"Oh!" Her lips formed a circle as she gasped. "In all the excitement, I almost forgot. He went to track the other wolves, the ones who were in the pens, and make sure they were safe."

My heart jumped at the reminder of Calista, Leo and the others. I needed to catch up with Felix before it was too late. Nudging Keerla's shoulder, I steered her towards the front door of the residence, the one we'd never been allowed to use before. "Come on. Let's go and see how all of this ends."

Chapter Fifty-Four

~Felix~

Conflicting instincts pulled at me as Evalina broke from the group on our way out of the house. I needed to protect my mate but I also needed to be there for my Alpha, not to mention my Luna who had literally been offered as some kind of sacrifice to the local dragon population.

Weighing the situations, I decided to follow Vaughan outside while remaining close enough to the door that if Evalina called for me, I'd hear her.

Calista was still alive; that much, I knew, because if anything happened to her, Vaughan would have felt it. He'd be in intense physical agony thanks to the bond that tied them together and the marks they'd given each other when they accepted that bond. His clenched fists and rigid posture hinted at his simmering fear, but the fact that he still stood upright, roaring at the fae king, made it clear that the worst hadn't happened.

We still had time to make sure it wouldn't.

"Can any of you teleport like the elves?" Vaughan demanded.

"N-no," the king stuttered out. "None of us have that ability."

Vaughan's growl rolled through the clearing like thunder, shaking the trees. "Then I want your fastest men to show me the way. They'll take us all the way to these dragons' nest if they have to. We're not stopping until we find them, and by the Goddess, so help me, if a hair on her head has been harmed..."

"Vaughan, look!"

Evalina appeared in the doorway with another fae woman beside her, cutting off my Alpha's threat as she pointed to the sky behind him. Her other arm awkwardly juggled the box with Tarron's heart inside, but everyone seemed to have forgotten about the box. All of us, fae and werewolf alike, turned to look in the direction she indicated.

Above the trees, three immense forms darkened the skies, their purplish-gray bodies glinting against the soft pink sky. The rhythmic beating of their wings sent gusts of wind rippling through the clearing, and though I had never seen a dragon in the flesh before, it didn't take a genius to recognize the flying lizards.

Were dragons technically lizards? I'd have to check when I got back to my books and pinboard. I had a whole bunch of new species to add to my list of the ones I'd encountered in person.

"Ready your fire!" one of the fae soldiers called out. "Everyone else, take cover."

Several of the men pulled weapons off their backs, glimmering bows that looked like the same weapon that had been used to sedate me on my first visit to this territory.

"No, wait!" Evalina cried out, running from the door to stand in front of the soldiers to catch their attention. "They're not alone."

It took me a moment to see what she meant. Almost lost in the bulk of the creatures' scales and wings and talons, there were smaller forms on their backs, forms that looked more than a little familiar.

"Callie!" Vaughan's roar carried equal parts relief and desperation as the small blonde figure on the middle dragon raised a hand in greeting.

What the hell?

Vaughan turned to the king, still with murder in his eyes. "If any of your men fire on them, I will personally ensure that they never use a weapon again."

That could mean any number of things but the vague threat did its job. The king held out a hand to his men. "Hold your fire. Lower your weapons."

Reluctantly, the men obeyed, and we watched as the three dragons began to descend into the open space in front of us. Wind from their flapping wings blew through my fur, and I watched in awe as Calista, Leo, and all the others, including a fae man I'd never seen before, slid down off of the majestic creatures. The movement was as nonchalant as if they had just been out horse-riding in a meadow rather than soaring through the skies on the backs of mythical creatures none of us had ever seen before.

You're just jealous, Kai teased.

Damn right I am. I want to ride a dragon.

Some of the men were naked, meaning they must have shifted at some point, but Calista remained clothed. She only managed a couple of steps forward before Vaughan reached her, his long strides easily eating up the space between them. His hands went to her face first, then her shoulders, his eyes scanning her as he searched for any sign of injury.

"I'm fine," I could hear her say, thanks to my wolf's superior hearing. "What's going on here?"

"I need a little more than 'I'm fine'," Vaughan protested. "What happened with the dragons?"

He shot a wary glance up at the beast who glared right back down at him.

Calista stepped forward, speaking loud enough for everyone to hear. "We were making our way back to the portal when the dragons approached us. We had nowhere to hide, which I'm sure was Tarron's plan when he summoned them. Luckily, a new friend intervened and managed to negotiate with them."

She gestured to the fae man, and the woman who had come out of the house with Evalina ran forward and into his arms, nearly knocking him over in the process. "Pavla!"

Evalina's face beamed with delight as she watched them.

"Turns out they have a bone to pick with Tarron too," Calista continued. "Once we established we were all on the same page, we agreed that if they brought us back here, we'd turn him over. Where is he?"

Her eyes scanned the assembled crowd while I tried not to chuckle. Tarron miscalculated using the dragons to attack the werewolves, the same way he miscalculated using me to get Evalina to agree to his plans. The man got greedy and he paid the price, but unfortunately for the dragons, it meant they'd already missed the fun.

"He's here," Evalina replied, holding up the box she still held. Her slim arms were beginning to tremble from the strain of carrying it for so long. "What's left of him, anyway."

The eyes of the lead dragon narrowed on the box and it let out a huff of breath through its nose, discharging a puff of smoke that completely enveloped Vaughan, Calista and the others standing nearby.

"What is that?" the dragon asked, its eyes still fixed on my mate. The rasp of its voice made my own throat hurt.

It can talk? Kai asked, his tone full of envy. *Why can't I?*

A question for another day, buddy.

Having had enough of sitting on the sidelines, I padded forward and shifted back to my human form next to Evalina.

"I'm not sure what the box is made of, but it's nice and shiny, as you can see." I gestured towards the box like an assistant on a TV game show displaying the prizes. "And inside, you'll find the still-beating heart of the jackass we're all happy to see dead. What did he do to you?"

The dragon let out another heavy puff of smoke, its nostrils flaring as it did. "He stole our eggs."

"To be an antidote for the illness he caused among the elves," Vaughan added, his eyes bright with understanding. "Dragon eggs were their payment for kidnapping Felix."

"He had his fingers in everyone's pies, didn't he?" I mused. "Well, I'm afraid that we already killed him, but if you'd like to take the box for safekeeping, I think it would fit in nicely with your hoard."

Personally, I couldn't think of a safer place to store the heart and make sure no one went near it.

The dragons exchanged glances, seeming to confer silently in a way that made me think they might also have some kind of telepathic ability.

"You can't barter away my son's heart," the king tried to protest, but his words had no urgency to them. He must have realized, as everyone else did, that the balance of power had shifted. Tarron had too many enemies, and the king should count himself lucky that he wasn't also being asked to pay the price for his son's scheming.

"Give us all a ride back to the portal and the box is yours," I offered. Vaughan rolled his eyes, muttering something about priorities, but I stood firm. When else would I get to ride a dragon?

When the dragons nodded their agreement, I held out my hand to Evalina.

"Are you ready to get out of here?"

"Absolutely."

Her smile was sweeter than victory, promising everything I'd ever wanted and things I never knew I needed, all wrapped up in one perfect package.

Chapter Fifty-Five

~Evalina~

The change in the big werewolf at my side couldn't have been more pronounced. In a matter of minutes, Felix went from the deathly-serious protective mountain-of-a-man who cut out Tarron's heart to grinning down at me with childlike excitement, his blue eyes bright with anticipation.

"Have you ever been on a dragon before?" he asked, his voice laced with boyish glee. The spark in his eyes was so bright, I couldn't help but smile back.

"No, never. This isn't exactly typical for a day in Etta. Nothing that's happened since you showed up has been typical."

Every moment with him felt like an adventure and I had a feeling it had a lot more to do with him and his outlook on life than anything else.

Being around him would never be boring.

"Let me take that for you," he offered, holding out his big hands for the box with Tarron's heart in it once we reached the side of one of the dragons. They weren't as huge as the ones in my childhood stories who lived at the very top of the world, but their backs were big enough to hold four grown werewolves.

I handed it over gladly, relieved to have the weight off my arms. Whatever metal had been used on that box, it wasn't light.

Keerla appeared at my side, wrapping her arms around me in a fierce hug before I could say a word. "You're leaving now, aren't you?"

"I am." The words were harder to say than I expected, and though I didn't add 'forever,' I knew she understood. "Thank you for everything.

And thank you too, Pavla." I reached out a hand to the man at her side, who took mine and squeezed it in return. "Take care of each other. Be happy."

"We will," Keerla promised, but her eyes had already moved to the man at *my* side, her gaze travelling up and up and up until it reached his handsome face. "I'd tell you to be happy too, but I think you've got it covered."

"This is Felix," I said, my cheeks burning from the innuendo. "He, uh, usually wears clothes."

My mate's deep laugh rumbled through my body. "Nice to meet you both. I'm afraid we need to get going, though."

After giving me one more hug, Keerla stepped aside, Pavla close behind her. Felix looked up at the massive dragon beside us, its scales shimmering in the sunlight, and frowned.

"Well, shit. I can't help you up if I'm holding onto this."

Looking around, he saw that Vaughan and Calista had already climbed back up onto the beast in the middle, apparently as eager to get out of there as we were. Felix got his Alpha's attention with a shout.

"Vaughan, catch!"

With strength I could barely imagine, he tossed the heavy box high into the air. Calista ducked while Vaughan reached out to snatch the airborne box, its weight making a dull thud against his hands when he caught it. He scowled at Felix as soon as he had it safely in hand.

"You could have hit Callie!"

"Nah, she's smart enough to get out of the way. If anyone got hit, it would have been you."

Unperturbed by Vaughan's muttering, Felix used his now-empty hands to lift me up over his head, high enough that Leo, already seated on the dragon's back, could help me the rest of the way up. He pulled me behind him, and once I got settled, Felix scrambled up behind me, his arms wrapping around me and his naked body pressed tight against my back.

"What do I hold onto?" I wondered aloud, my fingers sliding across the dragon's slick, cool scales. The creature's powerful movements beneath me sent vibrations through my legs.

Felix's arms tightened around me. "Don't worry. I've got you."

A few moments later, when the dragon's wings began to flap and we lifted off the ground, I realized that he did, in fact, have me. Keerla and Pavla waved from below, their figures shrinking as we rose higher, and my chest tightened with one more bittersweet pang as I waved back.

Felix felt solid and strong behind me, providing a stability to go along with his sense of adventure that appealed to every single bone in my body. With his powerful thighs clenched tight around the creature's back, we stayed rooted firmly in place even when the wind ruffled my hair as the dragon accelerated, heading over the trees back towards the portal to the terrestrial world.

This man had turned my world completely upside down, to the point that leaving everything I ever knew not only felt right, it seemed inevitable. Where he was, I would go.

The trip back took a mere fraction of the time it had taken on foot, and almost too soon, the dragons began their descent over the open plain, towards the shimmering portal that gleamed in the setting sun. I had no idea how much time had passed since we left to find Felix, but with my adrenaline waning, fatigue began to set in.

The dragons dropped us off next to the portal and Vaughan handed over the box to them. We all stood and watched as they took off again and headed to their mountain home, carrying their new treasure.

"What will happen to the prince's body?" Calista asked.

"I should have ripped it to pieces," Felix scowled. "If we hadn't been interrupted, I would have."

"The royal family has a crypt beneath the residence," I explained. "It will probably be placed there."

Calista's lips pursed. "So, theoretically, someone could retrieve the heart from the dragons and reunite it with the body?"

"I suppose they could, but who would want to? The elves know of his scheming and the soldiers who saw everything today will know of it too. Gossip spreads fast among the fae. Tarron will be the talk of the fae world, just like he wanted."

"We want to hear all about what you discovered," Vaughan said, giving me a supportive nod. "But can we go home first?"

That sounded like the best idea I ever heard.

On the other side of the portal, night had fully fallen and my eyes weren't as sharp in the darkness as the werewolves' were.

"Let me carry you," Felix offered, his voice soft as I stumbled over a tree root, the uneven ground blurring beneath my exhausted vision. "You've had a hell of a day. Let me look after you."

Mentally, I retracted my earlier statement. *This* was the best idea I ever heard.

Strong arms lifted me from the ground with solid strength, and nestled against my mate's warm body, lulled by the rhythmic pace of his walking, I soon fell into a deep, contented sleep.

Chapter Fifty-Six

~Felix~

I couldn't remember the last time I felt so weary, my exhaustion so heavy it seemed to settle in my bones. The effect of the silver chains and cage and the physical battering that my body had taken, not to mention the emotional upheaval I went through thanks to Tarron's threats and the possibility of losing my mate after I only just found her, had my body begging for sleep. Evalina and Calista were both passed out in the back seat of the SUV, their faces soft in sleep as the blankets beneath their heads shifted with each bump in the road. Vaughan drove us back to Crimsontooth territory while I sat in the passenger seat, doing my best to keep my eyes open and help him to navigate through the dense forest.

"What happened with the elves?" I asked him once we were back onto a dirt road, the headlights carving a narrow path through the forest's shadows.

"Weirdest experience of my life," Vaughan grumbled. "And after the month we've had, that's saying a lot."

"But what happened?" I pressed. Getting information out of Vaughan was like pulling teeth but I knew that eventually, if I asked enough times, he'd tell me.

"I might have gone in guns blazing," he admitted, shooting me a sheepish smile after glancing over his shoulder to make sure Calista didn't hear him. "Told them we know how to close and open the portal at will, and I'd make their lives a living hell if they didn't take us to you. Threatened to send through bears and lions and all sorts of other creatures they don't have over there."

I couldn't help the snort that came out as I pictured the scene. "Interesting strategy. And it worked?"

"No, not really." He let out a self-deprecating chuckle of his own. "The guy in charge said I must be a friend of yours since we both liked the sound of our own voices so much, but after some discussion among their leaders, they agreed to take us anyway. Tarron really pissed them off so helping us was a way of getting back at him. They certainly didn't offer to help because they liked me. They also insisted that we close the portal on our land so no one else wanders through when they're not supposed to."

He shot me a meaningful glare that I had to admit I deserved.

"During their debate, they did say something interesting, though," Vaughan added. "A few of them mentioned that there had been an increase in 'unnatural' happenings in the area lately."

My ears perked up the same way his must have. "What kinds of happenings?"

"They didn't elaborate, but it made me think about the spirit, the Ravenstone scientist, and all the other madness we've faced lately. Maybe there's something in the air?"

"Across worlds?" I wondered. "It would have to be something pretty big."

"That's what I'm afraid of," my Alpha confirmed grimly. "At this rate, I don't know if our pack can survive someone else finding their mate."

Warmth swelled inside my chest at the reminder that I had a mate of my own. With all the drama of the past few days, it hadn't really had a chance to sink in. Just a few days ago, I sat in Vaughan's office, trying to ignore the jealousy I felt over his mating. Now, all that remained was gratitude. "Can you believe we got so lucky?"

Vaughan's eyebrows shot up. "Lucky? We nearly got killed, more than once."

"Vaughan. Come on." I gestured to the back seat with my head, grinning at the sight of Evalina curled up back there. "Take off the Alpha hat for a second and look at them."

Grudgingly, he threw another look over his shoulder at Calista and Evalina, and his scowl instantly softened. "Yeah, all right. We're pretty damn lucky."

"Eyes on the road," I reminded him cheerfully when the vehicle began to drift towards the trees still lining the forest trail.

Snapping his head forward again, Vaughan sighed. "I'm serious, though, Felix. I thought the way Calista and I met was crazy enough, but after what happened with Sav and now you and Evalina, it feels like a pattern and I don't know what to make of it."

"It might just be a coincidence," I pointed out. "On the plus side, finding your mate has shut down all the talk of mutiny within the pack."

"Has it, or has it just pushed it further underground?" He sighed again, his hand reaching up to push his hair back off his face, the way he always did when he felt anxious. "I can't put my finger on it but I have a feeling the worst is yet to come, and after what happened today, that scares the shit out of me."

"These things aren't connected," I stated as confidently as I could. "The spirit Calista was hunting had been around for hundreds of years. Jasper got exiled months before he met Savannah. Tarron had been plotting to increase his power for years and had his eye on Evalina since her birthday. None of it has anything to do with our pack."

"It has to do with our mates," he pointed out, voice heavy with concern. "Someone connected to each of these situations is mated to someone within our pack. One, or even two, I might have been able to explain away, but three insane situations in such close succession? It's too big of a coincidence to me. There has to be something else behind it."

"Like what?"

His hand brushed his hair back again, this time in frustration. "I don't know. Nothing *seems* connected, like you said, but I still think there's something there. I have no idea what it could be and it's driving me crazy."

Even though I didn't fully agree with his theory, I believed him when he said it worried him. With that in mind, I slipped into my Beta mode. "What do you want to do about it?"

The tension in Vaughan's shoulders slackened slightly, as I expected it would. Focusing on the practical always made him feel more in control. "We should start by putting our feelers out. Find out if there's still any discontent in the pack now that I have a mate, and find out if anything strange is going on in our neighbouring packs. We've been spending a lot of time away from the pack recently and there might be things we've missed."

"I'll get on it first thing in the morning," I promised. "I'll get the team together and make a plan."

"Thank you." Vaughan blew out a deep breath. "I'm really happy for you, by the way. In case I haven't said it yet."

"You didn't have to. I know you love me." I threw him a smug smile that made the corners of his mouth twitch. "She's amazing, Vaughan. You haven't been able to spend much time with her yet but she's incredible."

"Of course she is," he agreed easily. "She's your mate. I wouldn't expect anything less. But..."

He trailed off and my smile fell. "But what?"

"She's still invisible to most of the pack. How are we going to deal with that?"

"I have no idea," I admitted, drumming my fingers on my armrest. "It doesn't bother me, but it limits who she can interact with and I don't like that idea. I want her to be able to do anything and everything she wants to do."

"Maybe Calista will have some ideas," he suggested. "Or those online message boards you're always messing around with."

"Hey, those boards are helpful. They saved my life today."

We spent the rest of the drive exchanging more details of what happened to us in the fae realm until I felt I had been there with him and he knew everything I'd been through. When we finally reached the Crimsontooth pack house, most of the staff were asleep. After carrying a sleeping Evalina back to her guest room and putting her to bed, I stopped in to check on her mother in the room next door.

A male figure sat slumped on one of the chairs, one I recognized very well but didn't expect to see there.

"Dad?"

My father jolted upright, as if I'd woken him, and visibly relaxed when he recognized me. "Felix." He stood up and ushered me back into the hall, closing the door behind us so we didn't wake the sleeping fairy. "How did everything go? Is your mate okay?"

I had given him a rushed summary of events that morning, and someone else must have told him about my capture. His warm hand patted my shoulder, his pleasure at my safe return plain to see.

"We're both fine," I assured him. "I'm about to go to bed but I wanted to see how Evalina's mother is doing. Why were you in there?"

He shrugged his broad shoulders. "It felt like someone should be watching over her."

"But you can't see her."

"No, but she could see me. I figured it would help her not feel so alone in a strange place."

That was my father in a nutshell: the kind of man who would sit and keep an invisible woman company. Everything I ever learned about kindness and empathy came from him.

"Get some sleep," I instructed gruffly, my emotions already strained after the stress of the day. "I'll introduce you to them both properly tomorrow."

With a bleary nod, he headed down the hall and I stepped back into Evalina's room. Just like I did on her first night there, I stripped down and shifted, letting Kai curl up on the bed next to Evalina to be close to her. Her caramel and apple scent seeped into every cell of my body, easing all my tension, and my mind finally switched off as I slipped into a deep, dreamless sleep.

CHAPTER FIFTY-SEVEN

~Evalina~

As sunlight filtered through the curtains of the room in the Crimson-tooth pack house, I woke to the comforting warmth of a wolf curled beside me, just like the last time. This time, though, I didn't scream. The familiar earthy scent of Felix's wolf, mixed with Felix's unique pullaberry smell, reached me before my brain fully processed the change of venue. The last thing I remembered, I fell asleep in Felix's arms. I must have slept through the whole trip home and him putting me to bed. I still wore my dress from the previous day, a quiet reminder of Felix's unwavering respect for me.

Felix would never do anything to make me uncomfortable. He'd proven that over and over again in the few days since we met. I felt I knew him as well as I'd ever known anyone, and yet I still had so much to discover.

For the time being, I simply enjoyed his presence, running my hand through the wolf's fur and resting my head on his warm, furry chest.

Almost immediately, the wolf beneath me began to transform, until instead of fur under my head, my cheek connected with warm, muscled skin.

"Good morning," Felix murmured. His large hand caressed my hair the same way I'd just done to his wolf. "How are you feeling?"

"A little numb," I admitted, the weight of everything still settling over me as I snuggled deeper into his embrace. He was completely naked while I remained fully clothed, but somehow, it didn't feel strange.

Nothing about him ever felt wrong.

"I think it's going to take a while for everything to sink in, about what Tarron did and what he wanted, and that he's gone now."

"It's a lot to process," he agreed. "But you slept okay?"

"I slept wonderfully. Your wolf makes an excellent heat source."

Felix chuckled. "Kai's happy to be whatever you need him to be."

"Kai?" My head tilted to the side as I repeated the name curiously. I didn't remember him mentioning anyone by that name before, and I didn't understand why he would in this context. "Who's that?"

"That's his name. My wolf." Felix grinned at me, clearly amused. "I guess I forgot to mention it."

That statement only gave me more questions. "He has a name? I mean, a different one than you?"

His warm laugh sent my stomach fluttering, like always. "I better back up a few steps. My wolf is completely separate from me even though we inhabit the same body. Some shapeshifters can alter their physical form but keep the same consciousness. Werewolves are hybrids, half wolf, half human, and we co-exist inside my head at all times."

My eyes widened as I tried to wrap my head around it. "So, normally, you would have a werewolf mate who has a wolf of her own, so your wolf has a mate too?"

"That's more common, yes, but I don't like the word 'normal'. None of us are normal, and I'm lucky enough to get a completely unique, exceptional mate."

His passionate explanation made me smile, but concern lingered as I thought through all the implications. "What about Kai, though?"

I would never turn into a wolf, so he would never have a partner. That didn't seem fair.

"He's just as happy as I am, I promise." Felix's hand ran through my hair again, leaving deeply soothing tingles in its wake.

"He's not disappointed?" I asked one more time.

He leaned down to press a kiss to my forehead. "Not." His lips brushed one eyelid. "At." Then the other. "All."

Tilting my head up with his fingers beneath my chin, he captured my lips in a soft, sweet kiss, his warmth chasing away the lingering numbness inside me.

It didn't take long for the kiss to turn from sweet to needy. My lips parted for him, and when his tongue pressed hungrily against mine, I couldn't stop the moan that hummed in my throat. Felix's chest rumbled in reply, his kiss growing even deeper. When every touch felt electric, it didn't take much to go from sparks to full-blown flames of desire.

The bulk of him pressed into me, rolling me over so my back hit the mattress and his broad frame covered me. With no clothes to restrain him, I could feel his cock hardening against me, its firm pressure promising a wealth of pleasures that I understood much better now than when we first met. My nerves weren't as strong as the first time we were alone in bed together but my excitement made up for it.

"I think it's time for your next lesson," Felix whispered, his hands stroking my face so tenderly, I felt both delicate and powerful at the same time. "Do you want to set the pace this time?"

I had no idea what that meant, but I trusted him implicitly. "Yes?"

The way his grin lit up his face never failed to make my heart soar. "Let's try it and see how you like it."

With tenderness that seemed entirely at odds with his size, he undressed me, laying soft kisses on each inch of skin he exposed, until we were both naked. He also put on another of the condoms, as he called them, before returning to the bed. Rather than settle between my legs like he did the last time, though, he rolled us over again so that he lay on his back and I balanced on top of him. My legs naturally fell open around him to steady myself and the pressure of his stiff cock against my core, even without any penetration, set my whole body humming.

"Your knees don't quite reach the bed, do they?" he asked, his hands slipping beneath my knees to feel the gap between them and the mattress.

"That's not my fault," I protested. "You're very wide."

His laugh echoed around the room. "And you're very short. But adorable all the same."

My eyes narrowed at him. "I'm a perfectly average height for a fairy. You're the giant."

"As long as we fit together where it counts, I don't care how tall you are," he assured me, still smiling. "Sit up and put your feet on the bed."

Following his instructions, I shifted my body so that I sat upright on him, my pussy settling even more firmly on his cock, and planted my feet on either side of him. With a gentle nudge, he encouraged me to raise my hips, and reached between us to raise his cock, placing it against my entrance. When he had it where he wanted it, he reached for my hands, lacing his fingers through mine.

"Now, sit down on me. As slow or as fast as you want."

Ah. That was what he meant by setting the pace.

Squeezing onto his hands for balance, I lowered myself slowly onto his cock, letting him fill me inch by inch until it felt that he couldn't possibly go any deeper. Perfect was the only word that did it justice: he filled every empty part of me, every part I never knew I needed someone to fill, but never felt like too much.

"Goddess, that's perfect," he groaned, his eyes hooded with desire as he gazed up at me. "*You're* perfect."

I could say the same about him. "What now?"

"Now, you ride me to your heart's content, my sweet Evalina. Give us both the pleasure I know you can."

Eager to learn, I pushed my feet down into the mattress, my thighs and core tensing as I lifted myself slowly upward, feeling his cock stroke along my inner walls as I did, and Felix groaned again.

"The way you're clenching... fuck. It's so tight," he gasped.

I paused in mid-action. "Is that bad?"

He let out a strangled laugh. "No, little fairy. It's so fucking good."

When I reached the tip of him, when it felt like he would fall out of me if I went any further, I reversed course and sank back down onto him again. The feel of him filling me a second time sent sparks zinging through my body, the pleasure even more intense than the first time. *Again*, my body demanded. *Again*, my mind agreed.

Over and over, slowly at first and a little faster with each pass, I lifted myself up and dropped back down, his cock sliding in and out of me, filling me with deep satisfaction each and every time.

"Roll your hips when you hit bottom," he instructed gruffly. "Rub your clit against me."

Obediently, I did as he said, and moaned as the sparks between us hit that sensitive spot. Every rise and fall took on a new, tantalizing component. Between that and the incredible feeling of him inside me, my need soon reached an almost agonizing peak.

As if he could read my mind, Felix squeezed my hands. "Are you close?"

I nodded, not able to force the words out, and although I remained on top, he took control. One hand went to my waist while the other slid between my legs, finding my clit. His thumb rubbed against me as his hips thrust upwards, slamming into my body hard, with only his steadying hand on my waist keeping me in place.

Held in his firm hands, I let go, letting the sensations fill me, coiling tighter and tighter until it all burst in a flood of ecstasy. My body clenched hard around him and Felix gasped out a string of syllables I couldn't decipher as he came too. His cock pumped deep inside me, and as his grip loosened, I sagged down onto him, lying skin-to-skin. His heart beat so strong against my ear, I thought it might burst right out of his chest.

"Evalina." After a few moments of only our panted breathing between us, he whispered my name so tightly, it sounded painful. "My wolf wants to claim you. I want it too, but I won't push you if you're not ready."

My heart swelled at the idea of being his. We hadn't known each other long, but time didn't matter compared to the connection I felt with him from the very first moment I saw him. I could love this man, deeply and irrevocably, but the word 'claiming' obviously meant something specific to him and I didn't know what that might be.

Raising my head, I looked straight into his beautiful blue eyes. "What exactly does that mean?"

Chapter Fifty-Eight

~Felix~

The need to claim my mate nearly overwhelmed me, blood pounding in my ears with the relentless drumbeat of instinct. I forced myself to ignore its roar and focused on answering her question.

"Werewolf mates claim each other by leaving their mark on their mate. I would leave mine on your neck, just here."

My fingers traced over the spot reverently and Evalina shivered in response. The sparks that already danced beneath my touch would ignite into something even more powerful after the mark was placed.

"What kind of 'mark'?" she asked, her voice still a little breathless from the pleasure we just shared.

"With my teeth." I bared them for her, letting the canines elongate just enough that she could see their points as they took their wolf form. "It will sting, but only for a moment. After that, it'll feel good. Amazing, even."

"Like the first time you were inside me?" she asked so innocently that I had to bite back a groan of longing.

"Yeah. Kind of like that."

Her eyes drifted down to my neck while she thought over my words. "My teeth aren't sharp enough to mark you."

"No," I agreed. "And even if they were, you would only end up biting me. Marks are specific to the werewolf species, and the wolf side plays an important role. Since you don't have a wolf, you can't mark me."

"Oh." Her expression fell, a shadow of the earlier disappointment I saw when she realized Kai would never have his own mate.

"It's not a problem," I hurried to assure her. "We'll still be mates. My scent will still change after I mark you. I might not have the physical sign, but everyone will know I'm taken."

"Other werewolves will know," she corrected me softly. "Not everyone."

She had a point, but maybe she also had the solution. "What do fairies use to symbolize their pairing? Like the amica bond your parents shared?"

Her eyes brightened, chasing away some of the disappointment. "I'm impressed you remember the term."

"I remember everything you say."

Her cheeks reddened with pleasure at my simple statement before she answered my question. "Usually, they wear a braid made by their partner. Your hair is too short, though."

She ran her fingers through my hair and I sighed in contentment at the pleasant tingle of the sparks across my scalp.

"I could get a hair extension," I joked, but Evalina only frowned back at me.

"A what?"

"Never mind." I cleared my throat to refocus my thoughts on the problem at hand. "Is there anything else they do?"

"If they can afford it, they exchange jewellery."

Now, we were getting somewhere. "Like a wedding ring?"

When she gave me another blank look, I reached over to the bedside table where I'd left my phone the night before. There were messages waiting for me with pack business to attend to but I ignored them to pull up some photos of wedding rings.

"This is what humans do."

I scrolled through the image feed slowly to let her take a look, and her eyes lit up when we reached one with a Celtic knot. "I've seen designs like this. They're almost like a lock."

A lock. Something she could control with her special magic. Maybe *that* was the answer.

"What if I got you some metal and you used your magic to make me a ring? It would be your mark on me, as special as mine on you."

She beamed back at me, as delighted with the suggestion as I hoped she would be. "I would love to try."

"Good." I gave her a kiss before lowering my lips to her neck, nuzzling at the spot that every fibre of my being urged me to mark. "Does that mean you're accepting me?"

Her soft intake of breath sent a shot of desire straight to my cock. "If I say yes, you'll mark me?"

I inhaled deeply, devouring her apple and caramel scent. "Yes."

"And we'll be bound together forever?"

My tongue pressed against her neck. "Yes."

"And you... want that?"

It killed me to hear even a sliver of doubt in her voice but I answered her patiently while continuing to rub against her neck with my nose.

"More than I've ever wanted anything. More than I *could* ever want anything. I know it's happening quickly, especially since you don't have a wolf that feels it the same way mine does, but I promise you, Evalina, I will never change my mind. I will never regret it, and I'll do everything within my power to make sure you never do either. Your home will be here with me. Your mother will be welcome here. I'll provide everything you need, and most of all, I will love you with everything I have. But if you need more time..."

"No," she whispered, and my heart nearly stopped.

"No?" The word caught in my throat, my chest tightening with the unbearable thought. "You *don't* accept me?"

Evalina pulled back from me, her eyes meeting mine in a wide panic. "No! No, that's not what I mean. No, I don't need more time because yes, I accept you. I want you to claim me. To mark me. To love me, and to do all that other stuff. Because I... I love you too."

Thank the Goddess.

Relief swept through my body as I pulled her back down for another kiss, a deep, lingering one that translated all the words we'd just spoken into a language our bodies would understand. My hands roamed across her naked back, tracing the curves of her delicate body and savouring the connection between us. Her need soon mirrored mine, our emotions intertwined as deeply as our bodies, and my mouth lowered to her neck as I let Kai join me, our consciousnesses working together in perfect harmony for this most primal of werewolf acts.

With my canines extended, we clamped down on the marking spot, piercing Evalina's skin as she let out a sharp cry of surprise. Regret stabbed at my chest over any pain she felt, but the sound quickly died off, replaced by a moan as my tongue smoothed over the spot, lapping away the blood that seeped from the temporary wound and sealing it closed while the mark took shape.

Mine, Kai murmured happily inside my head.

Mine, I agreed.

In this, we were completely united. Evalina was ours, and nothing in this world, or any other world, would ever take her from me again.

Chapter Fifty-Nine

~Evalina~

Being bitten by Felix felt very different than I imagined it would when he first mentioned it. The sharp sting as his fangs pierced my skin hurt, but only for a few breaths. As soon as he began licking at the spot, warmth spread across my skin, radiating out from the injured area. As his tongue continued to move across it, the warmth morphed into something deeper and more heated, sending a throbbing urge through me that settled straight between my legs.

Again? We only just finished being intimate with each other, and already my body craved him as if it had never known satisfaction.

As if he could feel it too, Felix pulled back with a groan. "I would like nothing better than to spend the rest of the day in bed with you," he promised, his eyes filled with heat and promise. "But it's getting late. We need to eat. I need to check in with my Alpha and I'm sure you want to see your mother."

A gasp of horror nearly choked me. How could I have forgotten about my mother? She hadn't crossed my mind since I woke up and she must have been worried sick about me.

Without a word, I scrambled off Felix and across the bed, searching for my discarded clothes. Behind me, he chuckled at my frantic movements.

"She's alright. My father kept her company yesterday and if I had to guess, I'd wager he was there when she woke up this morning and has already told her that you're fine. Take a deep breath, Evalina. Relax. She's safe and you're safe. We're all safe now."

It had been so long since I felt truly safe, not since my father died, that I couldn't be sure I even knew *how* to relax anymore. However, I did as he said and inhaled deeply, letting his scent wash over me. Surprisingly, it did help to slow my heart rate back down to an almost-normal rhythm.

"Your father?" I repeated curiously when I could breathe again. "He can speak to my mother?"

"He can speak to her, yes, but he can't see or hear her," Felix explained. "He did his best so she didn't feel alone while we were gone. Hopefully, she didn't find him a nuisance."

Another bloom of warmth spread across my chest. "That was very kind of him."

"I think so too." Felix offered me a smile that mirrored that warmth back to me. "I think you'll like him, and I know he'll love you once he can see you properly. I bet he's in your mother's room now, so you can meet him if you like."

"I would love that." The affection that filled Felix's tone convinced me that I *would* like his father. Anyone who raised someone as wonderful as Felix and had his respect must be pretty wonderful themselves.

When we were both dressed, had eaten some food he called granola bars that he found in one of his drawers, and I had rebraided my hair, we headed next door to my mother's room. As Felix predicted, a middle-aged man sat in the chair in the corner, his deep, steady voice filling the room as he read aloud from a book. My mother lay in her bed, propped up on the pillows and looking better than I had seen her look in weeks. Months, even. The colour had fully returned to her cheeks and her hair shone in the sunlight, draping down elegantly over her shoulders. A smile softened her features as she listened to the deep rumble of the older man's voice.

That smile disappeared when she glanced over towards the doorway where we stood, only to be replaced by a beaming, joyful grin as she pulled back her covers and leapt from the bed, running over to me and throwing her arms around me before I could get a word out.

"Lina, you're okay." Her hands patted my head before she stepped back to glance down at my body, needing to see it for herself. "What happened?"

"It's a long story." I still had to decide how much I would share about everything Tarron had said and done. "How are you?"

She dismissed my concern with a wave of her hand. "I'm fine. Archer has been wonderful at distracting me from my worry."

As if summoned despite not hearing a word we said, Felix's father walked over to join us, his book still clasped in one hand. The family resemblance couldn't be denied. His once-blond hair now appeared mostly silver, his face creased with lines that Felix's didn't have yet. But his blue eyes sparkled with the same energy as his son's, and his broad frame remained just as solid.

"Evalina, this is my father, Archer." Felix's eyes gleamed with pride as he made the introductions. "Maudi, I believe you've already met."

"We have," my mother agreed, her face still flushed with pleasure at our return as she gave the werewolves a graceful nod of her head.

"Evalina." Archer said my name with almost as much affection as Felix did. "You're even more beautiful than Felix described."

Reaching out, he grasped my hand and brought it to his lips, placing a gallant kiss on the back of it.

Felix, my mother and I all stared at him in stunned disbelief. I was so taken off guard by the warmth of his hand around mine that I couldn't utter a word.

"Wait... you can see her?" Felix finally stuttered.

Archer blinked as he looked down at me, as if it only just occurred to him that he shouldn't be able to. "I think I can. She has long, shiny, brown hair, adorable pointed ears, and is wearing a pale blue dress that looks like something out of a movie. I'm not hallucinating, am I?"

"No, that's what she looks like," Felix confirmed, glancing down at me as if to double check. "But I don't understand. Can you see Maudi too?"

He and I both turned to my mother, but when Archer tried to follow our gaze, his eyes glanced right over her. "No, I'm afraid not. I saw the bedsheets move when she got up, but I can't see her at all. Only Evalina."

"Did something happen when we returned to the fae realm yesterday?" I tried to guess. "Did going through the portal again make me visible?"

"I don't think so," Felix said slowly, considering each word as it came out of his mouth. "You'd already been through twice before that."

"But what else has changed since yesterday when no one could see me?"

As soon as I spoke the words, a new thought came to me and my hand flew to the tender spot on my neck where Felix had placed his mark.

His eyes followed the movement and he gave a nod of agreement, a new smile spreading across his face. "I think it must be the mark. It binds you to me and, by extension, to this world. You're one of us now."

A teasing tone edged into his final words but I didn't think it was a bad thing at all. It actually sounded rather wonderful.

"Well, that solves one problem," Felix announced, his grin broad and infectious. "Now, we just need to figure out how to do the same for your mother."

"And for Jermyn," I added, thinking of the other fairy who had escaped with us. He'd slipped my mind during all of the activity of the previous day, but with things settling down, I should check in with him too.

"We'll see if Calista has any ideas," he promised. "We should go speak with her and Vaughan. Maudi, would you like my father to stay or would you prefer some peace and quiet?"

Again, his tone was teasing, not quite serious, and my mother smiled in return. "We were just getting to the good part of the story. I'd like to hear the ending."

"She wants you to keep reading," Felix relayed to his father and Archer bowed his head obligingly in my mother's general direction.

"I'd be delighted to."

We left them to return to their one-sided conversation as I mulled over my mother's quiet smiles in Archer's presence. I hadn't seen her smile like that since my father's death. Maybe coming to the terrestrial world would be a new start for her too.

It had already changed my life in every way possible, and now, with Felix's mark on my neck and his hand in mine, I felt more ready than ever to carve out my place in this new world.

Chapter Sixty

~**Felix**~

The walk from the guest quarters to the Alpha's office usually took only minutes, but that day, it felt like we encountered half the pack on the way there. Everyone peered curiously at the diminutive woman at my side, their noses twitching as they picked up her unusual fairy scent as well as the scent of my claim on her, and their eyes lit up with delight as they offered their congratulations.

My pack really was the best.

Evalina smiled shyly as she tucked closer to my side, letting me guide her through the crowd of pack members asking her name and how we met.

"We'll do a proper introduction soon," I promised the curious onlookers. Maybe there had been *some* benefits to her invisibility since no one questioned me about her when they didn't realize she was there. "Right now, the Alpha needs us."

A path immediately cleared; no one would get in the way of the Alpha's request.

At the end of the hall, Vaughan's office door was closed so I sent him a quick message by mind-link. *I'm outside. Are you decent?*

Unfortunately, came his sarcastic reply. *Come in.*

The site that greeted me when I opened the door stopped me in my tracks for a moment. Calista was there, as I expected, standing at Vaughan's side, but so were Leo, Darius, Matthias, and a few of the other men from the security team. Everyone's faces were grim.

My body tensed, and my voice came out sharper than I intended. "What's going on? Is it the fae again?"

"No, but I need to fill you in," Vaughan stated, gesturing to a chair that had been left empty for me. "Have a seat."

"I can wait somewhere else," Evalina whispered, but I shook my head, pulling her along with me.

"You're the Beta's mate and that makes you part of the team. This is as good a time as any to jump in."

"But there's only one chair," she tried to protest, as if that mattered. I took the empty chair and pulled her down onto my lap.

"You always have a chair when I'm around." Her cheeks flushed a pretty shade of pink but she didn't make any attempt to get back up. "Everyone, this is Evalina, my mate."

Those who hadn't met her yet all said hello and offered their congratulations. Calista looked between the men and Evalina in surprise. "You can all see her?"

"We found one solution to the invisibility problem but it's not going to work for the other fairies," I said, giving Evalina a wink that had her cheeks flushing even darker. "We'll explain later. Fill me in on what's happening here."

"I got a call from Savannah," Vaughan began. "Wolves are gathering outside their territory. It suggests a coordinated attack is coming, maybe as soon as today. It looks like news of the new Alpha has gotten out and their enemies are going to try to take advantage of it, hoping that Amanda and Sav aren't strong enough in their positions yet to defend their land. They're not asking for our help just yet, but we need to be ready if they do."

"Fuck." Everything he said made sense; a change of leadership or any sign of weakness in a pack often acted as an invitation for others to push the boundaries. One thing seemed off, though. "How do people even know about it?"

"That's part of the problem: Sav thinks they must have a leak. No formal announcement has been made outside of the pack yet, so someone inside the pack must have passed the information on."

"In which case, the attackers could have other inside information too," Darius pointed out. "Locations of key targets, number of defenders, even security protocols for the Alpha. If we were in their shoes, I would assume they knew it all."

In that case, I only saw one course of action. "When do we leave?"

"*We* aren't going anywhere," Vaughan replied, gesturing between me and him. "Remember what we talked about last night? I want *our* senior leadership at home in case someone decides to try the same thing here. Leo and Darius are going to take a team up to support Sav and Amanda. Seventy-five warriors. They're loading up right now. If it turns out they're not needed, they can turn around and come back, but I'd rather get them on the way."

Vaughan's words from the night before repeated in my head, how he thought the way we found our mates signified some wider pattern that we didn't understand yet. We needed to explore his theory, but the idea of sitting at home while others from the pack went to fight on behalf of our allies didn't sit right with me.

"I could go and Leo could stay here," I offered. Our Gamma, though strong and capable, had always been more of an administrator than a warrior. If we needed a detail-oriented investigation, he would be far more effective than me, and I had more combat experience than he did.

It made sense.

At least until Evalina turned her sweet face to peer up at me and I saw the worry in her eyes. How could I leave her after everything we just went through?

Vaughan seemed to read my mind. "You *just* found your mate. Your place is here."

"No," Evalina spoke up, her voice soft but steady as everyone turned their attention to her. "Please don't change the way you would normally do things because of me."

"I'm not," Vaughan promised, his tone softening in a way that warmed my heart. In that one small act, my best friend made it clear that he would always protect my mate in the same way that Calista had my undying loyalty. Evalina was important to me so she was important to Vaughan too, even if they didn't know each other very well yet. "I made the decision based on what's best for the pack. Leo will go and Felix will stay. It's all arranged."

"We're leaving now," Leo agreed, and as soon as he got to his feet, the other men all followed. "We'll keep you both updated."

"I want hourly updates once you arrive, at a minimum," Vaughan instructed. "We'll prepare a secondary team to follow if you need more bodies, just say the word."

"Yes, Alpha."

The men all bowed their heads in a gesture of respect to Vaughan, and they gave me one more smile and nod of congratulations as they filed out of the office, leaving me and Evalina alone with Calista and Vaughan. With more seats available, Calista came around the desk to sink into one of the empty chairs, and Evalina started to stand up to do the same, but I quickly pulled her back down, wrapping my arms around her waist to keep her in place. She weighed next to nothing and I wanted her next to me.

Calista only smiled at my possessive gesture before returning to the subject of Evalina's new visibility. "How are the others able to see you now?"

I loved that she asked Evalina rather than me and I let my mate answer. "We think it must be because of Felix's mark, that it somehow ties me to this world. Does that make sense?"

Calista turned the theory over in her head before nodding slowly. "I think it does. And I see now why you think it won't work for your mother."

Vaughan snorted in agreement. "Any ideas what we can do for her, then?"

"And Jermyn," Evalina reminded them. "I should go speak to him today and see how he is."

The Alpha and Luna exchange worried glances that I knew meant trouble. "What is it?"

"Jermyn seems to have disappeared," Calista admitted. "The food left for him yesterday went untouched and when I went to his room this morning, I couldn't find him."

Evalina let out a small gasp of dismay. "Do you think something happened to him?"

"I don't see what could have happened," Vaughan replied. "The guest quarters were being watched. If he left, I think it's because he wanted to."

"Is that possible?" I asked Evalina, and she reluctantly nodded.

"I don't really know him all that well, and maybe he thought he would be happier on his own."

"Being invisible has its challenges," Calista pointed out, her tone thoughtful. "But it also has its opportunities. Maybe he went in search of them."

"There's not much we can do about it now," Vaughan added. "He wasn't a prisoner, so if he chose to leave, so be it."

That left only Maudi to worry about then. "My father is with Evalina's mother now but we need to find a way for her to communicate with people at a bare minimum until we find a more permanent solution."

"I agree," Calista said with a nod. "Although I haven't found a way to make her visible yet, I *did* have an idea about communication."

Evalina sat up a little straighter, her interest piqued, and her ass rubbed against my cock as she moved. My teeth dug into my lower lip to keep myself from groaning. Maybe keeping her in my lap *wasn't* the best idea.

Oblivious to my reaction, Calista carried on. "You know how people from the fae realm can interact with items from our world, and we'll see those items being manipulated? Like how you tracked Tarron with the paint, Felix? Well, I don't see any reason why we couldn't just give

Maudi a pen and some paper and let her write messages. We should see them just fine."

That time, I *did* groan, out of frustration. "So simple. How did I miss that?"

My Luna tried not to smile. "I think you've been a little distracted lately."

"I'll try it right away," Evalina suggests, turning back to me for my agreement. "You have other work to do?"

"I do." Piles of it, probably, especially with Leo going away.

"In that case, I'll go and make myself useful with my mother and I'll see you later, when you have time."

"I'll always have time for you."

She gave me a quick peck on the lips, but when she moved to stand, I pulled her back down. My hand curled around the back of her neck and I kissed her properly, ignoring the other two people in the room. If I had to wait a few hours to see her again, I needed something to help tide me over.

With her cheeks flushed and her lips slightly swollen, Evalina said goodbye to Vaughan and Calista and headed out of the office.

"So, when's the ceremony?" Vaughan deadpanned when the door clicked shut behind her.

"Let's figure out what the hell is going on around here first," I suggested. "And before we do anything else, Calista, could you get Evalina a phone? I can't mind-link her and I need to be able to check in on her when we're apart."

"Of course." She gave me a knowing smile before standing up and giving Vaughan a kiss of his own and heading through the adjoining door into her own office next door. "I'll see you both later."

Vaughan's eyes lingered on her until the wall panel slid back into place and, almost in unison, we both let out long, happy sighs.

"We're so whipped," I laughed, and Vaughan's chuckle was equal parts agreement and amusement.

"Best feeling ever."

"You can say that again, Alpha."

Chapter Sixty-One

~**Evalina**~

After leaving Vaughan's office, I realized that although I knew what I wanted to do, I still didn't know my way around. However, it turned out I didn't need to worry. All I had to do was stand in the large entrance hall at the end of the hall, looking lost, and one of the large men by the door walked over to me, a friendly smile on his face. "You're Felix's mate, right?"

"Yes, that's right. How did you know?"

His smile grew wider. "Well, everyone's talking about the Beta's new fairy mate, and since you're the only fairy I've ever seen, I made an educated guess."

I supposed my chances of blending in were pretty low.

"And you have his mark on your neck," he added, his eyes dropping to my throat with a knowing look that made my cheeks blush.

"Right."

That reminded me that I still needed to make Felix something to wear in exchange for the brand he'd placed upon me, so when the man asked if I needed help, I had a small list.

"I need a pen and some paper, please, and some thin metal that can be shaped, if that's not too much trouble."

"Nothing is too much trouble," he assured me. "The pen and paper are no problem, and I'll send a message over to the jewellery store in town to see what they've got. It might take a little longer, but we'll get it for you."

"Thank you. That's very kind." Having people willing to help me would also take some getting used to. Life in the Crimsontooth pack would be very different from my life in Etta. "Could you send it to the room my mother is staying in?"

"Of course."

Glancing up the large staircase, I asked for one more favour. "And can you remind me where I can find that room?"

He chuckled softly. "The pack house is a bit of a maze. Up the stairs and to the left, second door on the right."

"Thank you." I turned to go before realizing I didn't even know his name, and I spun back. "I'm Evalina, by the way."

He bowed his head politely. "A pleasure to meet you, Evalina. I'm Connor."

"Nice to meet you too, Connor."

Feeling more at home already, I skipped up the stairs and returned to my mother's room. Felix's father still sat in the chair by the bed, still reading his book to my enraptured mother. They both turned to look at me as I walked in and I got the distinct feeling I had interrupted something.

"Felix is busy so I thought I would come spend some time with you," I explained almost in apology. "Is that okay?"

"Of course," they both said almost in unison, though Archer couldn't hear my mother.

"I can go if you'd like to be alone," he offered but I quickly shook my head.

"Please don't leave on my account. We're actually going to try something to see if my mother can communicate with you. Not just you, but all terrestrial beings, as a short-term fix until we figure out how to make her visible."

"That would be wonderful," Archer said, and from the way my mother smiled at him, I could tell she agreed.

We made small talk for a few minutes until one of the staff knocked on the door with the pen and paper I'd requested.

"Try writing something on it," I instructed my mother, passing the supplies to her. Archer gave a startled laugh when she took them from me, and I realized that to him, it must appear they were floating in thin air.

In her beautiful script, my mother wrote *My name is Maudi* before looking up at me expectantly. "Now what?"

Taking the paper from her hand, I passed it to Archer. "Can you read that?"

A smile that reminded me strongly of his son's spread across his face. "I can indeed. It's a pleasure to finally hear from you, Maudi."

My mother's cheeks flushed and she quickly scribbled something down on the next piece of paper. That time, she handed it directly to him, and Archer plucked the paper from her, chuckling as he read it over.

"She says I should tell you some of the stories I told her last night about Felix as a young boy."

"I could tell you myself, but Archer tells it better," my mother added, and I grinned at them both.

"I would love that."

For the next hour, Archer regaled us with stories about Felix as a boy, usually getting into some kind of mischief, until another knock sounded at the door and another staff member appeared, this one bearing a small box.

"The jeweller has sent over some leftover gold shavings. If these weren't what you wanted, let me know and I can ask for something else."

I peered into the box and the narrow strips of golden material inside. "This is perfect. Thank you."

"What's that for?" my mother asked when the woman left.

"I'm going to try to make something for Felix. Do you mind if I go next door to my room so I can spread this out on the bed?"

"Not at all," she assured me, and I left her and Archer to their notes and stories.

Back in my room, I laid out the scraps and matched them up by size as I tried to decide what to make. I could design a necklace that covered the same spot on his neck where a mark would go, but I worried it might choke him when he shifted. Similarly, a ring like the ones he told me humans used might fall off his finger when his hands changed to paws.

Maybe something for his wrist would be best? That should stay on in either form.

Laying two of the gold strips next to each other, I imagined them intertwining, weaving around each other to form an impenetrable lock, and energy began to build in my chest. As I watched, the metal began to move, fashioning itself into the exact image in my head.

It seemed my magic wasn't limited to simply opening or closing things after all.

Pouring all my focus into the work, I built up a chain, layer by layer until it formed a knotted, golden rope. I barely realized how much time had gone by until Felix appeared in the doorway and my stomach flipped at the sight of him standing there, tall and strong and smiling at me as if I were the greatest thing he'd ever seen. How on earth did I get so lucky?

"It's time to eat," he announced. "Normally, I eat downstairs with the other members of the leadership team, but if you'd rather stay here, we can have something brought up."

My stomach growled as soon as he mentioned food, confirming that I had indeed lost track of time. "I'd like to meet more of your friends," I told him. "But first, will you come try this on?"

I held up the chain and Felix immediately stepped forward, his eyes bright and interested. "You made this?"

"For you," I confirmed. "Instead of a mark. Hold out your hand."

He offered me his arm and I wrapped the chain around his wrist, its golden colour gleaming beneath the overhead lights.

"It shows that you're bound to me," I explained, starting to babble when he didn't say anything. "A symbol of the link between us. If you don't like it, I can do something else."

His eyes jumped from his wrist to my face. "Don't like it? Are you kidding me? It's incredible."

He leaned forward to capture my lips in a sweet kiss before glancing down at his wrist again.

"How does it close? There's no clasp."

"Like this."

Summoning my magic again, I directed the ends of the chain to wrap together, melding themselves into a perfect, unbroken circle around his wrist.

Felix's eyes were filled with awe when he looked back up at me. "That was so fucking cool."

His enthusiasm earned him a giggle. "The downside is you can't take it off. Only I can remove it."

"That's perfect," he stated firmly. "I never *want* to take it off. Our bond is forever and this is too. It's perfect, Evalina. Thank you."

He kissed me again, deeper and harder that time, and as his tongue slid into my mouth, my body instantly caught fire with the sparks only he provided. By the time he pulled back, I was panting for air and my body ached for him all over again.

"You know, maybe meeting your other friends can wait."

A knowing smile spread across his face. "Should I order some food for us?"

"In a minute. First, I think I'm ready for another lesson."

Chapter Sixty-Two

~Felix~

If I ever doubted the Goddess' ability to match fated mates, meeting Evalina made me a believer. Our bond stretched between worlds and species, connecting two people who couldn't have had more disparate lives, and somehow recognized that we would be perfect for each other.

Because this woman was *perfect* for me, and her asking me for another 'lesson' in the bedroom made me feel like the luckiest man alive.

"What would you like to learn?"

Evalina's ice-blue eyes held my gaze, determination and longing strongest in them with only a hint of uncertainty underneath. "You said there are many ways we could bring each other pleasure," she reminded me. "Can you show me how to do something special for you?"

Instantly, my mind conjured a vivid image of her sweet lips wrapped around my cock and I had to bite my lip to keep from groaning out loud. "Everything we do together is special."

Her lips pursed in dissatisfaction at my answer. "That's not what I asked."

I supposed not, and if she wanted to do something just for me, who was I to argue? I would have plenty of time to focus on her later.

The rest of our lives, actually.

"You remember how I used my fingers on you?" I asked, and she nodded, pink creeping up her cheeks. "Well, you can use your hand on my cock too."

Evalina's eyes dropped to the front of my pants where my cock had already begun to swell simply from being the topic of conversation. "Show me."

"Yes, ma'am."

With a wink, I pulled off my pants as fast as possible, making her giggle with my enthusiasm. My shirt followed for good measure, leaving me naked and at her command, which I already knew would always be my favourite place to be.

Taking my cock in my hand, I began to slowly stroke it up and down. "It's the movement that feels good. A firm grip but not too hard. Start slow and build up the speed gradually."

Her eyes followed the motion of my hand carefully, studying it as if preparing for an exam. "Can I try?"

"Anytime you want, Evalina."

I let go of my cock and a moment later, her small, soft hand wrapped around it instead, sending a cascade of sparks through my body that nearly brought me to my knees. I sucked in a breath so sharply that my mate looked up at me in alarm. "Is that wrong?"

"N-no. It's good. So good."

Her expression relaxed and a hint of mischief crept into her pretty blue eyes as she realized just how much control she had over me with a simple touch. Her hand tightened around my shaft, the combination of the pressure and the sparks exquisite, and I let out a low groan.

"I don't think you need much teaching. You're a natural."

Her pleased smile shot straight to my heart. Every single inch of me, inside and out, belonged to her, and nothing would ever be more beautiful to me than that smile.

Slowly, her hand travelled down my length until she reached the head, and when she twisted her wrist to move back up again, the friction felt so good, my knees almost buckled. Obviously, experience didn't matter nearly as much as the woman who had her hands on me. Sparks followed her fingers everywhere they touched while she continued to stroke me, and blood pumped hard into my cock, leaving me light-headed.

"Felix?"

I didn't realize my eyes had closed until I had to open them to answer her. "Yeah?"

Her gaze remained fixed on my cock, her hand still exploring me. "You used your mouth on me along with your hand. Can I do the same?"

"You can do whatever you want to me," I groaned, the mere thought of it sending another rush of blood straight to my groin.

Evalina's giggle was the sweetest sound I ever heard. "I mean: is it something people do?"

"It is."

"And you'd like it?"

A growl rumbled in my chest before I could stop it. I honestly couldn't tell if it came from my wolf or from me. Maybe both of us together. "Yeah," I managed to gasp. "I'd like it, but only when you want to."

Her tongue traced over her lips as she continued to watch her hand on my cock. "I want to see how you taste."

Fuck. Did I already mention this woman was perfect?

On her knees on the ground, she'd be too short to reach my cock comfortably, so I lay down on the bed instead, spreading my legs to let her fit between them. Evalina eagerly crawled up into the open space, her hands running up my legs, leaving another trail of sparks behind them. If she wanted instruction, I'd give it to her, but her instincts were so damn good that I didn't want to offer any suggestions unless she asked.

She didn't ask. Instead, after trailing her fingers over my cock again, her head dipped down and her tongue darted out to tentatively follow the path her fingers just followed. I sucked in another breath, doing my best to keep my eyes open since the sight of her touching me rivalled the feel of it in how much it turned me on.

Every swipe of her tongue felt magnified. Every press of her lips as she kissed her way down my shaft sent another shiver of pleasure through my body. I couldn't have moved if I wanted to. My heart pounded. My fucking *toes* curled. No one had ever affected me the way she did and no one ever would; I knew that for a fact.

By the time she lifted my cock and brought the head to her lips, my limbs had turned to jelly. Her eyes met mine and no thought existed in my head but the connection between us. She took me in as far as she could, her hands covering the area her mouth couldn't, and I saw stars. My orgasm came on embarrassingly fast, but when I saw my mate's satisfaction in the pleasure she gave me, I didn't regret it.

"How did I do?" she asked after licking up every drop.

For once in my life, speaking didn't come easily, but I managed to push the words out. "You're going to be teaching me in no time."

I reached for her and she came to my arms without hesitation, curling into my side as if she'd been born to fit there.

Which she had. Just like I'd been made for her.

~The End~

The Story Continues...

If you enjoyed the book, please take a moment to leave a review.
Thank you!

The fourth book of the *Rocky Mountain Wolves* series, Wishes in the Moonlight, returns to the Ravenstone Pack, where an unexpected visitor makes life interesting for the new Alpha. Coming in July of 2025!

KEEP IN TOUCH

For more about my other books and to keep up-to-date with new releases, find all the links here:
https://linktr.ee/melodytyden